A. Ye

# Becoming Real

Book One of
*The Becoming Chronicles*

In the Sydney heatwave of November 2019 a grisly scene of torture and murder is uncovered in a suburban street. Clint Ryal, journalist for the online newspaper the Sydney Saturday World is one of the first on the scene. Two naked people were chanting religious verses and waiting, in front of a burning house, for a UFO to take them to New York. The remains of Tadeas Costa are found burning in the backyard, seemingly killed by his wife Emma Costa and her lover Piripi Nosi. Clint's coverage of the case for the Sydney Saturday World gives him a reputation that is resented by his office rival George Bakker and his controlling manager Kelly Harper.

Clint's last name, pronounced Real, has caused other people mirth throughout his life. During the following year while the murder-accused await their trial, and through loss and heartache, Clint Ryal discovers who he really is and who his friends are. He investigates a religious cult, the Order of the Solar Temple. He unpicks the links between the Order and Tadeas Costa's murder. In the midst of a global pandemic, Clint finds himself on the trail of his absent father, Bekym Ryal. Clint loses the person who raised him and learns the history of his grandfather, Sunil Ryal. Sunil escaped from Iran when the Shah fell in 1979 and was only able to save his son Bekym; a fact that has haunted him throughout his life. Clint's mother, Pearl O'Leary, a product of her own dysfunctional upbringing, attempts to reconcile with her son after failing to be there for him when he was a child. Clint is rejected by his girlfriend and fired from his job with the newspaper.

On a post-pandemic trip to America in January 2021, Clint meets and confronts his father. In New York, he meets Lilla Adams, a detective with the NYPD who captures Clint's heart. Clint's oldest and best friend, Arash Esfandiari, forces Clint to abandon his pursuit of love with Detective Lilla Adams for reasons of national and international security. Clint turns his back on his old friend as well as his father. His friendship with Vishesh Devi is strengthened as other people in his life reject him or are left behind. Back in Sydney, Lubanzi Abara, attorney for Piripi Nosi, intends to defend his client against the charge of murder on the basis of Piripi's cultural upbringing. This may result in Emma Costa being found guilty of the murder of Tadeas Costa while Piripi is not. Vanessa Raine and her lover Diana Darling Croswell are a formidable legal team for the defense of Emma but have troubles of their own to contend with. Clint uses his skills as a journalist to help the lawyers uncover the truth about the murder of Emma Costa's husband while he yearns to be with Lilla.

*For all those who have suffered during the Covid-19 global pandemic*

Praxeum Publishing, Wellington, New Zealand

Front cover illustrated by BetiBup Studio Design http://betibup33.com

ISBN 9798655496521
Copyright © June 2020 Angela Yeoman
All rights reserved.

## Contents

- Existing .................................................................................................................. 6
  - Chapter One .................................................................................................... 7
  - Chapter Two .................................................................................................. 17
  - Chapter Three ............................................................................................... 32
  - Chapter Four ................................................................................................. 39
- Thinking ................................................................................................................. 51
  - Chapter Five .................................................................................................. 52
  - Chapter Six .................................................................................................... 62
  - Chapter Seven .............................................................................................. 67
  - Chapter Eight ................................................................................................ 81
  - Chapter Nine ................................................................................................. 91
  - Chapter Ten ................................................................................................. 103
- Knowing .............................................................................................................. 112
  - Chapter Eleven ........................................................................................... 113
  - Chapter Twelve ........................................................................................... 124
  - Chapter Thirteen ......................................................................................... 134
  - Chapter Fourteen ....................................................................................... 145
  - Chapter Fifteen ........................................................................................... 157
  - Chapter sixteen ........................................................................................... 170
- Being ................................................................................................................... 179
  - Chapter Seventeen .................................................................................... 180
  - Chapter Eighteen ....................................................................................... 190
  - Chapter Nineteen ....................................................................................... 199
  - Chapter Twenty .......................................................................................... 210
- Becoming Just: Book Two of The Becoming Chronicles .......................................... 221

# Existing

# Chapter One

The co-accused had changed while sitting in remand awaiting trial for murdering Tadeas Costa. Piripi Nosi's head was a statue of buffed stone and jutting cheekbones, with ridges of hair shaved in lines across his head and a jaw that preceded him into the courtroom. He wore an open necked white shirt to reveal the tips of coils of a tattoo that Clint Ryal remembered seeing in its entirety on the night of the murder. His weight loss while in remand made Piripi's youth more evident; he was now aged only 20. Emma Costa, on the other hand, had an air of collapse. She had stopped dying and cutting her hair and it now hung in grey, unwashed strands. She had been a victim of the global Covid-19 pandemic during her period of remand and had spent weeks in hospital under guard and even longer convalescing. Even without experiencing a horrific illness Emma Costa, at 47 years of age, could be expected to be showing the effects of life's natural decline, and she was. Small, standing a little over five feet tall, her shoulders were slumped and her breasts dangled bra-less beneath a blue cotton top which gaped around a neck comprised of strands of wrinkles. Clint wondered if anyone on the outside cared about her now that her husband was dead. He wondered if he had been her only visitor at the prison.

The Supreme Court trial in courtroom 11A was about as packed as it could be post-pandemic, with every second seat still taped off to allow for physical distancing between people. Even though time had moved on and the world was now in March 2021, the globe was still running scared of new spikes of recurring Covid-19; most people were taking few chances of being infected. Some people in the courtroom still chose to wear masks or thin rubber gloves. Hand sanitizer was available for use when entering and exiting the court.

The long wooden bench at the front of the court faced the large room and was flanked on both sides by marble columns and the Australian flag which was blue. It had a union jack in one corner, a large star representing the commonwealth, and five other stars for the constellation of the Southern Cross. The Judge's associate and the transcriber were seated at each end of the bench, leaving a large leather chair in the middle for the Judge. Clint could see over the heads of the public and the reporters to the backs of the wigged and gowned attorneys and the prosecutor; they were facing the Judge's bench. The inside of the courtroom combined modern, light-coloured timber with ancient grandeur and gravitas, while the outside, coming up the steps from Phillip Street, looked every inch a building designed in the brutalist fashion; made of utilitarian concrete and glass.

Early March and it was sweltering outside. It was even scorching inside, despite the air conditioning. The excitement and anticipation of the people in the room was rapidly increasing the temperature. While waiting for the Supreme Court Judge to arrive, they were undoing top buttons and fanning themselves with pads of paper or anything else to hand. Clint spent time recalling Friday November 8, 2019; the day Tadeas Costa was murdered. Clint remembered the day well and not only because of the murder. Three other things occurred that day which impacted his life.

The first thing, earlier in the day, was when his boss Kelly Harper rubbished an article he'd written for the Sydney Saturday World about the fluid sexuality of young people. While the staff waited for Kelly to arrive, the silence was filled with sound: a wet rattle with each breath out through Bella's nose; the click click, click click of George's pen; the squeak of the chair back resisting Marisa's weight. Clint could feel his bum bones on the wooden chair, his shoulder-blades uncomfortable against the straight back. The scream of tension was palpable but undeclared. Outside sounds were also coming in: bursts of conversation, snatches of music. If he relaxed his ears, cars driving by sounded like the rushing swish and then pebbly ebb of waves over feet. People were living. Clint wished he was out there. Instead, he was there in that room in that suburb in that hot city waiting, waiting with those people, waiting for Kelly. She arrived in the normal way: late, banging the door, giving a high pitched laugh as her fat wobbled over strapless heels, clutching a pile of papers in one arm on the top of which balanced a salad of spinach and reconstituted chicken, a take-away coffee clutched in the other hand and a story spilling from behind two curtains of blond hair with black roots which limply framed a large nose powdered with crumbs of pale foundation.

"The tech guys are saying that we told them the deadline was Sunday morning not Saturday morning. Why they thought we'd release a paper with 'Saturday' in its title on Sunday is beyond me." Kelly Harper gave another derisive laugh. "Well, what have I missed?" She ripped the plastic lid off her lunch, opened a small plastic bag of brown dressing, concentrated hard as she squeezed and began to eat with a plastic fork.

No-one responded.

"The increasingly non-binary sexual nature of university students?" Kelly turned towards him. "Really, Clint? Are you for real?" She chuckled at her own wit. Although his last name was spelt R-y-a-l it was pronounced Real. "This is a story?"

"Yes, I think so. An increasing proportion of young people feel comfortable enough in our society to come out about their sexual fluidity. Doesn't that indicate a society that is more tolerant than we're given to understand is characteristic in Australia? Our country has a legend of macho men and family violence. This is a positive story of change and progression."

"But who wants to read about this stuff?"

Clint tried to take a breath but there was no air. "Intelligent, caring people."

"The story is not a good fit. I can't see it helping us build the readership of the Sydney Saturday World. We are targeting professionals with time on their hands to read about their World on their I-pads over a flat white or two on a Saturday morning. A few of us, including me, have put a lot of money as well as our careers on the line for this business. Let's try and lift our game. I want you to use your contacts to cover the demise of student activism and the rise of the 'me' generation. We are up against deadlines this afternoon for a new story. Now," she turned her back on Clint, "You're doing the international stories, Marisa? The President's possible impeachment. Oh, and the Pope's condemnation of countries not accepting any more refugees; are you doing a pushback piece? Countries have their own priorities, after all, which don't necessarily have anything to do with the Pope's. Perhaps he could take some refugees into the Vatican." There was a laugh that managed to combine girlish coquetry with cynicism. But cynicism can sound like cruelty, unless you have a personal history of being down-trodden, Clint thought. "And the social pages Bella," Kelly continued, "Take me through what you have."

Clint eased his mobile from the pocket of his chinos and messaged Vishesh. *Need help with article for SSW please. Can you meet me at Uni? The Quarter. In 30 mins?* From where he was sitting, Clint could smell Kelly. It was the smell of a cat's yawn. To him, it would always be the smell of conceit. He turned his head away.

"I'll need to see all copy by close of play today," she finished. "We're going to release at 4am tomorrow. Let's meet after work today for a celebration."

Glebe Point Road was boiling. At midday there was no shade to be found on either side of the street. Crossing the A22 and approaching the University of Sydney through Victoria Park, Clint watched an ibis pull a disposable nappy from a bin. Drab ducks waddled towards the stream to get out of Clint's way. Even under the trees, people looked pink and perspiring in the heat. The job with the start-up Sydney Saturday World was Clint's first proper job since graduating as a journalist. He wondered if it would be his last. Vishesh Devi met him at the library at the heart of the University Campus, known as The Quarter. They could plug in their laptops there and would have access to free Wi-Fi.

"Hey Ryal."

There was a one armed hug. Vishesh's designer jeans were slung low over slim coffee-coloured hips and his short white tee accentuated bulging arms and tight pecks. His high tops were unlaced. Designer sunglasses perched on the top of dark hair that was cropped on one side but which touched his shoulder on the other. He was draped in a black satchel. Pyramids of black onyx spiked from each ear as if to ward off demons and, when he spoke, the piercing in his tongue was visible. Clint, wearing chinos, a light green cotton shirt with rolled up sleeves and lace ups felt a bit conservative next to Vishesh but told himself sternly that everyone was allowed to be who they were. How he dressed was fine.

Vishesh lectured at the Department of Peace and Conflict Studies while working on his PhD. The Department was housed away from the main University campus with the Great Western Highway in between as if the Department was contagious. Vishesh had talked about job options;

diplomacy or the United Nations or the World Bank, but it was unlikely that he would ever tear himself away from the academic life in which he thrived. Clint and Vishesh had met at the University a couple of years ago at a course on peace journalism. Fabulously gay, with a live-in boyfriend, Vishesh was not averse to the pleasures of women from time to time and had been one of Clint's sources for the article on sexual fluidity which had affronted Kelly.

With only a few hours to make sense of the complex issue Kelly had told him to write about, Clint was grateful for Vishesh's help. After two hours of research and drafting, he knew he could not write the article his boss wanted. Instead of the stagnation of student activism in Australia or, in fact, anywhere in the world, activism seemed to be alive and well although its face looked different today because of social media.

*We should all want young people to be politically active*, Clint wrote, *because we want their engagement in the world. We need to encourage them to be free thinkers and we should want them to want to change the world because the future they had been promised is not one they can see on the horizon. The impact on future generations of previous generations' lack of interest in climate change is one significant example.*

When Vishesh left for a three o'clock lecture, Clint carried on. By five pm, he had done what he could to make sense of the facts while trying to ask how it was possible for rising activism to sit side by side with a 'me' generation, and how and when the two might clash. Emailing his story to Kelly and saving it into the newspaper's document management system, Clint had packed up feeling wrung out. There was a knot in his gut. Kelly would not be happy. He should start thinking about other job opportunities but not now, not tonight, because the only jobs he could think of right now if Kelly fired him without a reference were labouring or supermarket check-out guy, even though he had a Masters in Journalism. He decided not to go back into the office for the celebratory drinks, aware that his absence would be another black mark.

As he walked back up Glebe Point Road, the rush hour was swelling and the cafés filling with pre-dinner drinkers. It was no cooler. Almost at Rozelle Bay, Clint was turning right into Cook Street when his mobile buzzed against his thigh. Propping one leg on a low brick wall to check the message, he drank in the look and feel of the houses in this stretch of town; their slim porches, the tiny strips of front yard and the curved veranda rooftops to keep the glare out. Gentrified houses were paved out the front with large matching pots of lemon trees or yuccas, while those that were rented out had an abandoned look with old bikes and sagging armchairs cluttering the porches and dead grass around the front railings sprouting long dandelions.

*I know I said I'd come round tonight, but I'm not going to make it. Sorry Clint but I don't think you and I are a hit. Best if you look elsewhere before we get in too deep. Really sorry. Lou*

That was the second memorable thing that happened to him on November 8, 2019, Clint remembered. He had met Lou when she was taken on as a temp at the Sydney Saturday World. He really liked Lou, enjoyed how smart and funny she was and loved how her curvy body felt under his hands. He had looked forward to getting to know her better and had wanted her to meet his grandfather. Resting one elbow on the leg propped on the wall, Clint had wondered at the time if it was possible for that day to get any worse. Now, as he looked back to that day, Clint marvelled at the naivety and self-entitlement of the man he was back then. Of course things could get worse, not just on that day but in the weeks and months to come.

Standing still in the sun thinking about Lou had made him too hot. People were walking down the street towards him and so he wiped his wet face, pulled his leg off the wall and carried on down Cook Street, trying to feel numb and ignore the various despairs churning in his gut telling him he was a failure. The shortcut into Leichardt Street through Ricketts Avenue was decorated with red bougainvillea flowers and spikey green aloe plants. Leichardt Street curved around and down to meet Oxley Street and the waterfront. Clint could see his flatmates Bian, Shane and Megan on the porch at number 16 trying to catch a cool breeze off the water. Shane and Bian were clutching cans of beer. Megan was on the phone. The owner of the tired Tuscan-like house was standing on the balcony around his half of the house, gazing out over the bay. Dr Graydon Audain, now in his 80s, had divided his house into two apartments after his wife died and lived a mellow life of books, opera and expensive wine, nicely paid for by the rent coming in from the tenants in the bottom half of his house. He had fluffy white hair and a set of wrinkles that showed he'd spent his life thinking and laughing. Clint liked his landlord; he reminded him a bit of his grandfather Sunil.

Bringing with him the confusion of the things that had happened to him that day, Clint leapt up onto the tenants' porch. Megan was now off the phone and was pulling on the police gear that would have her sweating within seconds. She was telling Shane, her fiancé, "I've got to go. Fire and Rescue attended a house fire. They've put it out but there are two naked people in the front yard waiting for a UFO to take them to New York, and a dog has unearthed what might be a human bone in the backyard." Shane stood up to give her a hug goodbye. She hugged him back, disentangling a wood chip from his hair and shaking her head in disbelief at what some people got up to. "It's a bloody bad time to put additional strain on Fire and Rescue right now when fires are raging in the suburbs and all across New South Wales. It's the hottest, driest summer in living memory and summer hasn't even really started."

Shane was in his work gear: denim shorts, a grubby tee of uncertain colour and steel-capped work boots over green and grey socks that had seen better days. He'd clearly collapsed on the porch in exhaustion after a day on the building site and hadn't managed to move since. Shane's ginger hair was matted with sawdust and sweat, and his bronzed face streaked with dirt. A tool bag was dumped beside him. Megan had the policewoman thing going on: six foot, fit as a fiddle and a laid-back temperament which completely suited her job of talking down people when they were on the edge. Shane topped her by a couple of inches and had the physique of a body builder. They relaxed most weekends by going for long runs early in the morning followed by boxing workouts. No-one was surprised when an engagement ring appeared on Megan's left hand.

"Human bones? A UFO? You have got to be kidding. What a story. Can I come?" Clint had a sudden vision of a scoop that would make even his boss Kelly sit up and take notice of his talents. He could smell the fragrance of eucalyptus as people trod on fallen leaves in the playground next door as they took the steps down to the waterfront for an early evening stroll. A flock of raven flying overhead made 'caa' noises to tell anyone who would listen that they were looking for a roost.

"Okay, if you keep back from the scene. We don't have to go far: its number 14 Forsyth Street which is almost round the corner. My partner said he'd pick me up but it'll be quicker to walk. I'm going to meet him there."

The story on the fire which Clint wrote later and emailed to Kelly received the response *Good story. Just in time for this edition. Thanks.*

That almost sounded like praise and Clint had felt a childish sense of having done something right.

*A house fire, two naked people and, in the back yard, a bonfire concealing parts of a skeleton; whether this is animal or human is yet to be determined by forensics. The bones were unearthed by a dog urgently scratching in the yard of number 14 Forsyth Street. It is possible that the bonfire was the cause of the house fire, although the emergency services have said that it is too early to tell. The dog was carried to safety by firefighters. Hard working families and students studying for exams in the gentrified suburb of Glebe, who were brought briefly outside by the commotion, asked "how could this happen here?"*

*Praise must be given to the firefighters who quickly got the fire under control, with the adjoining house suffering only minor damage. Smoke is still rising from smouldering black heaps and the neighbours have retreated inside, watching from inside their homes and behind closed windows to avoid the acrid smell. The smell of destruction and the scorch marks on the neighbouring house indicate the damage that the fire might have done had it not been quickly and expertly contained.*

*Police have evacuated the residents of the three closest homes in case hot spots flare up, and have now cordoned off Forsyth Street. The forensics team has moved in, wrapping the perimeter with tape and warning people to keep out. Senior Sergeant Pole has made a statement to the media asking people to stay away while the investigations of the fire services and the police continue throughout the night. Flood lamps have been erected to help with the examination of the scene.*

*The burned house is said to be owned by Mr and Mrs Costa. It is not known at this time if either of the people at the scene goes by those names. They were waiting, as they said to the police, for a UFO to take them to the headquarters of the Order of the Solar Temple, a religious cult which, they said, was based in New York. Your reporter on the spot will bring you more on this story in future issues of the Sydney Saturday World.*

The dazed and naked people were draped in blankets soon after Megan had heard their stories, with Clint hanging back but listening avidly in the background. Glassy-eyed, the young brown-skinned man was stiff and distant as if observing the scene from outside his body. Clint observed a swirling black tattoo on the man's right shoulder, with tendrils of inked fire creeping up his neck. The woman with short brown hair and grey eyes was old enough to be his mother. Not under arrest at that point but certainly helping the police with their enquiries, both were led away to separate police cars parked down the road outside the grey house with a cow painted on its front door. As she went, the woman had raised an arm, pointed directly at Clint and had said softly, almost lovingly caressing each syllable. "Become Real. Becomereal; becomereal; becomereal."

The black frame of number 14 Forsyth Street was still smoking. The other houses in the row looked undamaged other than the shared wall. By walking up Avon Lane on the other side of the burnt house Clint saw the top of an ancient Jacaranda tree at the end of the long backyard, scorched to the top and along the branches of purple flowers which were drooping over the stone wall.

## Chapter Two

Later that evening after he'd visited the site of the fire and delivered his story to Kelly, Clint was thinking about what to have for a late dinner. It had already turned to night time outside. It was then that his phone rang. He wondered briefly if it could be Lou saying that the evening without him had felt like a mistake and could they talk. But it was a call from an unknown number and it turned out to be the third unforgettable thing that happened to Clint that day.

"Hello?"

"Is this Clint Ryal?" It was a woman's voice.

"Yes."

"Grandson of Sunil Ryal?" Clint was on his feet, stomach knotting.

"Yes."

"I'm ringing from the Emergency Department of the Auburn Hospital. Your grandfather has been admitted after a fall. He is fine but will be staying at least overnight while we run some tests. He asked that we contact you."

"But he's okay?" Clint's voice was constricted: a darkness pressing on his vocal cords. "I'll come. Should I bring anything?"

"He's in the best place right now and has everything that he needs. We have a shop on the campus if you want to buy anything additional. Do you know where to find us?"

"Oh yes. Yes, thank you. You're near the Omar Mosque." It was one of the mosques Sunil visited. Clint was already walking to the door, with all thoughts of dinner gone.

"That's right. I'll tell your grandfather that you are on your way, shall I?"

When Clint arrived at the hospital, his grandfather was sleeping. The wisp of his white hair looked dead on the pillow and Sunil's body under the white cover looked tiny, almost wasted. His ears and nose looking larger than Clint remembered and his eyebrows were so slouched they crowded out his eyelids. There was a dark and swollen bruise down one side of Sunil's face and his hands were bandaged; he must have tried to stop himself as he fell. His grandfather looked nothing like the man with smooth olive skin Clint remembered from his childhood. His face was grey; leached of colour and vitality. Clint felt ashamed that he hadn't noticed the decline from the man Sunil used to be. It must have been going on for years. Kissing his grandfather's crumpled forehead, Clint pulled up a chair to sit next to the bed. He wanted to be the first person Sunil saw when he awoke.

A nurse at the desk had taken some details from Clint. "Do you know the year your grandfather was born? He doesn't seem to have much in the way of identification in his wallet, not even a driving license. Luckily, he had a money card with his name on it. He also had a photo of you in his wallet with your phone number written on the back, so we were able to reach you."

"My grandfather never sat for a license in Australia, so far as I'm aware. I know he left Iran in about 1979 and was about 35 years old when he left, but I don't know how exact that is. Is he going to be alright? Do you know what happened?"

"We're still interpreting his tests but the doctor will be around shortly, doing her rounds, and should be able to tell you more. We've put him into a single room just down the corridor." The nurse was young with white skin over prominent bones and she spoke with an Irish lilt. She popped a pen back into a pocket in her byzantine blue wraparound uniform and smiled with kindness. Clint turned away hastily, scared of tears. It had been a hard day and tenderness was sure to undo him.

Sunil had recently taken to wearing a kufi. He said it was to keep his head warm as his hair thinned. It sat now on the bedside drawers, a few flakes of dry skin clinging to the black fabric. He'd never been an orthodox believer, so far as Clint knew, but perhaps wearing the skull cap was a way, along with attendance at the mosque, for him to celebrate his Iranian heritage. Sunil's shoes sat side by side near the end of the bed. They were also black and had seen better days; broken down at the backs and lopsided from walking on the outside of his feet. The leather had stretched and the shoes looked too wide at the mouth. The laces were frayed. The tenderness around Clint's heart swelled at the humanness and the vulnerability of his grandfather. He'd just been worrying about a newspaper story and whether a girl liked him but Sunil had spent 40 years separated from his country and his family, trying to make ends meet, losing his son and bringing up his grandchild on his own. And now he was old. Clint's trials abruptly fell into perspective and he felt ashamed. The slight body stirred under its cover and Clint jumped up, reaching for Sunil's hand.

There was a cursory knock on the bedroom door and a crowd of white-jacketed people walked in. A tall doctor wearing yellow boots and a matching band on her wristwatch shook Clint's hand and told him her name was Doctor Ferguson. She examined Sunil's chart without removing it from its hook and placed two fingers on the patient's wrist as he groggily came around.

"Hello Mr Ryal. You've had a nasty turn and a fall, and you're in hospital. Can you remember what happened?"

Sunil's eyes flickered towards Clint and there was a small smile before his eyes rested on the doctor. "I was on my way to the mosque. Three men came at me. ISIS. I fell over."

The doctor frowned. "They thought you were from ISIS? They attacked you?"

Sunil moved his head as if to shake it and then stopped with a wince. "They said *they* were ISIS and that I was not worthy in their eyes. But they were kids playing tough. They just gave me a fright."

Clint squeezed the mottled hand. He thought there was something his grandfather was not saying. There was a story to be told but not now, not in front of this crowd.

"Well. The tests indicate that you have not had a heart attack or a stroke. It may have been a panic attack that made you fall over. We'll keep you in for the night and check you in the morning. We've got you on a drip to keep you hydrated. I don't think you drink enough water Mr Ryal." She smiled at him. "And we'll give you something to help you sleep." Turning, she nodded at them before leaving the room, her silent entourage in tow; her yellow boots making no sound.

The Irish nurse returned, checked Sunil's drip and injected a liquid into the tube. It must have been something to help him sleep. It was late now and dark. Clint rested his cheek against Sunil's.

"I'll be back in the morning grandad. Sleep well."

Sunil gave a tiny nod and a quick smile, his eyelids fluttering but not opening.

It was late when Clint returned home after visiting Sunil in hospital but his landlord Graydon was still up and leaning out the window of his top floor turret. He was smoking a thin cigar, backlit by a large lamp. Although Graydon had moved inside his apartment since the sun had gone down, he was still staring out to sea. Clint wondered what his landlord thought about as he stared into the distance for hours at a time. An almost full moon was partially obscured by threads of cloud, and stars popped out from behind the branches of trees as Clint walked up the steps to 16 Oxley Street.

Graydon was thinking about cause and effect. He had time these days to ruminate about his great passion and life's work, Middle Eastern history. He wondered if the descendants of Sir Mark Sykes and Francois

Georges Picot had ever looked sadly at what their forebears had done during World War I when they divided up the Ottoman Empire to suit British and French interests. The Sykes-Picot Agreement neglected to allow for the growth of Arab nationalism, resulted in the demise of the Ottoman Empire and created the conditions for the current troubles in the now named Middle East. Thousands of years of tribal, sectarian and nomadic history had been ignored. How could two men, two countries, wield so much power over other countries and not seem to consider the possible implications?

And then in 1919, soon after the end of World War I, the heads of state from England, France, America and Italy used their power at the Paris Peace Conference to agree on the Treaty of Versailles. That Treaty effectively required Germany to pay so much in reparation for the harm caused through World War I that the country was brought to its knees economically over the next couple of decades. The world knows what happened next. The only way Germany could improve its economy was to go to war again and to disenfranchise some groups of people to the benefit of others. The conditions were ripe for dictatorship, devastation and genocide.

When he was younger, Graydon had made a point of tracking down and attempting to meet the great grandchildren of Woodrow Wilson, who was the President of the United States in 1919. He also sought out the descendants of David Lloyd George, who'd been Prime Minister of Britain in that year. He wanted to hear their views on the fateful Treaty of Versailles which their ancestors had devised. Graydon was already engaged to be married to Selma when he first met Margaret Owen McMillan, great granddaughter of Lloyd George. She was a budding historian and an expert in international relations who was frank in her acknowledgement of the impacts of the Treaty. She was professional, brilliant, funny and fascinating to talk to. They had met after a lecture she gave in Sydney to a packed audience and went on to meet again over lunch before she left the country to return to Canada where she worked. At no time over the next 50 years of correspondence did he indicate his total devotion to her. Margaret, in turn, gave no indication of any interest in him other than professional collegiality. She was totally private about her personal life, deflecting any questions he might ask about partners or children.

Graydon was aware that, all through the years of their marriage, Selma could sense that he only ever partially belonged to her, but that was enough for her. Dearest Selma; he missed her. She was happy to run the house and be the perfect faculty wife, hosting parties, mucking in to edit his research papers and accompanying him on sabbaticals. They never did manage to produce children, though, and that made her sad. She would have been delighted, Graydon thought with a smile, to know that half their wonderful old house was now full of young people.

Clint stepped through the door to the bottom apartment. The lights were out in the bedroom shared by Shane and Megan. Megan would still be dealing with the events at 14 Forsyth Street and Shane knew not to wait up; it could be hours before she returned. The glow from under the door to Bian's room went off as Clint closed the door quietly and crept into the kitchen. Clint liked Bian. She was Vietnamese and had first travelled on her own to New Zealand when she was only 16, to train as a hairdresser. Bian had enormous courage, Clint thought, learning English from scratch, learning a new trade, and surviving on her own in an alien culture. She was also the tinniest woman he'd ever met. She was a small package of perfect limbs, huge dark eyes and long black hair which, being a hairdresser, she was constantly tinting with different colours and tying back in different ways. She dressed with artistic flair, wearing many layers of garments teamed up with huge-soled soles.

The toaster was full of crumbs and Clint spent time emptying it, aware that all his movements were laborious and far away as if he was dreaming or looking at the world through water. As the four slices of toast popped up one after the other, he grabbed the peanut butter and began to eat in greedy mouthfuls. He filled the kettle and made a cup of tea with a teabag, drinking it black and strong like his grandfather. The woman at the house fire had said his father's name, Bekym Ryal, Clint was sure of it, and then his grandfather had been scared half to death by people saying they were from ISIS. Were these two events related? And even if they weren't, what did either of them mean?

Fatigue undid Clint's arms and legs as he stood to put the dishes in the dishwasher but his head was buzzing too much for sleep. The dishwasher had finished a wash cycle and so he unpacked it and put the dishes away before stacking it with his dirty dishes. The kitchen was grubby and the door of the microwave had been left slightly ajar revealing splatters of what looked like bolognaise sauce. He toyed with the idea of surrendering to his neat freak instincts, his need to turn chaos into order, and give the kitchen a clean. He was often at the butt end of some good natured teasing about his need for cleanliness and tidiness, but even Clint's flatmates had no idea that one of his greatest joys was filling up the basket next to the toilet with large rolls of soft white paper. As a young child in his mother's house, toilet paper had been rare. The sense of abundance and control Clint could feel when he observed a basket of toilet rolls was enormous. That feeling of abundance was always tinged with a feeling of indulgence however, because a significant majority of people in the world were so poor that toilet paper was likely to be a luxury. Looking around the kitchen in the small hours of tomorrow, however, even Clint knew that he was done in. The cleaning would have to wait.

As he turned the knob on the wooden door to his bedroom, Clint could smell Arash. It was the smell of raspberry jam. He saw the backpack first and then his passport and a pair of soft black leather gloves lying on the dresser, followed by Arash's body with its neatly shaved head sprawled on the floor in a sleeping bag, reflected in the full-length wall mirror.

"Behold, Arash the Archer," were the first words Clint had heard Arash say while striking a pose on the fort in the school playground. That was about 20 years ago. It had been Clint's first week at Blaxcell Street Public School and he was cowed by the big boys, the taunting girls, the bullies, the teachers, the unintelligible rules; he understood nothing. Sunil had thought he was doing the right thing enrolling Clint in a school teeming with Arabs and other minorities, but Clint wouldn't have fit in anywhere. Brought up without a father and taken from an unsuitable mother, Clint was damaged. Arash looked like Clint only bolder, browner and bigger. He wasn't afraid of anything or anyone. He understood everything.

"The earth was quiet, the sky was quiet
As if all the world was listening to Arash
Little by little the sun appeared from behind the mountains
Thousands of golden spears were thrown to the sky's eyes."

At age five, Arash already knew sections of the famous poem about the Iranian hero Arash the Archer, and he said them aloud while standing on the top of the fort. "Come down," a teacher had yelled. "You're meant to play *in* the fort, not on its roof. You could fall and hurt yourself." Arash had smiled at her knowingly and then thrown himself off the roof towards the ground like a circus performer, accompanied by screams and running feet, but he landed like a crouched cat on the matting below, unharmed. There was a scene and some shouting. Arash had grinned at Clint across the playground. When he was older, Arash could quote Siavash Kasri's entire poem off by heart; his voice soft and warm, commanding attention.

Clint looked at the gloves. Maybe they were an affectation but they suited Arash. He had once told Clint that all the best archers wore gloves and that every moment of every day was an opportunity to be an archer. They were so soft they were like another layer of skin and so old they exuded an ambience of gallantry and adventure. Climbing into bed, Clint was aware that he had relaxed now that Arash was here and he would probably sleep. His failure at work, his grandfather hurt and in hospital, the loss of Lou; everything would all be alright.

The friends went to the hospital together the next morning. All Clint's flatmates were either at work or, in the case of Megan, still asleep, by the time they woke. Clint and Arash first ate cereal and drank tea before they set off, with the sun expanding through the kitchen window.

"Where have you been? It's November now and I haven't heard from you since July." Arash had gone without warning and not responded to emails. Clint heard his voice as querulous, reedy and complaining.

"Iran, mostly."

Clint waited.

"I wanted to see what it is like." Arash said. "See if I could find out why our grandparents left in '79 when the Shah fell. Think about whether there is anything to go back to."

"And?"

"Big divide between the poor and the rich. Internet censorship. Women hidden. Blatant propaganda. Protests against the government and the supreme ruler Ali Khamenei have been going on for over a year now. People detained and never returned. But the men on the street were friendly and keen to try out their English with me. Confusing place." Arash paused and Clint waited.

"You know, it is rumoured that protesters across Iran, including children, are summarily being killed by the Iranian regime's security forces. They fire live ammunition into crowds of unarmed protesters. Its only just started and I fear it is going to get worst."

"What are the people protesting about?"

"To begin with, they were protesting the increased cost of gas. Iran is one of the most oil rich countries in the world and has subsidised petrol prices for decades. But it has suffered economic problems since the revolution in 1979; economic problems it can no longer ignore. And so it has reduced the subsidy on petrol. But I wonder if this is just the beginning."

"What do you mean?" Clint was taking mental notes and wondering if he should write an article for the Sydney Saturday World.

"Now the protests have started, it's like a scab has been knocked off and pus is oozing out. Many people hate the current regime; it is very repressive."

"What do you think will happen?"

"That's a tough question, and I don't think my opinion is worth much, but either the government will become more oppressive, resisting change and keeping its citizens behind the Islamic curtain, a bit like North Koreans locked behind the Communist curtain, or it will erupt into decades of revolution. Neither is very appealing. Both will result in humanitarian abuses and hundreds of thousands of deaths."

"Would you go back?"

"I'm glad I went but I can't see a place for me there."

Which didn't exactly answer the question, Clint thought. He wanted to ask Arash why he had not responded to his emails or messages during his trip and why he hadn't said anything about where he was going before he left, but he didn't. It felt shrewish; like the stereotypical nagging wife. They ate their cereal.

"I did some research while I was there about your grandfather, Sunil Ryal, and mine, Meyrzad Esfandiari. I couldn't find any record of mine. But could Sunil have been an advisor to the Shah? There is a list of men that were being hunted down by the new regime in early 1980. Amnesty International was given a copy of the list. I got in touch with them and they let me read it on their premises. They wouldn't let me take it away with me."

"Where on earth did you visit Amnesty International?"

"Beirut. I flew there before I went to Tehran."

"My grandfather, an advisor to the Shah? A wanted man?" Clint laughed. It was absurd. The Sunil Ryal he knew had never shown any interest in world affairs or government. He kept himself to himself and lived a small life mourning the disappearance of his son Bekym in silence while raising his damaged grandchild.

As they rode on the number 370 bus to the hospital, swaying around corners at the mercy of the hanging straps, Arash said he was looking to buy an apartment in Sydney. He'd given up the lease on his rental before leaving for the Middle East.

"After I've paid my respects to Sunil, I'll start the hunt."

Clint felt the grin splitting his face like a five year old. It sounded like Arash might be settling down a bit and Clint liked the thought of that. Sunil Ryal was sitting in a chair next to the bed when they arrived. He was dressed except for his shoes and was breathing heavily. He acknowledged their arrival with a pressing of hands and two nods.

"I'm going to take you home in an Uber grandad."

"The bus will do. The bus will do."

"Not today you stubborn old thing." Sunil smiled. He likes me teasing him, Clint thought.

"Good afternoon young Clint." Graydon bowed his head slightly and touched his wide-brimmed sunhat in mock salute with his left hand.

"Hello Graydon," Clint had helped Sunil back to his apartment in Wingello Street after the hospital discharged him and had left him having a nap. He had made his way back to 16 Oxley Street and was at the bottom of the steps when his landlord stepped out onto the stoop. There was something very likable about their landlord. He had long ago asked them to call him by his first name, protesting that to call him Dr Audain would make him feel like he was lecturing a class in Middle Eastern history again and that, he'd proclaimed in mock horror, was ancient history.

His chocolate Wowauzer woofed joyfully, ran for Clint and attempted to climb his leg, clawing at his chinos. "Alice you naughty girl, come here." Graydon struggled to clip a lead onto her collar as if one of his arms wasn't working properly. "We are off for a walk in the late afternoon sun. We might stop for a beer at The Galley on the waterfront. My lovely wife used to call beer my 'pain killer' and I could do with one right now." He closed the door leading to the top half of the house and stepped down off the stoop, keeping his gaze on Clint. "Saturday afternoon, Clint. Beautiful day. In the prime of your life. I'm sure you have other things to occupy you, but would you humour an old man and his flighty mistress Alice and walk with us a while? We wouldn't, of course, trespass too much on your time." Clint hesitated. "It would be a kindness if you held Alice's lead," Graydon continued. "I had a fall this morning and seem to have put my shoulder out." He indicated his right arm with a nod of his head; it was held stiffly at his side. "Even if I use my left arm, there is jarring."

"Of course," Clint said immediately, taking the offered lead, "It would be a pleasure. You're such a lovely girl, aren't you Alice." He bent to scratch her head and rub down her back, while she licked the small amount of skin exposed around his left ankle. "How did you have the fall?"

"Ah. I was, to use the vernacular, mugged this morning, dear boy." Graydon's voice was light and still jaunty but Clint looked up at him sharply.

"Good grief. In broad daylight? How did it happen?"

There was a minute of walking single file down the steps from the children's playground to the waterfront; Graydon waited until they were on the flat before he replied.

"I took Alice up to Glebe Point Road for a coffee at Madame Frou Frou's. Bought the Daily Telegraph on the way. Old habits die hard. A real newspaper, dear boy," he explained to Clint's raised eyebrows. "The real McCoy, not an online version." Clint snorted and Graydon gave a small smile. "After coffee I untied Alice from beside the front door and began to walk towards Leichardt Street. Three men had been sitting at the other outside table and they left the café at about the same time as me. As I turned into Leichardt, they followed and then surrounded me. They looked a bit like you, dear boy."

"What? Like me? What do you mean?"

"Oh, just that they looked Middle-Eastern, nothing more. No need to be alarmed. They had Australian accents but Iranian features. They were, I'd say, still young men. At first, I thought they wanted to acknowledge my research in Middle Eastern history. They called me Professor Audain and seemed to know a lot about me."

"But what did they really want?"

"They wanted to know if I knew where someone called Bekym Ryal might be." Graydon looked straight ahead as Clint glanced at him and slowed his pace. Alice wound the lead around his legs. "I said I'd never heard of a Bekym Ryal and one of them shoved me. I'm sure they didn't mean to hurt me but I'm not as steady as I used to be on my feet and I toppled over on the uneven ground."

Clint looked around, wondering if the men were following even now.

"I don't think they're watching us right this minute," Graydon said, "But no doubt they will approach you, at some point, or your grandfather. I wanted to warn you. I presume Bekym is a relative?"

"Yes. No-one close," Clint both lied and told the truth. He had gone cold even though it was still sweltering in the sun. He decided it was best to tell Graydon as little as possible in case the men questioned him again. They talked of other things after that over two beers at The Galley. Graydon let Clint direct the conversation.

On their return, Clint could hear Graydon talking to Alice about what they might have for dinner as he shut the other door that led to his part of the house. Lost in thought on his way to his bedroom to drop off his satchel, Clint reached out a hand to open the door and realised it was already ajar. Had he left it like that? That wouldn't be normal for him. Under the palm of his hand, the door swung silently in. The room looked untouched or, at least, it would have looked untouched to any other person. But Clint would never leave a drawer slightly pulled out in the chest of drawers; would never leave the lid of the clothes hamper askew. Could these small inconsistencies be due to Arash? Clint didn't think so; he had done a tidy up before they left that morning for the hospital. His heart hammered in his ears and his body tightened like a cello string. There was a slight noise and Clint stepped back into the hallway. The door to the apartment, through which he'd come and closed behind him, was swinging open as if someone had just slipped out.

## Chapter Three

A plea hearing for Piripi Nosi and Emma Costa was held at the Downing Centre Courts a fortnight after the events of November 8, 2019. Clint had attended in his capacity as a journalist for the online newspaper the

Sydney Saturday World; a role he had since been required to relinquish. During the two weeks since the fire at 14 Forsyth Street, Sydney's temperatures soared even higher than before and more fires were out of control, all around Sydney.

"Mrs Emma Costa, you are here today jointly charged with the murder of your husband, Mr Tadeas Costa. Today's hearing is to determine how you plead: guilty or not guilty. Do you understand?"

The small woman in the dock at the plea hearing with short brown hair and vacant grey eyes made no move to indicate she understood. The Registrar turned to her solicitor. "Ms Raine, to the charge of murdering Mr Tadeas Costa, how does your client plead?"

"Not guilty Mr Registrar."

The eyebrows of Registrar Douglas Everett contracted slightly and there was a pause while he stared over his reading glasses at the solicitor.

"Those are my instructions, Mr Registrar."

"And, Mr Piripi Nosi." The Registrar refocused his attention. "You are jointly charged with the murder of Mr Tadeas Costa, at number 14 Forsyth Street, Glebe, and with attempting to remove traces of your crime by burning Mr Costa's body."

A small murmur surged around courtroom 4.4, which was packed.

"Do you understand?"

Piripi Nosi stood with his shoulders back and his chin up, exposing the tips of the tattoo that curled up his neck, one hand gripping the wrist of his other arm, biceps bulging with the tension in his body and his eyes so wide the irises were small black pebbles in pools of white. As he turned his head towards the sounds in the courtroom, a hush and a stillness descended so quickly and so completely it was as if the onlookers had become stone or pillars of salt like Lot's wife.

"Mr Registrar, my client is unfit to plead and I request a fitness inquiry." The solicitor for Mr Nosi had risen.

The accused's head snapped around to watch his legal aid lawyer. The prison guards on either side of the accused moving an inch closer to their charge. Although Piripi was standing only a small distance away from Emma, the two were prevented from making eye contact by the positioning of their respective guards. All eyes in the courtroom were now on the immense figure of the criminal lawyer Mr Abara, his every move hinting at the power of the muscles under his well-cut suit. His black face shone, highlighting three raised scars on his forehead which looked like he had been branded. Lubanzi Abara seemed unaware of the stir his presence caused. As Australia's most well-known criminal defense lawyer, he was probably used to attention. A journalist to the right of Clint had wondered out loud what Mr Abara had seen in this case that convinced him to take it on through legal aid; certainly not a large pay day. The Registrar had nodded and set down a fitness hearing for Mr Nosi and a trial date for Mrs Costa; both to be heard by the Supreme Court. Both of the accused were declined bail and were remanded in custody to the Silverwater Correctional Complex.

"It'll be months before we know any more," Kelly said as she put down Clint's article about the plea hearing. "I don't know why, but murdering someone and trying to burn them in your backyard seems somehow more horrific than simply murdering them."

"Speaks to how even our next door neighbours could be rampant psychos." George Bakker, one of Clint's colleagues, responded, "People with weird tendencies might be lurking behind every lamppost in your street."

Kelly tittered. It was the usual Friday staff meeting in the airless room with the usual Sydney Saturday World staff.

"Let's release your story in this edition, Clint, and why don't you start on a piece for the next edition covering some of our most serious psycho killers, how many of them pleaded diminished responsibility or whatever it's called now, and where they are today? I wouldn't be surprised if Mr Nosi and Mrs Costa are found to be diminished in some way."

"Substantial impairment by abnormality of the mind," Clint interjected.

"I beg your pardon?"

"The Crimes Act was amended to change the language from diminished responsibility to substantial impairment …"

"Yes. Yes. That. And let's do a piece on Sydney's amazing lawyers. George, see if you can get interviews with Lubanzi Abara, Vanessa Raine and any other prominent criminal or family lawyers you can find. We could do a series of pieces over the next few editions about the lawyers that are helping keep us safe from the psychos hiding behind lampposts: their backgrounds, why they went into law, what keeps them going. You know the sort of thing. Make it clear that we are not asking them to comment on any current cases."

Clint wanted to do the bios of the lawyers. It was, after all, his story. He had been with it from the night of the fire. "I can interview the solicitors."

"Oh but you have enough on your plate and George is so good at this sort of thing."

George Bakker's pug face in glasses and topped with a bald head fringed like a Friar swam at Clint. George's face was screwed up in that way he had which purported to keep his glasses in place on his snout-like nose but which looked a lot like an ugly smirk. A few days later, Clint had to swallow his pride. George's articles were good.

"This is wonderful George."

Kelly's voice reached Clint from across the room. She was leaning against the divider next to George's desk and was holding printouts of his articles about Lubanzi Abara and Vanessa Raine. He'd loaded them into the newspaper's document management system earlier that day. George's head was pink and moist. If Kelly wasn't married with young children, Clint might have thought she was making a play for their colleague.

*Sitting in a high-backed brown leather chair, Lubanzi Abara is everything you'd expect of a Sydney barrister and not at all like Cleaver Greene in the TV series 'Rake', although the clients they represent might sometimes be similar. At least six foot tall, with a powerful physique honed at the gym, it would be fair to say that Mr Abara naturally intimidates the mad and the bad, as well as the simply sad. All of which he meets in his job.*

*Descended from immigrants originally from Namibia in Africa, Abara combines a distant heritage of peace-loving nomadic hunter-gathers and the experience of excelling at the University of Sydney's Law School; one of the best law schools in the world for both teaching and research. His former Professor of Criminology, Gail Mason, is tipped to be in the running for the Distinguished Criminologist Award to be announced soon, in recognition of her lifetime achievements and contributions to criminology. Her field of expertise is research into crime based on race, religion or sexual orientation; known as hate crime.*

*Lubanzi is known to represent those accused of hate murders, exposing in each case the family or gang influences, or even mental instabilities, which resulted in the alleged crimes. His clients generally do not plead guilty per se. Rather, they plead guilty with remorse, as a picture is painted of backgrounds that made them do it. They are shown to be victims themselves, open to rehabilitation and seeking a second chance.*

*What motivates this powerful lawyer to seek out and represent the underbelly of our society? Three fingers of scar tissue dominate Lubanzi Abara's enormous forehead, testament to the attack that nearly killed him when he was a student at the Law School. The perpetrators were a group of skinhead youths trying to find work, barely existing in homes of neglect and with a powerful hate of anything black or 'foreign'. Lubanzi famously decided not to press charges, opting instead for restorative justice and compassion. All of his attackers have since done time in jail for other crimes but Abara is adamant that he did the right thing in giving his attackers a second chance, even though the attack held his studies back a year while he agonisingly recovered his ability to walk and talk.*

*Mr Abara will not discuss his current representation of the young Papua New Guinean Piripi Nosi who is co-accused, with Emma Costa, of murdering Mrs Costa's husband Tadeas. "This case is before the courts and I am not at liberty to discuss it," he said.*

*At Mr Nosi's first appearance at court for the plea hearing, a fitness inquiry was requested. Depending on the outcome of that inquiry, his trial might focus on 'substantial impairment by abnormality of the mind'. If it is found that an accused did not understand what he or she was doing at the time of a crime and did not intend to commit a murder, a murder conviction may be reduced to manslaughter which generally carries a lighter sentence. Substantial impairment is a partial defense used by people suffering from a mental condition which falls just short of qualifying as insanity and is only used in some Australian states including New South Wales. In 2001, for example, Malcolm Robert Potts was found guilty of the manslaughter instead of the murder of his father following a frenzied attack with a knife. The attack was found to be due to a relapse into an early stage of schizophrenia.*

*Some courts take a more jaded view of the substantial impairment defense. In 2014, Craig Daniel Catley was found by a jury to have committed manslaughter rather than murder when he beat and then stabbed his mother to death. This decision was handed down despite the Judge making his views clear that he doubted that any psychosis the offender had suffered or continued to suffer played a very great part in the offense.*

*Mr Abara has used the substantial impairment clause effectively for previous clients including in the trial last year of Simon Ernest Barrow who strangled a woman to death while they were having rough sex. Lubanzi Abara's ability to achieve a similar verdict for Piripi Nosi, if that is the intended line of defense, will become evident over the following months.*

Feeling aggrieved, Clint didn't bother to carry out Kelly's command to research perpetrators who had received lesser sentences due to abnormality of the mind; George had already done it. Whatever he thought about George Bakker and his methods, however, the bio of Vanessa Raine was just as impressive as the piece on Abara.

*I met Vanessa Raine in her downtown Sydney corner office. As a senior partner at Sturgess, Diamond and Co, she is entitled to an office with views over Hyde Park, St. Mary's Cathedral and the harbour. She settled herself with her back to the window and its views, however, and asked me how she could help. Ms Raine has a calm and centred quality which inspires confidence. She is a formidable and highly sought after defense lawyer who has frequently been able to persuade prosecutors to discontinue criminal proceedings altogether or to accept significantly reduced charges. Vanessa has a track record of successfully defending clients, particularly women, accused of serious and complex crimes.*

*One well-known way of beating a murder charge is when the accused acts in self-defense. It has been argued, however, that traditional self-defense favours men, who are more likely to kill in the heat of the moment. For women in abusive relationships and suffering from battered women syndrome (BWS), fighting back against a violent and physically stronger partner is not an option and so they might resort to a 'pre-emptive strike'. That might involve an attack on their partner while that person is sleeping or in a docile state. BWS includes symptoms of learned helplessness in a cycle of violence. In 2015, for example, Jessica Silva was given a suspended sentence in a New South Wales court and was allowed to avoid prison after she killed her former partner who had abused her repeatedly throughout their relationship.*

*Ms Raine, her long flaming hair piled on her head and her oversize glasses dominating her pale face, was a media sensation in a case two years ago in which she defended Elizabeth Donna Meadows who confessed to hitting her former husband with the brick propping open her back door. She did not immediately seek medical assistance for him, taking their son for an outing to the zoo first and only calling for an ambulance on their return, when she found that her estranged husband was still in her house and was in a comatose state on the floor. He later died in hospital. Mr Meadows had left Elizabeth six months previously for another woman but had a habit of returning to see his former wife and their son without warning. Mrs Meadows was found to have endured years of severe and systematic psychological abuse by her husband, who exhibited a deeply entrenched narcissistic personality disorder, leaving her almost unable to function. Elizabeth Meadows was found guilty of manslaughter but, like Jessica Silva, was handed down a suspended sentence and so avoided prison.*

*Vanessa Raine is currently defending Emma Costa against charges that she, along with co-accused Piripi Nosi, killed her husband and burned his body in the backyard in an attempt to hide their crime. It remains to be seen if this case also rests on a defense of BWS. It is usual and necessary for lawyers to be given time to build their cases before a trial begins and so it will be many months before more can be revealed.*

## Chapter Four

Clint was sitting at his desk in the hot office a few weeks after the flurry of events in November 2019. He was thinking about the fire at Forsyth Street, the plea hearing, his grandfather's visit to hospital, Graydon's fall and Lou dumping him. Mostly, he was thinking about Lou, missing Lou and wishing she would contact him. A message bubble popped up on his screen from Linda at reception: *Woman here asking for you Clint. Won't give name.* For him? Was it Lou? No-one ever visited him at work. *On my way*, he messaged back. Grabbing his mobile and access card, Clint took the stairs at a run.

Pearl O'Leary was a bundle of parched denim-clad sticks perched on the edge of a plastic waiting room chair, blue chips at the end of tight fingers around a fluffy pink handbag from a two dollar shop and one knee bouncing up and down craving a smoke. She gave a nervous start as her prominent green eyes lined with black pencil found the matching green eyes of Clint's. He took her elbow, lifted her effortlessly off the seat and murmured "Let's go outside for a smoke." They were down the stairs and on the pavement within seconds, Clint's heart thrashing. He steered her down the side alley of a neighbouring building until they stopped behind a row of khaki plastic rubbish bins with brightly coloured lids.

"Mum, what are you doing here?"

She fumbled at the pink bag; reaching for something to anchor her. It was as if she was all at sea being tossed in winds that unaccountably came from all directions and was not able to look up at the stars as a guide in case she met the look in her son's eyes. Pearl found a pack of smokes and a neon red lighter in her bag and lit up with a sigh that might usually accompany sinking into a chair on the porch after a long day of toil. She smoothed the shirt on his left arm; the cigarette clenched between two fingers of her right hand, trembling with the effort of not clutching him close, her eyes fixed on his open top button.

"I." Her voice broke and she started again. "I read your article on my phone. About the fire at the Costa's house." She took a shaky inhale.

Clint was surprised she followed his career by reading his articles. He could feel the beat of his heart slowing but his throat had closed over with the effort of resisting. He wanted to lay his head on her shoulder and ask her to make everything alright, to be there for him, to make him less empty. All things he could never ask of this wasted woman.

"You have a question about the fire?"

It was the most he could manage. Clint tried to make the words friendly but they sounded to his ears like a scrape of metal on metal; two cars trying to squeeze past each other in a tight space and not managing it without damage.

"Um. Information really. Emma Costa went to high school with me and your dad. Well, Reynolds. Emma Reynolds she was then before she married Tadeas Costa. And then, when I was pregnant with you, Bekym moved out and went to live at the Costa's house for a while as a boarder, you know. Emma has always called him Become, as a joke, instead of Bekym. And then he took off or disappeared at any rate. Anyway, I thought you might want to know. She might still be in contact with him. I had forgotten her until I read your story about the fire."

The words came in a rush. Her eyes were moist now and were looking at Clint's chin. He could feel the tightness in his jaw, his back teeth hurting as they ground together, and he moved his jaw a little in an attempt to relax.

"It might be helpful?"

She was appealing to him now. It had been an opening for her to make contact and to show him she cared, to make amends somehow, to help him. Pearl ground the butt of her cigarette with the heel of her right foot in a silver plastic sandal, knowing that this was the end of something even before it had started.

"Thanks mum," he whispered and lifted an arm of lead to pull her towards him, to give her a hug. "I am glad to know."

Pearl leaned into him like the carcass of a bird, looked at him as she stroked the right side of his face with her left hand as if to say thank you, I love you, I'm sorry, then turned and stumbled away. She reached the pavement where the bright light and lunchtime crowds halted her briefly and then she plunged forward and was gone. Clint leaned against one of the plastic rubbish bins, his head in his hands, and realised that his mother had not made a single complaint nor mentioned her poor health; she had not asked him to fix some situation or drama for her; and neither had she asked him for money. His visits to see her had trailed off as he had got older because of her incessant need to take, take, take, even from her own son, as if she was a bottomless well of unmet need that no amount of succour could fill. This visit was exceptional. What did that mean?

Pearl O'Leary was the child of Irishmen as far back as Irish history could go. When she was a young girl, her wild black hair, green eyes, alabaster skin and lilting voice had captivated all who met her, especially men. Her father and grandfather, both named Paddy O'Leary and descended from Paddy O'Leary the First who arrived in Sydney in 1850, had loved Pearl with the gruff hearts of Irish labourers. They made sure she was watched over by her brothers in the school playground and gave her the tastiest parts of the stew at dinnertime. Her father, Paddy the Younger, was born just before World War II and was mercifully too young to fight. In the middle of eleven brothers and sisters, he needed to leave school at 14 to earn an income for the family. He found a job on the Yennora railway, maintaining the tracks, thanks to his broad shoulders, quiet wit and the strength of character that showed in his green-eyed stare. As his brothers and sisters grew up, married and dispersed to farms in New Zealand and the mines in Perth and up North, Paddy the Younger stayed living with his parents. His mother finally moved from faded to dead after too many children and too little attention other than her husband grunting over her at night. Paddy the Older lived on, drinking a couple of flagons a night at the Yennora Oasis Hotel or its car park if he'd gone for a piss up against the concrete wall and found his mates drinking outside. He was sometimes shouted a whiskey or two to sing *Oh Danny Boy*, which set off the entire pub.

It wasn't until 1970 when things changed. Paddy the Younger, now in his 30s, found a job in the newly opened Yennora Distribution Centre using the forklift to shift bales of wool. He had spent time with many women over the years, the first being Sheila with her dark brown hair permed and teased into a bird's nest and who sometimes visited the rail gang. She had lured him behind the smoko shed with the promise of having something to show him. Whipping off her top she pushed him to the ground, undid his trousers and pulled out his old boy. She worked him with her mouth, her dangling breasts slapping against his testicles before climbing onto him and whooping as if riding a bucking bill, urged on by the cheers of the men inside the shed. She wouldn't take any money from him, saying that the men in the gang had already paid her. He'd not settled on a woman until he met Aideen who worked in the office at the Centre and wore tweed skirts and button-up blouses that strained across her abundant breasts. She had the black hair and milky white skin that their daughter Pearl was to inherit. The name Aideen meant fire and she had a fiery tongue alright to go with the name. The Aideen of legend was said to have died of a broken heart when her husband died, which Paddy (both the Younger and the Older) thought sounded just fine.

Aideen appreciated her husband's way of saying hello as he came home from work and nuzzled up behind her at the sink. Each day she would watch the clock and wait with longing, the dinner on and the table set. With one big hand he'd lift up her blouse, expertly release her bra clasp and spread thumb and fingers across the span between her generous nipples, roughing them a little, while slipping his other hand up between her thighs. When she was wet and stifling her moans, he would take her then and there with her panties pulled to one side, even with Paddy the Older in the living room watching TV and maybe turning up the volume just a little as he reached for his first flagon and the children peeking around the door before fleeing as their father roared at them that he'd take the belt to them. With his big hands clasped around her hips he'd move her up and down, his trousers unbuttoned but held up with suspenders, until she bit down on a tea towel to suppress her cries and clutched at the sink.

Paddy the Older passed soon enough with his nose red and his trousers wet and the old house became theirs. Sandwiched between an old car yard and the main road, the brick house had been built to last by Paddy the Older's father Liam. It had three bedrooms upstairs, a front porch accessed from the hallway between kitchen and sitting room and a lean-to out the back which now housed the toilet, bath and wash house. It had at one time managed to house Paddy the Older's family of 13, although this may have contributed to so many of Paddy the Younger's siblings finding ways of leaving home before they'd officially reached adulthood. Liam O'Leary, who had built the house, had learned his labouring skills from *his* father who was the first Paddy O'Leary in the family in Australia.

The story went that, during the potato famine, Paddy the First had walked more than 150 miles from Ennis in County Clare to Dublin to find work, aged only 15. A tall man, whose stick-like limbs were caused by starvation not genes, Paddy found work as a scullery hand and deck cleaner on board a ship called The Australasia. The job didn't pay real money but offered him food and a bunk. To a man whose stomach walls were meeting, that was something. The ship left Dublin in 1849 bound for Hobart, Van Diemen's Land which soon after changed its name to Tasmania; carrying 200 female convicts. The ship laid-over at Sydney Harbour on the return trip and Paddy the First heard tales in the taverns of gold being found on the other side of the Blue Mountains. He disappeared into the hills to live off his wits with a blanket knotted around him and a handkerchief in one hand filled with salted beef and stale ship biscuits. It was later said that he could never stomach salted meat or dry biscuits again. Paddy the First found that Bathurst was teeming with men, their horses, their thirst for gold, and their need for a drink when successful or when thwarted. Hotels and inns were opening quicker than they could be counted. Paddy was given a job at the Bonnie Laddie, which paid him in board and meals. He washed the dishes and beer glasses as well as fed the pigs and chickens.

As he was throwing out the potato peelings to the pigs on his first day of work, Paddy remembered the drink his own father used to make with potato peelings. He'd need a bucket, some yeast and some molasses. Paddy the First thought on this for a few days as he watched the hotel owner and publican, the stout and whiskered Mr Alexander Warren, to gauge his general disposition towards creative entrepreneurship. Assessing Mr Warren's temperament as one that was prepared to listen to ideas, he approached his boss with the scheme of making cheap liquor using Mr Warren's ingredients and Paddy's labour; going 50/50 on the proceeds. Paddy the First had been watching the customers and could see that after three or four beers, there might be some interest in a cheaper alcoholic option. Mr Warren tucked his fingers into the armholes of his waistcoat as the boy gave him the spin. Leaning back, he rubbed his belly, which Paddy had noticed was generally a good sign, and suggested one variation to the proposal and they solemnly shook hands. Mr Warren, a shrewd man, had proposed that the cost of the molasses and yeast be deducted before the proceeds were divvied up. And so it came to pass that Paddy the First began to make real money.

Anyone man enough to fence off a piece of land out in the countryside beyond the town fringe and erect a house, was held in regard. While others were pitching their tents, fighting over the discovery of gold and then pissing the proceeds away, Paddy the First remained a teetotaller and saved every coin; he was determined to own his own land. Eventually the Governor granted him land on the route between Bathurst and the Blue Mountains. He built a fine house in brick; long, low and in a U shape, forming a courtyard for the shelter of the horses. Vegetables were grown in raised beds that clung to the footprint of the house to take advantage of every little bit of shade in the day. The entire outside of the U was wrapped in a porch with a curved tin roof to keep the glare out. He offered overnight accommodation in one leg of the U as well as a hearty breakfast to those taking their gold back to Sydney for a payday. Although he lost track of his age, Paddy the First was probably still in his 20s when he became ready for a wife.

At the height of the gold boom in Bathurst, there were pretty girls to choose from. He had his eye on Johannah with her porcelain skin, black hair, hazel eyes and a dimple in her chin. Johannah Ahern had completed a seven years prison sentence in Hobart for stealing a coat for her sick mother. Eventually she received a certificate of freedom along with a dire warning that if she ever put a toe out of line, she'd be imprisoned again. She had found a man willing, for favours, to bring her from Tasmania to Sydney at which point she gave him the slip. She now worked as a bar maid in Bathurst. Like Paddy the First, she was a hard worker, quiet, and determined. He had been watching her and had decided that she would be his wife. With no Catholic Church in Bathurst at the time, Paddy O'Leary the First and Johanna Ahern were married with little fanfare by the Governor. Liam O'Leary was born nine months later, the first of seven boys and two girls and who would go on to build the O'Leary house in Yennora in Sydney and produce Paddy the Older.

Paddy the Younger and Aideen had six children, two strapping boys first, followed by Pearl and then three more girls. At the age of eleven and ten, the boys trapped their nine year old sister Pearl in the lean-to, held her down and felt between her legs like their dad did to their mum, to find out what it was all about. Fergus gave her a Chinese burn and Sean told her they'd break her arms if she told on them. She was scared of her brothers although she wasn't quite sure why and kept her distance from them after that; only visiting the lean-to when they were not at home or if some of the littlies came with her. But school was another matter. The boys were meant to look out for Pearl at school. Their dad worried that her good looks might attract the attention of the wrong sort of boys. It all happened without warning. One day Fergus ran up behind her at lunch time, teasing-like, grabbed her book bag, held it high over her head and ran backwards as she reached for it until they were near the bike sheds, so that Sean could trip her up, his thing already out and stiff in his hand. Fergus took care of the screaming with the book bag stuffed down on her face to muffle the sound.

Although he was already wilting, Sean's plan might still have gone ahead if a teacher hadn't been roaming the grounds on duty and had come across them. If it *had* gone to plan Pearl thought, years later, and even if he had raped her again and again over the years, she would probably have kept quiet because what actually happened was far worse. Fergus and Sean were taken to see the headmaster and whipped with a cane until they cried for their mother. Pearl had been told to sit outside the office; she could hear every sound. The child welfare services were called; a tall thin man with a moustache and a large woman with a tight bun. The tall man took the boys away in his car; they stared at Pearl with hateful, red eyes that blamed her as they were shepherded past her and out to the gate. The large woman, Miss Stevens, walked Pearl home even though school wasn't out yet. She sat for a long time at the kitchen table drinking tea with Aideen while Pearl was confined to the bedroom she shared with her three sisters; two of whom were still at school. The youngest toddled around her mother's feet in the kitchen, in nappies. Her father must have been called from work because Pearl heard him entering the house with his voice raised and scared. She'd never heard him scared before. That made her feel scared too.

Pearl heard the front door open and then shut. Her mother must have let Miss Stevens out; the front door was not usually used. There was shouting. And then there was quiet. The back door opened and slammed. Pearl wondered if her father was going to the pub to sit on Paddy the Older's stool. She sat on her bed but Aideen did not come to comfort her. Her sisters came home from school, standing white and scared in the bedroom door. Pearl must have slept because when she came to, shivering in her day clothes on top of her bed and her stomach telling her she had missed dinner, it was dark. Her sisters were asleep in their beds. Pearl's investigations found the boy's room empty. The door to her parent's room was ajar and Pearl could see her mother's body under the covers shaking and crying without a sound. Her father was not there and he never returned. Pearl later understood that the shame of it had driven him wild and he had left the family, his work and even Sydney, for good. Someone told her years later that he might have gone to New Zealand. The boys were taken to a reform centre and did not return either. Aideen, picking up the pieces amidst the disgrace and the shock, never spoke to Pearl again.

From then on, school for Pearl became hell. The story about her and her brothers spread like wildfire and became tangled in the telling. Her friends shunned her and complete strangers thought it was perfectly acceptable to taunt her, often using the word whore. There was no one she could ask what it meant. The unkindness, the unfairness of children, their parents and even her own mother stung her and left her confused. Pearl became quiet to try and avoid being noticed. She had trouble eating because her throat felt like it was closed by a giant fist. She lost weight. When it came time to leave primary school behind and start at Merrylands High School, Pearl assumed life would be no better but, slowly, she began to be drawn into a small knot of friends. It started when she realised she was walking to and from school along the same stretch of the street as that skinny Iranian boy Bekym Ryal. He was as quiet as Pearl. They walked apart but together for weeks before he asked for her name. After a while a short girl with light brown curly hair named Emma Reynolds began walking with them too. She told Pearl that she didn't know her parents and had to live with foster families. She didn't say much but Pearl understood. Sometimes, there'd be a bruise or a cut lip or marks up the back of her legs from what looked like a jug cord. Eventually, the three spent time together at break times too. The legend of Pearl and her brothers became old news, rarely dug up. The three left school as soon as they could, all aged about 16, and found work.

It felt like the way things should be when Bekym got a bedsit and he let Pearl stay with him. She loved him, his quiet and gentle nature, his jet black hair and sharp jaw, and his thin body like steel that he honed with exercise. By the time they were 20 and pregnant in 1994, Bekym had found computers and religion. These, along with his manic exercising meant he was rarely home and, even when he was, his silence began to depress her. The need for kindness as her belly began to swell was a driving force behind her nagging. And so he left to live with Emma and her husband. When baby Clint arrived, Pearl gave him his father's last name but Bekym had disappeared from Sydney by then like Pearl's father before him.

The woman from the welfare agency had to force Clint from Pearl arms when he was only four years old. He'd screamed until his throat hurt, while his mother sobbed. Tendrils of her black hair caught in his fist. He was delivered to his grandfather at Wingello Street and Sunil held Clint tight to his chest, sitting in his favourite chair. He sang in Iranian until Clint quietened and finally slept. When it came time to go to school, Sunil walked with Clint to the primary school and stayed a while on the first day, going in late to his job as a Grants Officer at the Cumberland Council. He'd started at the Council in the 1980s, initially sorting and delivering mail. Clint stayed at school at the afterschool programme until 5.30 in the evening when his grandad picked him up. It couldn't have been easy for Sunil who was already in his late 50's when Clint started school.

Clint never did tell his oldest and closet friend, Arash, about being taken from his mother and Arash never asked why he lived with his grandfather. It was something Arash would have struggled to comprehend. *His* mother did not do drugs or drink to excess or let men hit her son. Arash's parents were married and Mr Esfandiari, son of the refugee Meyrzad, worked for a bank and wore a name tag. They were respectable. Bekym Ryal on the other hand, son of the refugee Sunil, had abandoned his wife and son to their fates. Clint had over the years alternatively hated his father or, with compassion, wondered what demons had driven him away.

# Thinking

## Chapter Five

The year 2020 came around and the world became focused almost entirely on the global pandemic. Nevertheless, the fire and murder at number 14 Forsyth Street with its links to the religious cult the Order of the Solar Temple, the strange happenings to Clint's grandfather and his landlord Graydon, as well as Pearl's revelations about the link between his father, Bekym Ryal, and Emma Costa, continued to rotate in Clint's mind like a cow chewing its cud. He wasn't sure why he needed to make sense of it all; maybe so that he could write a story for the Sydney Saturday World that would knock everyone's socks off and cement him as a journalist of repute. But he was a long way off that.

While Sydney was gripped by Covid-19, Clint worked from home and searched for clues on the internet. He found information about the sordid and tangled past of the Order of the Solar Temple which had a leader at one time who thought he was the reincarnation of Jesus Christ. The founding members had believed they were heirs of the medieval Knights Templar with a mission to guard the Holy Grail. There had been mass murders and suicides involving guns, poison, suffocation and fire. There were claims of links to right wing terrorists and letters left behind proclaiming that the members had left the earth to transit to the stars.

There was a website advertising the Order today. Clint also discovered two YouTube videos with recent dates showing people in white gowns marked with a Templar cross and carrying swords, their faces blurred out, chanting and listening to sermons from a man in a black cloak and hood who might be their leader. The name of any modern-day leader of the cult was not identified anywhere, however, nor was there an address. One sermon focused on the aim of unifying the Judaic-Christian religions of Judaism, Christianity and Islam through the Order of the Solar Temple. The other talked of the redemption possible to all of us if we are in trouble. If we ask for help, the video stated, help would come; we just needed to cleanse ourselves, pray and then we would be lifted up. Clint assumed that this was a spiritual reference not a literal one, although he couldn't help thinking of Emma Costa and Piripi Nosi waiting for a UFO to take them away after the fire at Forsyth Street in November 2019. Was it meant to be literal advice or was it mistakenly taken as such by some of the Order's followers?

*Dear Sir,* he had written in the contact form on the Order's website. *I am a journalist for the Sydney Saturday World and am covering a criminal trial involving two of the devotees of your faith the Order of the Solar Temple. I know very little about your religion. I would appreciate it if you were able to either direct me to information or explain the religion to me over Skype or through another app. I am keen to accurately represent your faith to my readers. My contact details are below. Regards. Clint Ryal.* His email had gone unanswered.

After many searches through the Order's website, Clint noticed a small photo of a building which might be the Order's meeting place; it was taken from the street. He felt a twinge of excitement which he quickly told himself to dampen. There was no way he'd be able to work out where the Order met just from looking at an unknown street. Nevertheless, he increased the size of the photo and examined it minutely. It showed the lower floors of a solid building made of large slabs of sandstone which were intricately carved with flowers and grapes. The windows were covered with wrought iron bars and outlined by recurring patterns of small crosses. There were double wrought iron doors which stood slightly open. A person in a long black cloak, their head covered in a hood, held out both hands in which sat a ball of red light. Clint assumed it was intended to represent a fiery sun or just fire; both were meaningful to the Order. Being of a pragmatic nature, he wondered if it was run on batteries. No street names were visible and there was no name on the building. However, Clint noticed a small part of the adjoining building in the photo. There was a sign and some words. In mounting excitement he tried to make out the words. It was impossible. A magnifying glass, that's what he needed. Clint pulled on protective gear and rushed out the house, to pound on the adjacent door leading to the landlord's part of the house.

"Graydon, Graydon, are you there?" He knew he had to be careful. They were in lockdown, for God's sake. His landlord was elderly and could easily get sick, but there was a chance he might be able to help Clint without risk to his health.

"Is there a fire?" Graydon threw open the door wearing a thick blue bathrobe, clutching Alice to his chest and looking wild. His white hair frizzled like Einstein's.

"No, no. Sorry to scare you." Clint made sure he stood well back from Graydon. "I know we're in lockdown but I wondered if you had a magnifying glass I could borrow. It's urgent."

Graydon peered at him. "Well young Clint. I do, as it happens, have several magnifying glasses. I would be happy to oblige. Wait there and I'll bring one down."

"Thank you Graydon. Thank you. The most powerful one, if that's possible. I'll only need it for a while."

His landlord nodded and shut the door so that he could release Alice without her running out onto the street. Clint hopped from foot to foot impatiently while Graydon found what he was looking for. When he returned, he was without Alice; he must have shut her upstairs.

"Here you are young man. Take all the time you need with it. There is no need to return it in a hurry." Graydon laid it on the doorstep and retreated so that Clint could pick it up. "Are you alright? Is everything going well in the flat?"

"Oh yes. Yes." Clint said. "Everything is fine. I'm just doing some research for work and there's something I can't quite make out on the internet. I thought this might help. Oh," he stopped and thought to ask, "And how are you? Is everything alright for you during lockdown?"

"I'm spiffing, thank you, absolutely spiffing. Run along then and good luck with your research." Graydon gave him a broad smile and shut the door with a wave.

Clint rushed back to his computer and peered through the magnifying glass. Yes! The sign on a delicate wrought iron fence, in front of a row of thriving boxwood shrubs, said PowWow. Plugging the name into the search engine, up came the information he was after. PowWow was a boxing gym and wellness centre in East 19th Street in Manhattan, New York. It seemed to offer commuters and busy executives a place to have a power nap, press their clothes, have a bath and recharge with a coffee. It also offered CrossFit and boxing training. And, Clint thought, the building next door to it could possibly be the place of worship for the Order of the Solar Temple. Other notable landmarks in the vicinity were the New York City Police Department, Mt Sinai Beth Hospital and two parks - the Gramercy and Stuyvesant Square. Clint thought he might explode with discovery. After a while, however, he decided he had nothing of substance about anything and needed to wait until he could explore New York in person. But, he reminded himself, it will be a while until country borders are re-opened and air travel between Sydney and New York gets running again.

In the meantime, and because Arash had talked to him about the powder keg that was Iran, Clint kept an eye on events unfolding in the country of his grandfather and his father. Earlier in the year, Iran had shot down a commercial Ukrainian aeroplane, killing nearly 200 passengers. The country said it was a mistake. People marched in the streets in protest chanting "death to the dictator." The US had killed the commander of the Islamic Revolutionary Guard Corp, Qassem Soleimani, and so the IRGC sent missiles into US bases in Iraq followed by speed boats to harass American warships in the Gulf. Clint then watched as Iran failed to adequately respond to or contain Covid-19 and let it spread rampant through the country. It was hard to get a reliable handle on the numbers infected and dead. The USA and Iran continued to make runs at each other like a couple of dogs marking their territories. At the end of April, the IRGC successfully launched a military satellite into space, close on the heels of advances in Chinese and USA ballistic missile and anti-satellite capabilities. America was worried.

Sunil Ryal decided to tell his grandson everything. He had managed to get through months of the pandemic without being infected but now, in late April, he had a fever and was beginning to have trouble breathing. This might be his last chance before he was taken to hospital from which, given his age, he was unlikely to return. The Islamic fundamentalists hadn't been able to get him, but Covid-19 might. Clint could hear the shortness of breath when his grandfather called him, and knew what it must mean.

"I'll call an ambulance," he'd said trying to sound calm but wanting to scream *no*.

"Not yet. Come. We need to talk first. Call an ambulance from here."

When he arrived, the elevator seemed to be stuck and so Clint hastened to the concrete stairwell. He had walked up the stairs many times with Sunil who had always refused to use the elevator. They would take their time so that Sunil could lean one hand against the wall and breathe. There was usually the smell of urine and meat roasting. Sunil's apartment on the fourth floor of the complex in Wingello Street off Railway Terrace comprised one large bedroom and an open-plan space for the sitting room, dining nook and the kitchen. The bathroom at the end of the hall was tiny but still managed to contain a bath with an overhead shower together with a basin and toilet. Clint had lived there with his grandfather from the age of four until he went to University but it wasn't until he was about 11 or 12 that he realised that he was sleeping in the room that should be his grandfather's bedroom while Sunil slept on a pull-out couch in the sitting.

"You must have the bedroom," Sunil had explained when Clint pointed out what an imposition he was. "Every child needs his own space to grow and dream and the ability to shut out the demands of others by closing and locking a door." His large hand had covered Clint's head, stroking it with a look of great sadness in his eyes. "I did not take enough care to give your father what he needed. I was too hard on him. I must not make that mistake again. A boy without a mother needs extra care."

"I have a mother."

"Yes. But not really. And Bekym did not at all."

"What happened to his mother, my grandmother?" the younger Clint had asked, not adding 'your wife'.

"She stayed in Iran. Ah, but it does not do to dwell on the past," he had said quickly as Clint had opened his mouth to ask more. Why did she stay? Didn't he want to bring her with him? What had happened?

Today as he raced up the stairs two at a time, Clint remembered Arash's idea that Sunil had fled Iran in 1979 as a wanted man. Clint, pulling on a face mask and disposable gloves, entered the apartment and took Sunil's hand as he sat in his favourite beige-coloured and barrel-backed chair near the window, breathing hard. Clint sat near him.

"I need to tell you why I left Iran in 1979. Why I only had Bekym with me." He motioned with his hands for Clint to be quiet and listen and he began to talk. Between coughs and deep breaths, with his eyes closed, Sunil slowly told his grandson the story he knew he'd wanted to hear for a long time.

"It was 16 January 1979. I remember that it was a Tuesday. I would normally be at work but I had taken the whole month of January off after my wife Maryam pestered me to spend some time with our family.

On that day I was at the Grand Bazar near the Shah's Palace in Tehran, known as Golestan Palace. I was with my son Bekym. It was his birthday and he was turning five years old. He was having a treat with his pedar without the women in the house tagging along; his mâdar and three older khwâhar, sisters, you understand?" Sunil took a moment to breathe heavily and to remember. "The Bazar is beautiful: colourful mosaics line the walls, it is a labyrinth of tunnels teeming with people and filled with carpets, bundles of cloth, dried fruit, produce, spices … ah the fragrance. The colours are like a field of wildflowers and the noise, ha, the noise is the din of humanity from all walks of life, people who are living, living life with energy and wonder." Clint's grandfather let his head drop back on the head rest of his chair as his nostrils flared. Clint gazed at his face which had relaxed with its glimpse of happiness. "We went to a restaurant near the section selling jewellery. Bekym and I had discussed what we would eat. He wanted a kebab and I would have the stew with rice. It was a birthday treat. In one corner of the restaurant, at a table covered in woven cloth and overlooked by an enormous sword hanging on the wall, some of my colleagues from work were huddling. They beckoned me over …"

"Your work." Clint interjected, not able to stop himself. "Where did you work?"

"I, we, worked as advisors to the Shah Mohammed Reza Pahlevi." Sunil's head lifted up. There was a fiery look of pride in his eyes. "A visionary. In little more than a generation he had led the White Revolution that changed Iran from a traditional, conservative and rural society to one that was industrial, modern, and urban. But too much had been attempted too soon and our government had failed to deliver all that was promised. And the reforms had disrupted the wealth and influence of landowners and clerics. 1978 is remembered for its demonstrations against the regime of the time, fuelled by Khomenei from his residences in Iraq or France. It was all about taking control through religion. I love Australia with its separation of state and religion; so tolerant." Sunil gave himself time to think. "In September 1978, the Shah's men had fired on the protestors. Things had gone from bad to worse." Sunil stopped again.

"Would you like a glass of water grandad?"

He nodded and Clint jumped up. After putting a cool glass into a trembling right hand, Clint pulled a kitchen chair opposite his grandfather and sat, hunched forward, his eyes on Sunil's face. After a long drink, Sunil reached down to place the near empty glass on the small coffee table nearby. He closed his eyes again.

"A few days before Bekym's birthday the Ayatollah Khomenei declared that a revolutionary Islamic Council would replace the Shah and his government. It wasn't until 16 January that I heard from my friends at the Bazaar that the Prime Minister Bahktiar had persuaded the Shah it was time to leave the country. He had flown to Egypt that morning. Khomenei would formally take charge of Iran at any moment and his men would come for us. I had not anticipated that. I was so blind; so full of my own supposed brilliance. I thought I was irreplaceable and that I would be seen to be useful to any regime, no matter who was in power. I was so stupid."

His grandfather's eyes opened and met Clint's. Sunil's gaze was straight, without defiance or defeat. There was no look of supplication although his voice pleaded for Clint to understand his ignorance, his fault. He could finally tell it how it was. "As I was hearing this, a teenage boy ran up shouting that Khomenei's men had been spotted entering the bazaar. They knew where we were which meant that they had already been to our homes and interrogated our families. Our families had already been taken. I reached for Bekym's hand and we ran. All my friends ran."

Sunil took a deep rattling breath and blew the air out through his lips as if to slow a heart that was racing with the pain of what might have happened to his wife and daughters. This time, Clint stayed still and quiet. Arash was correct; Sunil and his colleagues had been political advisors to the Shah. Human rights abuses, disappearing detainees, military responses to protests; at the very least Clint's grandfather would have had knowledge about these things and may even have orchestrated some of them. Okay, they probably weren't as bad as things that had been done under the subsequent regime but, nevertheless, some bad things had taken place.

The escape of Sunil and Bekym had involved fleeing to the Gurbulak border, seeking asylum in Turkey and living in a refugee camp for at least a year before being accepted as part of Australia's refugee quota for 1980. With no passport and no way for officials to verify who he really was, Sunil must have had a difficult time. His ability to speak a number of languages, including English, might have helped with his acceptance into Australia. He never heard what happened to the members of his family who had been at home on 16 January 1979; his wife Maryam and his daughters Jaleh, Mina and Fatemeh. But he knew that whatever had happened would have been violent and prolonged and it broke his heart to think about it.

"And the attack on you in November last year, the one that happened on the same day as that house fire and murder in Forsyth Street, and you ended up in hospital?" Clint asked him as the details of his past seemed to be drying into sharp points that stuck in his throat.

Sunil nodded. "Three men. They looked Middle Eastern but sounded Australian. They said they were ISIS. At least I think that's what they said. You know that Khomenei's Iran established the militant Hezbollah in Lebanon, inspired Syrian fundamentalist Islamic positions and was the first country to call itself an Islamic State? It provided the fertile ground for what became, eventually, the Islamic State of Iraq and Syria; ISIS in short. For all intents and purposes, the old Khomenei and the new Khamenei were and are aligned with ISIS, maybe through their

Revolutionary Guards and the Ministry of Intelligence. Anyone creating unrest, especially those with a link to the old days of the Shah with his close ties with America, will be seen as a threat."

"But I don't understand. What did they want with you? You're not leading an uprising in Iran. You're no threat …"

"Bekym." Sunil said the name as if it was too heavy to hold in his mouth; it spilled out. "I don't know, but his name must have come up somewhere. I think they're after me to find Bekym. Much good it will do them. I've tried to find him. I always thought I would see him again and tell him I love him." There was no bitterness, just sadness. "And there are protests in Iran. It seems there is a backlash against religious fundamentalism. I don't know if Bekym is involved, but maybe those men do."

"I have tried to lead a life founded on Islamic principles." Sunil gripped his grandson's hands encased in their disposable gloves. "I regret my involvement in anything that may have harmed people when I advised the Shah but I know that politics is never straight forward. Look at what the President of the United States is doing, rolling the dice with Covid-19 and accepting that more than a hundred thousand people will die. It is little different, Clint. It is little different. I have made my peace long ago with my guilt but the only reason I carried on living was for Bekym and then for you. For what other reason should I lead this grey, tiny and forgotten life of no consequence?" He was rambling now with shuddering gasps. Clint, with shaking hands, dialled for an ambulance.

Sunil fell in and out of consciousness as the paramedics strapped him into a stretcher and took him away. Clint was not allowed to accompany him or to come and visit him but was told to get tested and to self-isolate for two weeks. They would ring him with any news. When they did ring, the news was bad. Struggling to breathe for weeks, even with a ventilator, Sunil finally gave up and died. Clint was surprised he had resisted death for so long. He sat alone in his bedroom, crushed, the phone still clutched in his hand but the line dead.

## Chapter Six

Sturgess, Diamond and Co. was a great place to work; Vanessa Raine enjoyed her intelligent and committed colleagues. The firm was small enough to feel like a family while also large enough to feel like she was part of a business that was going places. Vanessa had spent the lockdown of 2020 working hard on the Costa/Nosi case. As spring announced itself outside her windows and restrictions were lifted, her partners at the firm told her in no uncertain terms that she needed to take a break before she began the sprint to the trial in early 2021. She decided to visit her parents in Canberra. She had been in regular contact with her parents during the lockdown but Vanessa wanted to see her father in person and give him a hug. He was delighted to see her. As they were eating rare roast beef with a green salad and crispy small potatoes for Sunday dinner, Vanessa asked her father a question she had been mulling over.

"Is there room for consolidating some of the pieces of intelligence and security laws in this country?"

"Why do you ask, Van?" He had grinned at her grimace. No-one but Paul Raine could get away with shortening her name to 'Van'.

"Well crikey. There are goodness knows how many laws governing, what, half a dozen primary intelligence organizations? And why do we need all those organisations anyway … the ASIO, the ASIS, the AGO, the ASD, the DIO …?"

"I take your point. But security and intelligence are complicated matters. There's internal national security as well as border security. There's military intelligence and cross-country intelligence sharing. And then there are the complexities of balancing intelligence-gathering with the right to privacy."

"So tell me about Australia's Secret Intelligence Service; ASIS. The acronym is suspiciously like the Nazi's SS, by the way, but with 'intelligence' in there somewhere." Vanessa had given her father a small wicked grin.

Paul Raine had shook his head and laughed. "You take the cake, Van. You know I can't tell you anything much about ASIS. All I can tell you is already publically available on the ASIS website. The organization mainly protects Australia from external terrorism and people smuggling. It does this by keeping an ear to the ground, making sense of international intelligence and watching social and economic trends in other countries."

"I've looking at the Intelligence Services Act which provides the framework for ASIS activities. One of the organization's functions is to … hang on," Vanesa tapped her phone and brought the law up on an app, "…obtain, blah blah, 'intelligence about the capabilities, intentions or activities of people or organizations outside Australia.' Would that, hypothetically, include oddball overseas religions that are penetrating Australia?"

Her father neatly placed his knife and fork side by side on his plate and wiped his mouth on a napkin. Paul leaned back and put his hands over the small round of his stomach. "Hypothetically?" He squinted at her, looking serious. "What is your interest in this?"

"You realise you're trying to answer a question by asking another question. You should be a politician." Vanessa mocked, worried about the serious look on his face and trying to interject some levity. "I'm working on the Costa/Nosi trial. You know the one; you will have seen it in the news …"

"Man cut into pieces and burned in his backyard," Paul had tipped back in his chair and stared at the ceiling trying to put the pieces together in his mind. "A naked couple, a religious cult and something about a UFO?"

"You've got it. Very succinct. I wish the defense was as straightforward. Anyway, I can't talk about the case, secrecy runs in our family, but that religious cult is very strange. And I have been told by my client it has its headquarters in New York of all places. If the government thought that the religion was a threat to law and order in Australia, would ASIS investigate?"

"Do *you* think it is a threat?" Paul had reached out and covered one of his daughter's hands with one of his own. He's trying to show that he's not blocking me, Vanessa thought, and decided to swallow the stab of annoyance at his question which was not at all an answer to hers. He is not exactly loquacious, she'd mused, but that must be a prerequisite for a Minister of intelligence and security.

"I don't know. There hasn't been a rash of murderous acts in Australia in the name of the Order of the Solar Temple, so far as I know. Yet. But something doesn't feel right. I can't put my finger on it."

"Well, don't worry. If there's anything in it, rest assured ASIS or the police will have it covered. Now, tell me about the firm. How is it going at Sturgess, Diamond and Co.?"

Cecilia had stood up and begun stacking plates. "Pavlova with passionfruit, strawberries and whipped cream?" she'd asked. She did not like it when her husband and daughter excluded her from their conversations.

Paul and Vanessa had both responded enthusiastically and waited until Cecilia was busy in the kitchen to resume their discussion in muted tones. The topic of Vanessa's love life was not raised. Paul and Cecilia had long ago stopped making enquiries. They had decided that Vanessa would tell them about anyone important if and when it happened, and it was pointless to pry in the meantime.

Diana Darling Croswell had joined the firm of Sturgess, Diamond and Co. through the graduate entry scheme. Diana both reminded

Vanessa Raine of herself and appeared to be her opposite. To look at, they could be sisters. Both were tall and slim, although Diana was slightly shorter, with skin kept away from the fierceness of the Australian sun and long red hair. Vanessa pulled hers back and up into piles held in place with clips while Diana left hers loose in waves that were formed around hair tongs each morning. Diana Darling, as she came to be known in the firm, had an impish quality about her and looked like she might peal with laughter at any moment. Vanessa, on the other hand, was the embodiment of professionalism at all costs with no hint of the playful. Reading Diana's application for a job at the firm and talking with her later, Vanessa had been struck by their very different backgrounds. She wondered what her parents would think about Vanessa being friends with Diana.

After leaving High School, Vanessa had studied at the College of Law in Canberra. This was a natural extension of her upbringing in Canberra and was approved by her father who had first sat on the opposition benches and was now the Honorable Paul Raine MP in charge of Intelligence and Security.

"It's a fine College," he'd told her when Vanessa had announced she'd been successful in her pick of College, "and a fine profession. It will be very nice for your mother to have you around for a few more years."

Mrs Cecilia Raine was on the Boards of numerous charitable groups and Vanessa didn't think she'd notice particularly if her daughter was around or not, but understood her father's code. It was he who would be pleased to have her around.

Diana Darling, on the other hand, had been brought up in a commune north of Sydney and had been home schooled. By the age of 18, she was dissatisfied with what the future might hold for her in the commune: partner, mother, healer, teacher, builder (if she insisted) or gardener. She had left the commune, worked in restaurants and written children's stories for the radio to make money while putting herself through the senior years of High School. Achieving a high Australian Tertiary Admissions Rank allowed her to go on to University. She chose the Macquarie Law School in Sydney and did well. Her application to Sturgess, Diamond and Co. indicated her desire to defend the most vulnerable women in need of support and noted the firm's track record in this area.

In their first case together, Vanessa and Diana Darling had defended the 19 year old Mirabelle Dixon of the charge of murdering her step-father, Findlay Thornbury. Mirabelle, undernourished and so timid that she flinched when the police or Vanessa spoke to her, had emptied her mother's beta-blockers into Findlay's beer. His heart slowed and then finally stopped as he sat in his La-Z-Boy watching formula one on the television. The family, thinking he had fallen asleep, tiptoed off to bed so not to disturb him. It wasn't until morning that they realised there was something wrong. The first responders, both the police and the paramedics, noticed a distant lack of grief from any of the family including the dead man's wife. Mirabelle's mother, as she tried to hide the bruises around her neck and down her arms, was the first suspect. When Mirabelle realised that her mother might be in trouble, she confessed. Initially, there was no obvious motive. When Vanessa interviewed her, Mirabelle insisted she thought she was playing a prank and it was all a mistake. Frustrated, Vanessa asked Diana to talk with Mirabelle as she watched through the one-way glass.

"You must be overwhelmed, confused." Diana reached across the table and gripped Mirabelle's nail-bitten right hand. "Your step-father is dead. You have confessed. I can only imagine how you must feel. Did he treat you badly, or your mum? Is it a relief that he's gone?"

Mirabelle was undone by Diana's kindness and her gentle touch. Tears trickled down her face as she nodded.

"Why don't you tell me about it? I promise you it can only make things better, not worse."

And so it came out. Findlay Thornbury beat his wife on a whim, when he was drunk, when he felt inferior and when someone laughed at him at his work in the chop shop down the road. And he fiddled with the children. He'd stopped raping Mirabelle when her periods started at age 14 and moved onto the younger children. They were scared of him, scared of life. She hated him. He was evil and her mother was powerless to stop him. She couldn't stand it anymore.

Mirabelle avoided prison with a suspended sentence but was required to live in a sheltered home for a year while attending counselling and learning a skill so that she could find work. She chose to train as a pastry chef and found her first ever job in a Sydney hotel. After their success in the case, Vanessa and Diana Darling had walked (or, rather, skipped joyfully, Vanessa remembered) back to Vanessa's apartment for a celebratory drink. Diana had never left. Since then, Vanessa had agreed in principle that they should meet each other's families but had been relieved when the lockdown prevented that. She had made some excuse about seeing her family on her own after the lockdown, but her excuses were wearing thin.

## Chapter Seven

Bian stood in the hallway listening to the husky voice of Leonard Cohen. It was accompanied by the enveloping treacle of a woman's voice and the soaring of a stringed instrument that she found herself riding. Tears glinted in her eyes. "So many graves to fill/ Oh love aren't you tired yet." She placed her hand on the handle to Clint's door, wanting to hold him and share his heart break. She knocked gently and cracked the door open as the song changed. "Suddenly the night has grown colder/The god of love preparing to depart." She slipped through and lay down next to him on the bed, hardly making a dent, and kicking off her slippers. The outsides of their hands touched as they lay together saying nothing.

The room smelled sweet despite weeks of self-isolation in his bedroom following his grandfather's death followed by months of continuing to keep himself to himself. Clint had kept the room aired and clean. He was burning something aromatic; maybe tea tree oil. The room was also very tidy, Bian noticed, there were no piles of clothes lying about like in her room. Clint was wearing a thin jumper that zipped up the front, chinos and socks as he lay on the bed staring at the ceiling. Bian had put on tights this morning under a short blue merino dress that never creased. She wore a black gauze wraparound layer over the top. Her long hair hung in ringlets around her face.

During the lockdown, Clint had worked sporadically for the Sydney Saturday World but, other than Covid-19, there was little to report. Bian had been out of work, not earning and waiting to hear if New Zealanders living in Australia would be able to get income support if they couldn't earn an income during the crisis. But she felt so privileged. The flatmates had decided to pool their resources so that all four of them could survive whether they were earning or not, and Graydon had suggested they stop paying rent while the lockdown was in place. Bian knew she'd be in a difficult position without all this support. She had only managed to get into Australia because she'd been lucky enough to be granted New Zealand citizenship after living, training and working in New Zealand for ten years. Hairdressers had been in short supply in New Zealand at one point and so the country's immigration department had made visas available to people who wanted to train in that skill. That also meant that they could eventually apply to become New Zealand citizens. Once she had become a New Zealander, the reciprocity arrangements between Australia and New Zealand had enabled Bian to hop across the Tasman Sea and settle in Sydney.

There was one thing Bian was sure of; although she was happy to visit her family in Vietnam occasionally, she had no interest in ever living in Vietnam again. Either New Zealand or Australia would be her home. If she had stayed in Vietnam, she would have been married off, like her younger sister, and expected to live in the home of her in-laws. She would have had no control over her finances and would have been expected to start producing children fairly quickly while continuing to work at a highly regimented jewellery factory in Ho Chi Minh City. Her life would have been mapped out for her according to the country's traditions. Despite the wars that had ravaged the country and the victory of the communists, those ancient traditions of reverence for family, clan and ancestors above all else, had solidified. Even before Bian had escaped, her family was thought to be not quite reverent enough, with her mother divorcing her philandering husband and returning to live with her elderly mother. Bian smiled when she thought of how tough her mother was. She had ignored what people said about her and she had started her own business doing manicures and sculpting beautiful nails. She also supported Bian in her plans to travel to another country on her own at only age 16, even though her escape reinforced the impression in the City that her family was not reverent.

As she lay beside Clint, Bian thought about the things they had in common: families affected by war or political unrest and the experience of trying to adapt to a new culture while seeped in cultural traditions that were so very different. In Sydney, they were also both now without family networks. Rolling onto her side, Bian looked at Clint. He had smooth caramel-coloured skin and green eyes. She wanted to follow his sharp jawline with a finger and smooth back his black, slightly wavy hair; maybe kiss the eyelids over those extraordinary eyes and hold him so that he could find some peace and drift off to sleep. As if he could read her mind, Clint also rolled over to face her and smiled sadly. He liked Bian and enjoyed her friendship. It was nice of her to comfort him. She put her arm over him, and he pulled her into a hug. They lay close while they talked about the pandemic, about Sunil Ryal and, eventually, about Bian's history.

"I was brought up in Ho Chi Minh City by my mother and grandmother. The city used to be called Saigon until the communists won the war. My grandparents first lived in Xom Lang, a little village in Quang Ngai province. This was during the war with North Vietnam. The village was said to be heavily used by the Viet Cong but my grandparents said they never saw any. They were farmers and lived a simple life. They had no sides in the war and cared nothing for politics. The Americans were in our country and were determined to keep communism out regardless of what we wanted. But most people didn't even know what communism was. The village of Xom Lang was called My Lai on the American maps. The US soldiers thought or pretended that the villagers were Viet Cong and so they shot 500 men, women and children. They gang raped and mutilated some of the women and even the children, burned the houses, killed the cattle and the buffalo used to till the fields and ruined the crops. Good American soldiers in the helicopters realised what was happening and helped some of the Vietnamese farmers escape to safety. My grandparents, with their baby girl, managed to get away and were taken to the city of Saigon. The baby girl was my mother. The tragedy in my grandparent's village is now known as the My Lai massacre."

"Bloody hell. What happened to the men who were responsible?"

"One soldier was later found guilty of killing 22 people and he served about four years under house arrest. No one else was charged."

Bian's matter of fact tone belied the horror of the event and how she must really feel about it. Maybe it is possible to make things more bearable by reducing them to their bare facts, Clint thought. He began absent-mindedly curling Bian's long black hair with its reddish highlights around a finger. Life was so unfair, he thought, no matter which country or which time period you looked at. There was always so much hardship and death. Clint's fingers on her hair made Bian feel both soothed and alive at the same time. She could feel her nipples growing hard and a fire growing in her belly.

"You know you speak English very well," he commented.

"You know we don't have to speak at all if you don't want. Would you like to kiss me?"

Clint laughed, the corners of his eyes crinkling. "You are also quite plain spoken. I think you are a woman who knows what she wants."

"I do," she replied. "I want you."

She lifted her lips to his and, pushing away the nagging voice in his head that this wasn't right, he lost himself in the sensual pleasure of her plump soft lips. It was a relief to stop thinking for a while, to just listen to Bian's purring moans and the wind outside the window. But later, limbs entwined under the covers and watching through the window as the sky turned dusky coloured at the edges, Clint felt he must be honest. He didn't want to hurt Bian, she was a lovely person. He stroked her arm.

"Bian."

She turned to look at him and turned the corners of her mouth down. "I think I know what you're about to say," she said resignedly. "But go on."

"Well. You are lovely. I really like you. But I'm not ready to commit to a relationship."

"What makes you say that?"

"I am in the middle of something; something involving finding out who I really am and what I really want. I'm not, um, emotionally available right now. Is that the right term?"

"Is that a cop out?" Bian sat up and retrieved her purple rimmed glasses from the bedside table. She stared at him, looking a bit stern.

Clint shook his head sadly. "I need to find my father and understand why he left me when I was just a baby. I need to reconcile myself with who my grandfather really was. He told me some truths before he died; things I had never heard before. And I need to understand how the Costa's are linked to all this."

"Who?"

"Oh, do you remember hearing about Emma Costa and Piripi Nosi? They were arrested last year for murdering Emma's husband Tadeas Costa and setting fire to his corpse in their backyard." Bian nodded, remaining upright. "Emma was a friend of my fathers. My dad lived with the Costas after he left me and my mum. I have a feeling that Emma Costa might know something."

"Like what?"

"Where he is now or even just why he left all those years ago." Clint was flooded with grief and he rolled over with his back to Bian. He didn't want her to see his moist eyes and trembling lips. How could his father leave his baby boy and never, not once, try to make contact. What sort of a man was Bekym Ryal? Where was he when his son needed him?

Bian sank down under the covers and curled around Clint's back. "And all of this somehow stops you from being emotionally available." She sounded doubtful.

Clint rolled over and looked her straight in the eyes. "Yes. It may sound strange. I don't even understand it myself. But I know I'm not here for you. This afternoon was lovely. You are gorgeous and kind and sweet; you helped bring me back to myself. But I am not the man for you."

"I can wait."

"Oh Bian. That never works does it? You're probably a few years older than me … I know what you're going to say, age doesn't matter, but … you must be ready for, and deserve, a really nice man who is there for you, wants to be with you, have children with you. I am not that man right now and I don't know if I can ever be. Please don't wait for me."

What he thought, but didn't say, was that he was also a bit scarred from his experience with Lou. He had given himself to her wholeheartedly and she had unceremoniously dumped him with a text, for goodness sake. He didn't think his heart was strong enough for that to happen again just yet, and he didn't want to get involved with Bian just because of the 'propinquity effect' when people who live or work together end up forming a romantic bond. There had to be more to it than that. Clint wanted to know he was in love through a bolt of lightning to the head and an ache in the heart. If that made him an incurable romantic, so be it. They were quiet together for a while, lying on their backs, their hands no longer touching. Without warning, dollops of rain thumped onto the roof. Clint recalled the news this morning that the drought in the Australian outback had apparently broken after three years; this must be the tail end of it. Eventually Bian got out of bed and pulled on her underwear and tights followed by her other layers. Clint admired how effortless she made dressing. She moved with grace. Wafts of vanilla soap reached his nostrils as she moved.

"Dinner time," she said showing Clint a brave face. "It's my turn to cook. I thought I'd do a green Thai curry. What do you think? See you in a bit."

"I'm so sorry Bi…" The door clicked shut just as Clint's mobile rang. It was his boss.

"Clint. It's Kelly. Lockdown's being eased. Just heard. I want Saturday's edition to be full of lockdown stories – people who've done things hard financially, those who have been on the front line of the hospitals, families who lost someone to the pandemic, and, oh yes, people who have been good sorts and helped neighbours and the elderly. Can you get onto that? I'm asking for stories from each of you; as many as you can manage." Kelly stopped talking. "Are you there?"

"Yes." Clint couldn't think straight. He felt confused and exhausted. "Stories. Right. Where to start?" He was talking out loud but was really talking to himself.

"How about your own experiences and those of your flatmates? Anyone get sick?"

"My grandfather. He's dead." Clint's chest stopped working and there was a tell-tale hitch in his voice.

"Oh great story Clint. I mean, sorry to hear that. Were you close? Writing from your heart can be very compelling."

"Right. Um got to go." He couldn't find enough air.

"Two days Clint. I'll need the stories in two …" Clint shut the call down and rested his head in his hands as he sat naked, chilly and shaking on the side of the bed, feeling small.

Clint decided to call Vishesh first to see if he was willing to be interviewed for a 'lockdown ordeal' piece. He had the idea that Vishesh and his partner Samuel (an older, kind, fair-skinned man who made buckets of money working very hard for an investment bank) would have had a fabulous lockdown making wonderful food, drinking fine wine, playing backgammon together and then going online to play cricket and bridge with their friends. They lived in Samuel's apartment in Darling Point overlooking the harbour. It took up the entire top floor of a heritage building that had been remodelled in the best possible taste and even had a library, a scullery and a temperature-controlled room for their cellar.

Vishesh agreed to meet on the waterfront below 16 Oxley Street and arrived wearing a brown oilskin in case of rain. They decided to sit on opposite ends of a bench in the early spring sun and Clint opened the voice memo app on his phone to record the interview. He hoped no one would come and sit on the bench between them and break physical distancing etiquette which most people were trying to keep in place even though the lockdown was over.

"So tell me how lockdown has been for you Vishesh," Clint opened, positioning his phone in the middle of the bench, "Have you been working from home?"

"Definitely. I've been conducting online lectures and tutorials and marking assignments without any trouble at all. It's quite straightforward to lecture on war and peace from a distance. It would be harder if I was teaching medicine or chemistry or anything with a practical component."

"So what have been the best parts of lockdown for you?"

"Ah. Wearing pyjama bottoms all day. Home cooked meals and having no option but to avoid takeaways; that has been good for the waistline." Vishesh did a little sit-down strut. "Oh and online exercise sessions."

"Have you got bored?"

"No way. There is always so much to do: books, movies, electronic conversations with friends, my novel." He grinned. "Never be bored."

"And what has been the worst thing about the lockdown for you."

"Oh that's easy; my boyfriend breaking up with me and kicking me out."

"What?" Clint reached over and stopped the voice memo. "No way. Vishesh. Oh God, I'm so sorry." He wanted to reach over and hug his friend but kept himself in check. "Why? You two have always seemed such a great couple."

"Well. Samuel got tired of my flings with women. He reckons I'm just playing at being gay and that I actually prefer women to men. We have become best friends over the years you know, not really lovers any more. I wondered if I was just falling out of love with him, it happens. But, on reflection, I think he might be right. I think I prefer women."

"Wow. That's big. How are you? Are you okay?"

"I miss Samuel and his friendship so much; every minute of every day." Vishesh's face twisted with the effort not to cry. "But the lockdown has meant we either had to stay together throughout it, which Samuel refused to do, or not see each other at all. So I moved back with my parents," he answered Clint's unspoken question. "I've wanted to call him, thousands of times, but Samuel has blocked my number. I'd say that's that."

"I'm so sorry Vishesh," Clint repeated, at a loss to know what to say or do.

"I'm okay. Going cold turkey hurt but I'm coming out the other side. My parents have been great. No recriminations, no advice, just solid love and support. I'm so lucky with my parents Clint. They are intelligent, erudite but such humble people. You know, they bought me and my three brothers up in a two bedroom apartment and they still own it. My brothers have, respectively, grown up to become a computer programmer, an engineer and a successful actor with parts in Bollywood movies."

Clint placed his right hand on his heart and gave his friend a look of concern and worry. "So how much of this can I use in my story for the Sydney Saturday World? I'm quite prepared to scrap it."

"No, no. I'd like you to use it all. Gays are people too, with all the same cares and woes. And I'd like it if Samuel and our, his, friends can see that I still care for him and them. I'm not bitter. I am so lucky to have had Samuel's love and to be able to share his life. He is quite right that I need to sort myself out. I'm just sorry I hurt him. You can print that too if you like but let's give him a pseudonym."

They walked along the waterfront, through the Bicentennial and Jubilee Parks and had nearly reached the Tramsheds before they turned back. They bounced ideas off each other about pseudonyms for Samuel (settling on Oliver) and for Vishesh (Amit, which meant friend) and then Vishesh talked about his hopes and dreams and plans. Clint let him talk, wondering if he'd ever be as far ahead as Vishesh in understanding his own heart.

Clint had decided he was not ready to tell the story of his own lockdown and the loss of his grandfather. He wondered if Graydon might agree to be the subject of his second lockdown story. Returning the magnifying glass was the pretext for banging on Graydon's door. He then then noticed, and rang, the bell.

"Are the dragoons after us young man? All that hammering and ringing; I wondered if we were at war," he explained in response to Clint's look of incomprehension.

"Oh no." Clint had the grace to look shamefaced. "Sorry. I didn't notice the bell until after I'd knocked. I have your magnifying glass to return. Thank you very much for lending it to me." He handed it over.

"Why thank you. I hope it was of some use?"

"Very much thank you. And …"

"Yes?"

"My boss has asked me to do some 'lockdown stories'; the human face of the Covid-19 suffering and all that. I wondered if you'd agree to be one of my stories. We could give you a pseudonym if you like, to give you some privacy."

"My dear boy, what a fabulous idea. Happy to help. Come in. Come in. I'll put the kettle on. We can keep a little apart if you like, to avoid the bugs, you know, and I have some hand sanitizer there by the door if you'd like to use it as you come in and go out." Clint obliged.

Graydon carefully opened the door to the sitting room with one foot forward, to keep Alice contained. She was jumping up at the inside of the door woofing merrily as she heard her master and a visitor approaching. "Down Alice, get down. Good girl." Graydon patted her back in big sweeps and then fondled her little face under the chin. Alice abandoned her master to rush at Clint who laughed and, crouching down, hugged the little dog tenderly.

"Tea or coffee Master Clint? Sit, sit. Make yourself at home."

"Coffee, thank you. Milk no sugar."

The sitting room was salubrious. The word jumped into Clint's head and felt right. The room and the things in it felt respectable and respected. The furniture was antique and anything with upholstery was done in either pale blue or deep red textured cloth. The art was grand. One painting looked like a Picasso, maybe even an original, and another that looked like the splatterings of a Pollock. Silver frames decorated photos of people and places, sitting on the upright piano and lined across one wall. A shallow blue bowl on a small table held an arrangement of flowers. Clint sat in a tub chair near the French doors opening onto the balcony. The view from up here across Rozelle Bay and the Anzac Bridge, with Johnstons Bay stretching beyond, was stunning. Today, the sky and water reflected deep blues and a flotilla of yachts was boldly under sail, released from the standstill of lockdown. One door to the balcony was open; the spring sun flavoured with the fresh smell of the neighbouring eucalyptus trees and the brine from the bay. No wonder his landlord spent so much time at the window.

"So have you been lonely in lockdown?" Clint asked, after they were both seated and sipping their coffee from small pottery mugs.

Graydon thought a moment. "I don't believe I have," he decided. "As you get older, your life narrows anyway to books and music, the radio, and the news and movies on the television. So lockdown is not much different from ordinary life for me. And I got out for a daily walk with Alice along the waterfront, saying hello to people from a distance. In fact, life in lockdown was not that dissimilar to life any other time. I enjoyed having my groceries delivered," he grinned. "And I am lucky that I am not in a rest home or needing daily help to look after myself." He offered Clint more coffee and topped up his own.

"Do you use Zoom and other apps to talk with friends? Or do you stick to the phone."

"Oh yes. I love Skype and Zoom. My ex-colleagues from the University forced me to learn how to use them so that I could join in conversations about the meaning of life, new developments in the Middle East, the impending apocalypse and so on. I have lovely friends all around the world to talk to."

His words reminded Clint that Graydon had been a professor in Middle Eastern history. "So do you keep abreast of what's going on in the Middle East today, in Iran in particular?"

"Oh yes dear boy. Iran is a fascinating country. The past desire for self-determination became mixed with fundamentalist religious views. Now we have a younger generation wanting a different sort of self-determination that is more tolerant, but vested interests will not want to let go. I fear that the fundamentalists will react with force in the not too distant future now that the pandemic is coming under control. For some groups of people to flourish, others need to be subjugated. It is the same in capitalist countries although they can mute that effect by offering welfare for the poorest of the poor and allowing all people to vote in the full knowledge that many or even most, don't bother. And in dictatorships, which is what Iran is of course, well …"

"Who is subjugated in Iran?"

"Women for a start. Most are treated as if they are slaves. Think of the economies that flourished due to slavery; there was America of course and England which grew wealthy off the back of shipping slaves to America and owning the cotton and sugar plantations there. And Nazi Germany used the free labour of Jews and blacks and gays and gypsies to shore up its economy. Iran is very clever when it comes to women. A token handful of conservative women have been allowed onto the Iranian Parliament. What else; let me think. Well, there is some discrimination in Iran against the Sunni Muslins, because Iran is largely comprised of Shi'ite Muslims, although that seems to be under control at the moment."

"If you don't mind me saying, you seem to have an equally scathing view of capitalist governments as you do of dictatorships."

Graydon twinkled his blue eyes and beetled his wiry white brows at Clint. "Something to do with old age I suspect. I have become less passionate about ways to improve the world and less sure of the motives of people who seek to improve it."

They agreed that Clint could publish Graydon's real name; he did not feel the need to hide behind a disguise. Clint's article talked about how many older people still have so much interest in the events of the world and how their ideas and thoughts keep them company. As well, they can offer so much to the people with whom they connect by phone or video-conferencing. For this reason, being in lockdown was not a trial for Graydon or, possibly, for many older people. Kelly was thrilled with both of Clint's stories. She could see that different market segments could be interested in these stories and that building a readership across the demographics would be helpful if the Sydney Saturday World was to stay afloat.

"More," she enthused. "Clint, I want you to keep going. Put your feelers out and come up with more and varied stories."

It occurred to Clint that he could do a story on how people in prison were coping during lockdown. He wasn't quite sure how to go about it but wondered if calling Vanessa Raine might be a way in. It was also a way in to Emma Costa, of course. He pushed to the back of his mind that he might have an ulterior motive for getting in touch with Emma's attorney.

Vanessa was delighted when she heard who was on the end of the phone.

"My client has actually asked to talk with you. This is serendipitous. I did a search of your name and found that you work for an online newspaper. I was thinking of ringing the main number there to try and track you down."

Clint was very glad she hadn't. The last thing he needed was Kelly hearing what he was up to; she'd probably insist that George Bakker do the story instead.

# Chapter Eight

"I'm Clint Ryal. Bekym's son."

He looked at Emma sitting behind a sheet of Perspex and at a distance from him. There was a guard in the room and Emma's lawyer Vanessa Raine was there too. It had taken months to get to this stage since Clint's conversation with Vanessa. After the Covid-19 lockdown the prison had re-opened very slowly to visitors and, for the first few months, only to immediate family. In the intervening months, he'd produced many lockdown stories for Kelly and managed to stay on her good side. The demand for lockdown stories was receding and Clint had already been diverted to fresh stories for the Sydney Saturday World, when the opportunity to visit Emma Costa and meet with the Prison Warden finally arrived in November. He decided to go ahead. Clint had asked Vishesh to accompany him because he didn't want to go alone and Arash was, again, not answering his mobile or emails. Vishesh offered to drive them in his mother's Toyota Corolla and pick Clint up on the way.

"Come in, come in" Clint had called through the kitchen window. "Just getting ready."

Vishesh was wearing faded blue jeans that hugged his legs and a tight black T-shirt under a black jacket made of the thinnest leather. He had replaced his onyx pyramid earrings with black rings. The fragrance of musk accompanied him into the kitchen. He looked sexy as hell. Clint smiled to himself as he laced up his shoes. His friend must be on the prowl now he was no longer living with Samuel. Who did he think he might meet at the prison? Wise to take a jacket though, Clint thought, I'll take one too. Although it's a hot day, the prison might be cold.

"Meet my flatmates. Megan, Bian, this is my friend from University, Vishesh Devi." Megan was pulling on her police jacket and preparing to leave for work. Shane had already left for the day. Today was Bian's day off from the hair salon.

"Hello, hello." Vishesh shook hands with Megan and then held Bian's for slightly longer than would be usual, Clint thought. She, in return, was eying Vishesh with interest. Clint felt a twinge of annoyance and jealousy; he wanted to say "back off" to Vishesh. Why did he ask him along anyway? Clint could have caught a bus or an Uber. Stop it, this is irrational, he told himself. I told Bian to find another man. We haven't been intimate since that one time ages ago. She is not doing anything wrong.

"I'm ready, Shall we go?" He felt confused and put out.

They stayed mostly on Parramatta Road then turned right into Silverwater. The prison was not that far from the suburbs of Guildford and Yennora. Clint looking back over his shoulder; his mother and her family, his father, his grandfather and even he himself had roots around here. The complex itself was huge and some of the buildings were very old. Beautiful mature trees provided shade and a sense of calm. Sparrows and wagtails were scratching for something to eat under the trees, bouncing around without a care. Parts of the complex looked like a park. Clint hadn't anticipated that a prison could look like this. One area was under construction, surrounded by wire fences. Clint was glad they had come early for their booked visit because finding a park wasn't easy and they had to wait for someone to leave.

The visitor room in the Women's part of the Correctional Centre was small and, once he, Vishesh, Vanessa and Emma Costa were seated, watched over by a standing guard, it felt full. They all wore masks and thin plastic gloves. There was a smell of boiled cabbage and disinfectant. Clint began to feel hot; his forehead broke out in sweat and his neck felt clammy. He took off his jacket and sat in his thin grey shirt with the sleeves rolled up. Clint could feel his hair, which had grown longer and increasingly wavy during the lockdown, sitting damp against his temples. Ms Raine had said on the phone that Emma had recovered from the Coronavirus but she was still waxy white with dark rings under eyes which looked too big for her face. The regulation orange jumpsuit she was wearing did not do anything for her complexion. She stared at him.

Since the initial plea hearing for Emma Costa and Piripi Nosi was held a year ago, a fitness hearing had taken place for Piripi Nosi. Following the pictures publically released of Mr Nosi in court with his wild eyes, some people had commented on talk back radio and in print that he had to be mad, didn't he? But he had been found by psychologists to be fit to stand trial. Like Emma, he had then entered a plea of not guilty. Both lawyers for the accused had sought separate trials, but that option had been denied. They had been successful, however, in being granted a Judge-only case because the considerable negative publicity about the case might make it difficult to find an impartial Jury and, anyway, because the complexity of issues expected to emerge were not able to be easily or objectively assessed by a Jury. This decision had acted on reporters like a rabbit dangled in front of a greyhound; they wanted to know more. While avoiding the palaver of a Jury trial, it did mean that everything would rest with the sole person assigned to the case, His Honour Malcom McNeill. Emma was now awaiting the joint Supreme Court trial which was set down for early the following year.

"You asked to see me?" Clint prompted. He wanted to sound like a kind doctor doing his rounds but his voice sounded impatient and defensive. He suddenly wasn't sure why he was here and already thought it was going to be a waste of time. His head drooped, not meeting Emma's eyes.

"I knew your father. He was a good looking man. You look a lot like him. Much more like him than your mum."

Clint's head came up; he had momentarily forgotten that Emma had been friends with Pearl as well as Bekym.

"We all grew up together in the 70s and 80s you know. Pearl and I mostly just wanted to leave school and our families. They weren't very nice."

She paused, her eyes gazing into the distance of the past, somewhere over Clint's right shoulder.

"Bekym was different to us. He lived with Sunil, your grandfather. He was lucky. He had a loving home."

There was no hint of bitterness in her voice. It was the same sort of matter-of-fact tone that Bian had used when she talked about the My Lai Massacre, Clint thought, as if the past was locked behind a Perspex shield just like the one between them right now. Emma pulled down the mask covering her mouth and nose and took a sip of water from a white plastic tumbler. Clint scanned the room looking for water; he could do with a drink. There was nothing obvious and no one was offering.

"Bekym went to the mosque. Just with Sunil to begin with. Then when he was older he went all the time on his own. Pearl and I thought he must be very religious and tried to ask him about it. But he wouldn't tell us anything. Bekym never said very much. When he found a job and a bedsit, Pearl asked him if she could stay with him. Her mother had started hitting her, you know. Bekym said yes because, well, he was kind. Pearl had the pull-out bed and he slept on the floor. Even then he spent his evenings reading that Muslim Bible thing. All this time, Pearl was trying to catch his attention. I don't know what happened, Bekym never said, but I think she might have drugged him so she could sleep with him. He never did drugs or even drank alcohol, usually. And he told me he didn't want to have sex with Pearl or anyone he knew right then. When Pearl told him she was pregnant and he was the father, he was so angry."

Emma shivered. Clint reflected on Pearl's manipulation of Bekym and thought it sounded exactly like something his mother would do.

"When Bekym was angry it was like nothing I'd ever seen. Anger is shouting and hitting, usually. But he went quiet. So quiet and closed off. Like ice. He left the bedsit and came to stay with Tadeas and me for a while but you could see he wasn't really there. He was often out at night courses or at the mosque or was working. When he disappeared I thought he might have gone back to his country. Iran, wasn't it?"

Her eyes flicked to the guard and then to Vanessa, before resting on Clint.

"Now I am not sure about this, but when Piripi came to live with us …"

Emma stopped for a moment, putting her hands over her mouth as her eyes filled with tears. The tears sat in large drops on her lower lashes, falling each time she blinked. She took her hands away and carried on in a constricted voice.

"He showed us some YouTube videos of the leader of the Order of the Solar Temple because we were interested in the religion, you know. You couldn't really see the leader because of the cloak and the big hood, but there was his voice. I thought I knew that voice; quiet but in charge, every word placed as if he was thinking about what to say before he said it. Later, I wasn't sure."

Emma pushed a strand of hair behind her left ear to stop it falling over her face.

"Piripi told me that the leader is based in New York. I don't know how he knew that. Probably found something on the internet." She stopped.

Clint kept his eyes focused on Emma and she looked straight back at him. "Why are you telling me this?"

His mask was making him itchy around his nose and he screwed up his face to try and get rid of the itch without touching his face.

She dropped her eyes to her hands which Clint now noticed were twisting in her lap.

"I saw you. The night of the fire. My Tadeas is dead and I'm in trouble. I want to do something good before I go to the electric chair."

"No, no." Vanessa put a hand on the Perspex barrier as the tears slid silently down Emma's cheeks. "We have no electric chair in Australia. There is no death penalty here. Remember? And, anyway, you are pleading not guilty." Vanessa put emphasis on the last two words. "We talked about this, remember?"

Emma didn't seem to understand or maybe she simply wasn't listening to Vanessa. Clint wondered how true it could be that Bekym Ryal was based in New York and leading a religious cult. None of it made sense. The guard was leading Emma away.

"Thank you for telling me Emma. Good luck with your trial," Clint called after her, making an effort to be polite. He felt sorry for her.

She stopped and looked back. "Gin," she said with a sense of urgency. "Gin, Gin." And then she was gone.

They were allowed to remain in the visitor's room for a while so that Vanessa could talk to Clint about how it had been for Emma during the lockdown and her illness.

"She must have picked the virus up off a guard or another inmate rather than from a visitor," Vanessa told him, "Because you are the only person to have visited her so far as I know. They managed to contain the virus to just one wing here, which is remarkable really once it had found its way in, and Emma was one of those who were the most sick. It was touch and go for her for a while, actually, even though she was very well looked after right from the first signs of the disease taking hold."

Clint's eyes flicked up from his notebook and met Vishesh's. Vanessa had taken that moment to check her phone. Clint was thinking that a lot of effort had been expended to keep someone alive who was on trial for murder and who had the threat of life imprisonment hanging over them. Vishesh's raised eyebrows indicated he was thinking something similar. Did that duty of care, that level of care, reveal something merciful about Australia and demonstrate the notion that someone really was considered innocent until proven guilty? It was something philosophical and maybe even wonderful that he could mull over in his article.

Vanessa Raine said goodbye, putting her hand on her heart to avoid shaking hands with them and walking out of the small room looking thoughtful. She had some new information about the religious cult to think about while building the defense of her client. Clint and Vishesh were shown into the office of the Warden for the Silverwater complex including both the men and women's units and the prisoners on remand as well as those sentenced. Alec Sherman stood up to say hello, raising his hands in a gesture of welcome instead of shaking them as they entered. He motioned them to settle at a round table to one side of the office.

"How can I help you Mr Ryal?" He was polite. "You work for the Sydney Saturday World I believe?"

"Yes I do. Thanks very much for agreeing to meet with us. This is my colleague Vishesh Devi." They inclined heads. "The Sydney Saturday World is doing a series of articles about how people coped during lockdown. I hoped to be able to write about how a prison coped with the pandemic. It can't have been easy."

"I have read your previous articles on the topic, Mr Ryal"

"Please, call me Clint."

"Clint. Very nicely done. Very human."

Alec Sherman's youth had taken Clint by surprise. At a guess, the Warden was in his early 40s, with smooth slightly sun-kissed skin and with hair that had receded so far back at the temples that he now gave it a Number 2 all over. The slight paunchiness under his chin and around his waist gave a sense of comfort in his role and his life. His immaculate suit, purple satin tie and palest blue shirt of quality cotton made Clint feel unkempt. He had a warm smile and soft calm voice. He clearly took things in his stride.

"Well, we have had a pandemic plan in place since the SARS scare in 2003, so it was straightforward to roll it out, but Covid-19 was different to SARS and that created its own problems."

Clint waited. The Warden began talking through the issues they'd found and the measures they'd put in place.

"Covid-19 was so very contagious and so fatal to people with other conditions; we have a lot here whose systems are weakened by drugs and poverty. We were worried what might happen. First, we tested everyone and then continued to do so weekly. Second, we required all new prisoners during the year to remain in self-isolation for the first two weeks of their stay. Third, all guards were tested weekly and were (and still are) required to wear disposable gloves and masks at all times. We also made sure that the same groups of guards have worked together in work-bubbles, if you like. Fourth, we kept the inmates to their own bubbles and staggered their meal, work detail and break times to ensure that the bubbles did not overlap. Cleaning took place between the use of facilities by each bubble. Fifth, all inmates were provided with masks, hand sanitizer and gloves. We have had fewer than 50 cases here and no deaths."

"And visitors?"

"Ah yes. You have visited Mrs Costa today I believe Clint ..."

He doesn't miss a trick, Clint thought.

"... so you will have seen the Perspex shields we have installed in each of the visitor rooms. And everyone in those rooms has been and is still required to wear masks and gloves. The rooms are disinfected between visits. During the worst of it, visitors were unable to visit at all. As you can see, visits are underway again now. We re-started visits for immediate family members only to begin with but have broadened access now, as you know. The car park was probably full. How was your visit with Mrs Costa?"

"Very good thank you sir," Clint had no intention of talking about that. "And the mental health of the inmates under more confined conditions and with no visitors? Are you able to talk frankly about that?"

Alec Sherman nodded his head in understanding of the question. "We put in place the advice from the federal government. One key element was to provide daily updates to all prisoners, even if there wasn't much to say, and to give them an opportunity to ask questions. They were worried about what was happening to their families and friends as much as themselves. We did daily updates for three months but we've scaled that back now that the worst is past. We also allowed more access to phones so that the prisoners could contact their loved ones in lieu of visits and we disinfected the phones between uses, obviously. A key aim of the regular updates was to provide hope; we didn't want the inmates to feel that things were out of control. I think we succeeded. There were actually fewer behavioural incidents than usual during the lockdown period."

This man is good, Clint thought, as they took their leave. No wonder he rose to be Warden at such a young age. Back at the car Clint threw his jacket on the roof and leaned against the hot blue metal, looking back at the complex. "The information for the article was useful," he said, "although Alec Sherman had sanitized it, no pun intended, but the rest of it from Emma ... What a load of old rubbish and what a waste of time."

Vishesh beeped open the card doors and slid into the driver's seat, "Whew it's hot in here. Let's get the air con going."

Clint bucked up. "Why the hell would my father lead a manky religious cult from New York if he was so devoutly Islam? None of it makes sense. And what the hell was all that about 'gin'. She's a bit thick and batty as hell if you ask me."

"Well, I've thinking about that. I wonder if Emma was saying Jinn J-I-N-N not Gin G-I-N."

"What do you mean?"

"Jinn are a part of the Islamic faith. I believe they are generally demons. Do you think that this Order believes in Jinn? Maybe the Order is a type of Islamic faith. Didn't you say you saw some information about the cult trying to join up the Judaic-Christian faiths? Emma and Piripi have both talked about Mr Costa being possessed by a demon. Maybe he was possessed by Jinn; is that possible?"

The car hummed for a while. "Why did Emma want to tell me all of that though?" Clint said at last. "What good is it to me? Emma thought the voice of a hooded man in New York, being broadcast from an unknown location, sounded like my father did 25 years ago. I've watched the YouTube videos myself although I, obviously, don't know my father's voice. There was nothing I could see that might indicate it was my father. I couldn't even tell what the man's accent was. It's all a bit far-fetched though, don't you think? Thanks for the lift and for coming with me. Would you like to come in and have a coffee?" They had reached 16 Oxley Street.

"Sure. Thanks." Vishesh's long legs unwound from the car and he bounded up the steps. Clint remembered Bian. While they were away she had made a lemon cake which they devoured with yoghurt and a pot of coffee, sitting out on the porch overlooking the water.

"This is blissful," Vishesh stretched out his legs and tilted his head to the sun.

"Aren't you lecturing today?" Clint asked.

"You want me to go?"

"No, of course ..."

"You caught me at a good time," Vishesh cut over him, grinning. "Lots of papers to mark but lectures are finished for the year."

"Oh, what do you lecture in?" Bian asked.

Clint took a pile of plates and the yoghurt inside. After tidying up in the kitchen he stepped into the hall just as a peal of laughter in two tones came from the porch. Clint decided to return to his desk in the bedroom to work. First he tried Arash on his mobile. It went straight to voice mail, again. Clint didn't bother leaving another message. Clint really wanted to talk to him. Nothing made sense without his point of view. But he kept doing this; disappearing without any warning. It was like his friends didn't really matter to him. He didn't know the address of Arash's new apartment and there was no response to email, messages or calls. Even without him, though, Clint felt compelled to forge ahead through the fog of his confusion to try and unravel the mysteries of the Costas, the Order of the Solar Temple and his father.

Clint got his next story to Kelly within the deadline and, as anticipated, Kelly was mad. Just when he thought she was coming round to him.

"George should have done that story, you know it, Clint. He's the one with the connection with Vanessa Raine." She had rung him within minutes of receiving the story.

Clint had no intention of telling Kelly that Emma Costa had actually asked to see him and that the planets had simply aligned. The story he was working on was one which would need to wait to be revealed; the time was not right.

"Let's talk about it when you're back in the office tomorrow."

## Chapter Nine

"Coming through," Megan carried a hot plater of nachos to the dining room table, weaving through the bodies. They were having a dinner to celebrate the almost-end of 2020. Megan and Shane were planning to celebrate Christmas with family in Perth and Bian intended to visit her mother and sister in Vietnam. This gathering was an opportunity for the flatmates and friends to celebrate together before they went their separate ways for a few weeks. Bian had invited Vishesh to the gathering. Clint had hoped that Arash would be able to come because he'd been answering emails recently, but Arash had responded that his firm was sending him to America for work now that the borders were partially open. Clint had asked Graydon if he'd like to join them, instead. The dining room-cum-sitting room felt full even though there were only six of them standing, milling around, talking. The French doors were open onto the porch in the hope of attracting any passing breeze; it was going to be another hot Sydney summer.

The theme for the dinner was Mexican and so Clint was wearing a Mexican hat purchased from a two dollar shop in Glebe. Megan and Shane had offered to do the cooking if Bian and Clint did the shopping. They all pitched in for the cost. It had felt a bit awkward shopping at the supermarket in the Tramsheds, just like a couple. Clint and Bian had avoided each other for weeks and, when forced to be in the same room, had been polite to each other in an exaggerated sort of way. It had felt brittle. Clint wondered if Megan and Shane had noticed. If they had, they hadn't said anything. Anyway, Vishesh seemed smitten by Bian and was round at 16 Oxley Street every few days; he was becoming a fixture. Clint assumed Bian had said nothing to her new man about her tryst with Clint and he certainly wasn't intending to say anything. Vishesh was his friend and he wanted it to stay that way.

"Where are you spending Christmas this year Clint?" Vishesh sidled alongside Clint holding a small white plate laden with corn chips and nachos smothered in melted cheese.

Clint had been wondering the same thing. It was the first holiday period of his life without his grandfather. The Islamic faith believed that Jesus was a prophet of God rather than the son of God so Muslims did not celebrate Christmas, but Clint and Sunil had taken the opportunity on December 25 each year to have a meal and a nice day together. Clint had often wondered what Pearl did on Christmas day but had never asked. He could not spend time with his mother anymore and did not want to put ideas in her head that might start something he did not want. "I might just go for a long walk and cook myself a curry for lunch," Clint responded.

"Would you like to come to my parent's place on Christmas day? Being Hindu, we don't celebrate Christmas in any religious sense any more than Muslims do, but we tend to get together for a meal at lunch time. I can assure you it will be curry and it can be fun. There are a lot of us, as you know, and so my parent's apartment quite quickly becomes chaos. Nieces and nephews make that inevitable." Vishesh grinned.

Clint beamed. "Thank you." He was grateful. Truth be told, he didn't really want to spend the day alone feeling sad about his grandfather. "That is kind of you. Would your parents mind?"

"My mother told me to ask you. She said she won't take no for an answer."

"So you're not going to Vietnam with Bian to meet her family then?"

"Not invited." Vishesh grimaced, looking self-pitying. "I would have loved to go but Bian feels it's too soon. She needs to warm her mother up to the idea of an Indian boyfriend. Would you like some nachos?" Clint helped himself off his friend's plate.

"Vishesh," he asked before popping a loaded corn chip into his mouth, "Would you be up to an adventure, a holiday if you like, after Christmas, with me? I have an idea forming."

"That sounds mysterious. Keen to know more at any rate."

"Graydon is sitting all alone," Clint noticed. "I should go and spend some time with him. Talk later about the adventure."

Their landlord was lounging in a tub armchair that had stuffing escaping from the arms. He was gazing with faraway but still twinkling eyes through the open French doors at the towering palms and fragrant eucalyptus stepping down to the waterfront. The palm fronds were imprinted against a blue background. Clint was reminded of his grandfather sitting in his favourite barrel-backed chair by the sliding door to the balcony in the sitting room of his apartment in Wingello Street. He wondered if Sunil's contemplations out of the Wingello Street window were about Iran and the people he'd left behind.

"Young Clint, I've been thinking about our talk a while back about Iran. Are you still following events in the country?" Graydon asked, as he raised his glass of red wine and saluted Clint.

Clint grabbed a stool and pulled it closer to the tub chair. "Definitely."

"Well, as we predicted, the second half of 2020 has seen significant unrest in Iran. It is in turmoil. I anticipate a crackdown by the fundamentalists soon."

Clint took a deep breath. "Graydon, I've been meaning to ask you whether as part of your study of Middle Eastern history you became familiar with the religions in the region."

"Oh yes, dear boy. Yes. The rise of Islam is a part of history. It is a religion that meets the deep-seated needs of many Arab people. Religious beliefs can so easily be manipulated by those in power, too, and that consolidates religion as integral to history."

Seeing Clint's look of inquiry, his landlord placed his empty wine glass on a small table and carried on.

"If you were a dictator, wouldn't you want to unite your people by creating an enemy; the infidel, for example, people who do not believe in the God in which you believe? Then wars can be fought in the name of religion when they are actually about power and territory and natural resources such as oil. As a dictator, it is so much better for your people to be fighting an external enemy than to be feeling restless about how you rule a country. Look at Margaret Thatcher. She became an unpopular Prime Minister making huge social and economic changes in Britain and creating significant unemployment as a result. And then the Falkland's

War came along to unite the seething masses of discontent against an external enemy. The PM was voted back in for another term."

"I see what you mean. Um. I have some questions about Islam for a case I'm following."

"For your newspaper?"

"Pardon? Oh, yes. It's a story for the Sydney Saturday World. Shall I get us another drink first?"

Clint poured Graydon a red wine; it the New Zealand Pinot Noir Bian had chosen at the supermarket. He grabbed himself another can of Tooheys. As Clint returned to his seat, Megan appeared with a bowl of guacamole and another of corn ships for the nearby coffee table, smiling at them as she rushed back to the kitchen. Graydon helped himself and Clint stood up to load up a corn chip with the delicious pale green dip too.

"So I'm trying to understand the role of Jinn in Islam. Do you know anything much about Jinn?"

Clint had re-read the Quran looking for the role of Jinn but chose to pretend he knew little. He wanted to hear what Graydon might have to say.

"Well yes. Jinn were a fixture even before Islam came along. They were absorbed into Islam, just as pre-existing beliefs have been absorbed into other modern religions. It's a technique used to make a new religion more acceptable, a marketing tool if you like. Jinn are mentioned in dozens of verses in the Quran which tell us that they were created from fire and will return to fire. They are mostly considered to be demons or bad spirits that can either look like a human or can inhabit a human to make them do bad things. Why the interest in Jinn, if I may ask?"

"I'm covering the trial of Emma Costa and Piripi Nosi for the alleged murder of Emma's husband back at the end of 2019. The trial date has been set down for March 2021, which is not far away, and so I'm trying to prepare." He was stretching the truth but Clint didn't think it mattered. If Kelly heard, however, she'd have his guts for garters. She really wanted her bright-eyed boy George Bakker to follow the trial. "The Costas and Mr Nosi followed a religious cult called the Order of the Solar Temple. And there is a possibility that they believed in Jinn, too. Have you heard of that cult?"

"I do recall that cult. It was popular in the 1990s, if my memory serves? It met the needs of people who wanted to believe they were special, hmm, reincarnations of the Knights Templar or some such. Members killed themselves or each other in mass apocalyptic events? The founders, from what I read at the time, were intelligent, highly manipulative and also deranged because they believed their own hype. In the end, it looked like they had been in it for any cash they could fleece from wealthy believers as well as ready sex from female believers. Gosh, has the religion risen like a phoenix out of the flames and started up again?"

"It's possible. But I'm struggling to see the connection between that weird cult and the Islamic conviction that demons called Jinn exist. Do you have any thoughts about that?"

"Well, it would be pure speculation, of course," Graydon scooped dip onto a large corn chip, "But the Order believed in an antichrist, did it not, and the demons of the Islamic faith are on the opposite side to God so are similar to antichrists, so it might not be too much of a stretch for a religion to equate the two. Especially if the leader of a cult had been Islamic or at least knew the Quran. As we've discussed, religions borrow from each other and from earlier beliefs and mythologies."

"The tacos are ready," Shane announced. "Shall we eat at the table?"

The group gathered with appreciation and Vishesh made himself busy filling water and wine glasses. From behind her purple rimmed glasses and long fringe, Bian watched Vishesh's every move. Clint thought about the Costa/Nosi case. He had not heard from Vanessa Raine again. He wondered how the preparation for the trial was coming along and what the defense might have up their sleeves. Clint also questioned if he had started off on a wild goose chase. Were there really a link between the Order of the Solar Temple and Islam? Was his father somehow involved? And did his father really have anything to do with either the unrest in Iran or the Forsyth Street murder? How did it all join up?

On the day that Clint and Graydon ate Mexican food and discussed the Order of the Solar Temple, Vanessa Raine and Diana Darling Croswell finally visited Summer Time together. They hired a compact dark grey Suzuki Baleno for the two hour trip so they could avoid the frustrations and close encounters that would accompany public transport and set off at 8am. Vanessa drove feeling a bit giddy with the freedom of a holiday and the prospect of coming out as gay for the first time, and to strangers. She hadn't even allowed herself to know it before she had met Diana Darling and it was only now, driving and looking straight ahead, that she was able to tell Diana this.

"Wow Vanessa, that's huge. I knew you were private but I had no idea that you were secretive. Being reluctant to meet family makes sense now." Diana reached over and placed a loving hand on her thigh. "I love you. Thank you for loving me too. And thank you for letting me and my family 'in'."

"In?"

"In to your life, heart; just in. And maybe we can share who we are and what we have with your parents sometime soon." It was really a question, but Diana had made it sound like a statement so that it was less threatening. Vanessa left it at that for now.

Diana Darling's parents and two of her sisters in their late teens, one carrying a baby, were waiting to meet them at the gateway to the commune. Vanessa parked the car just inside a wooden arch proclaiming 'Summer Time' in yellow paint. She steadied herself before opening the car door. Diana's mother, who asked to be called Petal Wild, took Vanessa in a long slow hug. There was a dreamy quality about her as if she was focused inwards rather than out. Diana later told her that Petal meditated a lot and was very mellow. There were slightly awkward hugs from Diana's sisters, Caro and Rosie, and a bear hug with Gerry Croswell who was wearing a blue embroidered kaftan, bare feet and a long beard. Vanessa was given baby Len to carry as they walked up the hard earth pathway to the main building. Len was wearing a cloth nappy and a sunhat. His tubby legs and the rolls of fat around his middle were smothered in sunscreen. The child didn't complain at all about being handed to a complete stranger as the three sisters led the way, arm in arm. Chickens wandered past, pecking around their feet. Len snuggled into Vanessa's neck and clutched at her hair. She fell instantly in love and wrapped her arms around him as he nodded off.

 The meeting house looked like an enormous yurt; round, cream-coloured and with a dome-like roof. Against the wall immediately opposite the doorway was a huge fireplace which curved with the building. To left and right were long curved tables and benches. Vanessa was encouraged to poke her head into an adjoining outhouse containing the kitchen. Bread was baking in pizza ovens, wood-burning stoves were being stoked in preparation for lunch and a number of people were preparing food. A kettle on one of the Aga was steaming. Once Vanessa and the family had settled, Gerry disappeared into the kitchen to make tea. He emerged with banana cake, an assortment of cups, a teapot steeping dried leaves that smelt pepperminty and a clay pot of honey with a wooden honey dipper shaped like a beehive on a stick.

 Caro and Rosie answered Diana Darling's questions about partners and work on the commune and which cabins they now occupied. Caro was sharing a cabin with three other teenage girls while Rosie, who had become attached to a man called Thomas, was sharing a cabin with her lover now that his wife had left the commune ("stormed out" Rosie said with a mischievous smile); Len was their child. Caro preferred working outside in the gardens and Rosie was now one of the carers in the crèche so that she could be with Len during the day. They were both bronzed and long-legged in shorts and T-shirts. Vanessa felt pasty white and overdressed in flared trousers stripped in black and white and a short black blouse made of sheer silk. The outfit helped to keep her cool in the rising heat but, on reflection, she could have chosen something else. Petal Wild sat next to Vanessa and took her left hand, almost absentmindedly.

"Watch out," Diana Darling grinned, "Mum can read auras. She just needs to touch you to feel your vibe."

"Ah." Vanessa watched Petal's eyes droop as if concentrating on a voice inside her head and then open wide again. She smiled serenely.

"Nice," she pronounced. Vanessa realised she had been holding her breath and let it go with a rush.

"I've passed?" she asked Petal quietly.

Petal simply smiled again.

"So how long have you and Gerry lived here, Petal?"

"It must be about 25 years now. We came when Diana was about Len's age." They both looked over at Len sitting in Rosie's lap and curled against her stomach, their breathing rising and falling in unison as he slept.

"What was here when you first came? Was this main building here? The sleeping cabins?"

"There was nothing here at all when we came. The land is part of a farm that belonged to a couple who wanted to share their good fortune with others in a communal way. They owned about 1,000 acres and carved off ten acres for the commune. They already had planning permission for many of the structures you see here today and just needed people to pitch in and build them."

Vanessa could hear a past tense. "You say a couple 'owned' the land; they don't own it now?"

Petal glanced at Gerry and then to Diana who was listening. "The couple have now both passed and the land has been left to their three children; they have decided to sell the lot, including Summer Time. It is going on the market next month. The children have asked us to leave once it is sold."

Diana Darling moved to sit on the other side of her mother and put an arm around her. It was clear to Vanessa that this was news to Diana. Petal patted her oldest daughter on the back. "Nothing to worry about yet. It may take ages to sell and, anyway, the new owners may be happy for Summer Time to stay where it is. We've always provided the big house with vegetables, eggs, goat's cheese, honey and pork. There are a lot of advantages to the owner of letting us live here."

"And if they want you gone from their land?" Diana asked.

"Ah well. We'll cross that bridge if we come to it."

The finality in Petal's voice had closed the conversation down for now. Gerry had said nothing all this time, sitting very still and staring at his hands resting on the table which were steepled as if in prayer. Vanessa met Diana Darling's eyes and knew they were thinking the same thing. How on earth would her parents, sisters and baby Len survive in the big bad world away from this sanctuary? Would they cope in a too-small council flat in a Sydney suburb that sat drugged in the heat of a wasteland, and treated like layabouts and scum? This was an unexpected turn of events and Diana looked worried.

After that they took a tour of the vegetable beds full to bursting with fresh produce and irrigated with a drip system from the nearby stream that must have been a real job to lay down. Hives stood in a multi-coloured row to the North on a rise near a stand of evergreen tea trees. A large area of land had been fenced off with mesh wire behind which clusters of white-bodied goats with brown faces and ears, topped off with small curved horns, could be seen munching on legumes.

"Oh look." Vanessa pointed to a fenced off area further down the slope where a dozen pigs were roaming.

"Those are Kune Kune pigs." Diana Darling stood beside her and took her hand.

"They are gorgeous, all different colours, and huge."

"I love them too. They lead a very happy life."

After that they needed to spend some time with the pigs and Len woke in time to pat them. Vanessa and Diana left the commune before lunch because Petal and Gerry had chores. Diana Darling drove on the way home.

"You are quiet." She glanced over at Vanessa who was leaning back in the passenger seat with her sunglasses on, feeling drowsy. "Are you alright? Thank you, by the way, for coming and meeting my family. You have no idea what that means to me."

"I loved meeting your family. Thank you for taking me." She reached over and rested her hand on Diana's shoulder. "What an idyllic place to grow up but so sheltered. Real life would be such an intruder there." She sat up straight and rubbed her eyes under her glasses. "Is there anything we can do to help Summer Time retain the land? Do they have a contract with the original owners? Do they have a lawyer?"

"All very good questions," Diana Darling said grimly. "It's lovely of you to want to help. I'll talk to mum and then let's see what we can do, if anything."

"Do they have phones there?"

"They have only one; a landline in the kitchen. They use it to order supplies and for emergencies. I'll call her tomorrow shall I?"

Vishesh and Clint were doing the washing up. The party had been a lovely idea and the Mexican food was tremendous.

"So," Vishesh prompted, "Is this a good time to talk about your plans for our big adventure?"

"Oh yes. Well, now that international travel is possible again, with some restrictions of course, how about we take a trip to New York after Christmas?"

"What? Are you mad? It will be the coldest month of the year. New York is the seat of Covid-19 in America and flare-ups are still happening. It's a bloody long way and think of the cost." Vishesh stared at him, puzzled and worried that his friend might have lost his marbles.

"That is all true. However … but you can't mention this to anyone, not even Bian. Promise you will keep this a complete secret?"

"Keep what a secret?"

"Promise first and then I'll tell you."

"Aargh. Alright then. Promise."

"I think I might have discovered the headquarters for the Order of the Solar Temple in New York. I'd like to visit and see if my father is there."

"Good grief. You're planning to walk up and knock on the door of a wacko religious cult which supports, or at least has supported, torture, murder, mass suicide, and other looney stuff including a belief in UFOs? And what if your father tells you to bugger off? What then? It's a lot of money to spend on a day-trip to New York."

"That is a risk I have to take. Can you afford the return airfare for yourself? I'll pay for mine, obviously, and I can pay for our accommodation, meals and any transport while we're there. I've been saving. I've got a passport. I've booked a place to stay. I just need to apply for a visa and I've held off booking a ticket until we'd talked. I'm almost all set. I have a few questions for my father and, if he is there, 'bugger off' won't be an acceptable answer." There was a resolute look that had settled on Clint's jaw and in his eyes. Vishesh was torn between a desire to laugh and total admiration for how balmy Clint was.

"You're on," he said after a few moments of thought and once he'd finished scrubbing a pan and rinsed it out. "Let's do it."

"Remember, complete secrecy. You promised."

"It'll be tough," Vishesh said laughing and shaking his head. "I'd love to share with the whole world how completely nuts you are. But," he raised a hand to stop Clint's protests in their track, "A promise is a promise. Mum's the word." He returned to the sink. Clint stacked plates into the dishwasher, grinning.

## Chapter Ten

Diana Darling squeezed Vanessa's hand as they unbuckled their seats belts and waited to disembark at Canberra. Jingle Bells began replaying over the speaker as people collected up their presents for loved ones. It was Christmas Eve and Vanessa and Diana were spending Christmas 2020 with Mr and Mrs Raine. Their tickets back to Sydney were booked for late afternoon the following day; Christmas day. A single night was the most that Vanessa thought she could manage.

"It won't be a relaxing or fun break. I, we, will be on trial. Our Christmas break will start once we are back in our apartment," she'd told Diana.

Diana had smiled at that. She loved it when Vanessa said 'our'. To her, that made them a couple whether Vanessa's parents liked it or not. She was also feeling very proud of Vanessa. Although property law was not her thing, Vanessa had gone out of her way to understand Summer Time's legal position and whether the commune-dwellers could be evicted under the law. The findings were positive. Summer Time had signed a lease for 100 years with payment of one dollar a year. Vanessa discovered that the property laws of New South Wales state that if a lessee does nothing to contravene the terms of the lease, then they cannot be evicted from the land during the term of that lease even if the land changes ownership. The new owner can offer to buy the lessee out of the lease but the Summer Time residents weren't interested in that. The deceased's children were not thrilled about the law but there was nothing they could do about it. Pearl and Gerry were about as happy as a mellow couple could be. Diana Darling had glowed with pride. Her lover was smart and caring. Diana felt was so lucky.

Paul Raine gave his daughter a long hug and then shook Diana's hand. Vanessa had emailed only that she was bringing a friend. Paul's mind had jumped to a boyfriend ("about time," he'd thought) but Cecilia had taken the idea of a 'friend' literally and so had made up two bedrooms. Vanessa and Diana both climbed into the back seat of Paul's car and Diana caught up Vanessa's hand to kiss it. "Ah, so that's how it is," Paul Raine thought and allowed himself a quiet chuckle. Cecilia was going to have kittens. Her husband was looking forward to the show.

"So Diana, are you a lawyer too?" Paul asked from behind the wheel.

"Yes I am sir. I work with Vanessa at Sturgess, Diamond and Co. It's my first year."

"Please, do call me Paul. The law is a great profession in my opinion. People will always need lawyers. They'll continue to buy and sell houses, for example, and crimes will continue to be committed. The pandemic revealed that, didn't it? Did you hear about that small group of people who decided to burn down cell phone towers during the lockdown? People trying to call for an ambulance could not get a signal. Someone died as a result I seem to remember reading. *They* sure needed a lawyer."

"And what about that man who knew he had Covid and who wheeled a trolley around a supermarket spitting and coughing on people!" Conversation flowed after that: the trouble people got themselves into; what made people tick; how Paul and his parliamentary colleagues had managed to keep working at a distance during the lockdown. Vanessa settled back comfortably and let them talk. She felt happy; it was the sort of happiness that wells up, bringing with it a few tears. She was with the two people she loved the most and both were on her side. They would be there beside her when she was confronted by Cecilia. It would be alright.

"Mum, this is Diana Croswell. Diana Darling, this is my mother Cecilia."

As soon as she had said it, Vanessa had the urge to explain that Darling was Diana's middle name but then decided not to. Her mother stiffened and glanced at Paul who had his head in the car boot retrieving the single suitcase the women were sharing for their overnight stay; he was grinning from ear to ear. Cecilia was wearing a fitted paisley-patterned dress with the hemline at her knees and with three-quarter length sleeves. She worked out and looked toned and tanned. She'd taken off her apron to welcome them. Her salt and pepper hair had been permed and sprayed into stiff curls and her nails filed and buffed to a pearly shine. Her lipstick was an immaculate muted shade of beige that matched her pumps. "First impressions," Vanessa could hear her saying in her head, "are so important" and she grinned too.

Diana was shaking Cecilia's hand and saying how nice it was of her to allow her to visit at Christmas, and should she put the presents under the tree? Diana was wearing some of Vanessa's faded jean shorts that were too large for her and so slipped down her hips, teamed with a pink top that stretched tightly across her bust and exposed her cleavage when she bent over to take the suitcase from Paul. She was wearing pink sneakers with no socks and her long red hair was artfully messed so that she looked like she'd just climbed out of bed after a passionate encounter. Vanessa was wearing a short 1950s dress in an off-the-shoulder pattern that exposed her white shoulders and long white legs, and drew attention to the ancient flip-flops on her feet. Neither she nor Diana had put on makeup. It was too damn hot.

Paul drove off to park the car in the garage and the group moved off the front step into the cool of the townhouse. Diana's immediate impression was of lots of glass, the colour white, and no curtains on the windows. The house overlooked the Molonglo River and it was only a short drive over the bridge, Cecilia explained, for Paul to get to his office in Canberra's Capital Hill. She placed their presents under a two-foot high sparkly white tree which stood on a white marble table. They had agreed to spend no more than $20 on any present causing Vanessa and Diana Darling to get highly creative: a window sticker of President Trump for Paul to put on a side window of his car and a book for Cecilia called My Mum: Style Icon which was on special at only $12. Vanessa had bought Diana the Ladybird Book of the Zombie Apocalypse, which was right at the top of the $20 budget, but Diana was keeping her present to Vanessa a secret.

"Would you like to dress for dinner and put your case in, um, your room?" Cecilia asked, "And then we can have cocktails. Vanessa can show you where to go Diana."

As they climbed the stairs, Vanessa felt her body start to shake with mirth. She managed to get into the bedroom, throw herself on the bed and stuff the pillow into her mouth before she exploded with laughter.

"Oh my God," she said at last sitting up and wiping away her tears. "What have I brought you too?"

"They are lovely well-meaning people Vanessa," Diana sat next to her on the bed and grinned. "Yes, okay, dressing for dinner took me by surprise …"

They both laughed again and collapsed into each other's arms. As they found clothing suitable for dinner, Vanessa thought not for the first time how different her life had been to Diana Darling's while they were growing up.

On December 25, Clint felt grateful again that Vishesh and his family had invited him for lunch. He had woken that morning on his own in 16 Oxley Street and been revisited by the loneliness and terror of his grandfather dying and leaving him alone. Vishesh's mother called out to him as he arrived at their open door. She was wearing a deep red and gold sari and was standing in the kitchen at the end of the hall, directly in line with the front door. He assumed she was trying to find some cool air. An Indian love song played beneath the squeals from the children in the sitting room and the shouts of men in the master bedroom where they were watching a re-run of cricket on the television.

"Thank you so much for having me Mrs Devi," he said, bending down to kiss her on the cheek and looking for a place to put down a dozen beers. Vishesh indicated a spot at one end of the bench and grinned at him from where he stood in only shorts and sandals, cutting meat into small chunks. His hair was slicked back and a gold chain hung to his well-toned abs. Today, he had no earrings in; perhaps in deference to his mother. Even so, he looked like a movie star.

"Hey Ryal."

"Do you think we will have enough food?" asked Mrs Devi looking at the basins and platters standing on every surface. She was short and well-rounded and had a sunny face that matched her disposition.

"It'll be a close thing," said Vishesh in a serious and worried tone. "But we could always ring for takeaways if we run out."

"You are a very naughty boy," Mrs Devi said with love in her voice as they laughed.

"This looks amazing," Clint said surveying the counter tops. "What are we having?"

"Okay." Vishesh pointed to each dish as he named it. "Vindaloo, malai kofta, biryani, dahl and mughlai chicken. Onion bhaji. Rice. Papadums. Chutney. Salad."

"That all sounds wonderful. What can I do to help?"

At that moment there was a shriek and a wail from the sitting room. "Would you mind keeping an eye on the children Clint?" Mrs Devi asked as she moved over to the pantry on the other side of the kitchen. "The men are ignoring them and the girls have disappeared."

"They've gone for a smoke," Vishesh whispered to Clint as he moved towards the door.

"I heard that," Mrs Devi raised her voice. "They are bad girls and will break their mother-in-law's heart."

The mayhem of a large family having lunch in a small apartment was wonderful to Clint. Having been an only son and grandson of a single mother and solitary grandfather, he had never experienced so much joy, noise and complete freedom.

"You are very lucky," he said to Vishesh afterwards as he washed the dishes and his friend dried them. They were becoming a good team in the kitchen. Vishesh's brothers had all gone home, taking their wives and children with them. Mr and Mrs Devi were taking the opportunity to sit on the sofa and doze for a while in front of a Bollywood movie.

"For my family?" Vishesh was reading his mind. "Yes, I am lucky. I have great parents and decent brothers. And they all accept me for what I am."

"What's that?"

"A bit queer," Vishesh chuckled. "So," he became serious, "All set for operation New York in just over a fortnight? Got your visa?"

"I'm all set, except for a really warm jacket. I plan to do the Boxing Day sales tomorrow to see what I can find. Want to come?"

"Great idea. I'm all set otherwise too. I've even started packing to see how little I can get away with taking. I reckon the less we are hampered by luggage the better, don't you? Then we could just take our bags on the plane and avoid a wait at the carousel. And so," he had a sudden thought, "Was your boss okay about you taking a week off in January? Last thing I remember, you were worried about asking her."

"Well, she was mad as all hell. I'm now officially unemployed."

"No. Bloody hell. Can she do that?" Vishesh put down the bowl he was attempting to dry with a very wet towel and looked at Clint.

"Well. Not really. I could challenge her but post-Covid-19 is a tricky time and so she only has to say she can't afford me and I'd be out on my ear anyway. Last one in and all that. Also she's given me three month's paid notice but said not to come back into the office, so I don't have to work out my notice." Clint stopped scrubbing clean a large bowl in the sink and looked at his friend. "The reality is that I did not enjoy working for Kelly or for the Sydney Saturday World and I just haven't got it in me to fight to get reinstated there. I plan to be careful with the money and decide what to do next while I'm on the flight back home from New York. Apparently Sunil left everything to me in his will, too, so I need to consider what that means for me once probate is finalised." Clint regarded Vishesh. "Maybe I'll retrain. I don't know. I am waiting for inspiration. Failing that, I'll get some career advice when we're back."

"And now, the last present."

Diana Darling had been in charge of handing out the presents after the turkey lunch. They had risen late and then lunched late, starting first with tiny mouthfuls of canapes involving miniature curls of salmon on kale chips, dollops of crabmeat on puffs of pastry, and tiny squares of wholemeal toast holding an asparagus and blue cheese mixture, all washed down with Pol Roger Brut Champagne which was served by Paul.

"Apparently this is the same Champagne served at Harry and Meghan's wedding, as well as William and Kates, so all we need now is a wedding," Paul had chuckled as he raised his glass to his daughter. She shook her head and wagged a finger at him.

The turkey was magnificent. It was succulent, stuffed with oysters, dripping in gravy and served with a radicchio salad with sour cream. There were shingled sweet potatoes rubbed with harissa and parsnip confit with pickled black currents.

"Mum, you are an extraordinary cook," Vanessa said as she laid down her knife and fork. "I wouldn't know where to start."

"Yes Cecilia," Diana agreed, "I cannot remember ever eating such magnificent food."

Cecilia glowed and brought out the desert: individual eggnog cheesecakes mounded with cream and dusted with dark chocolate flakes. With cups of coffee in hand, they had then moved to the sitting room to unwrap the presents. Diana, being the youngest, had been tasked with handing out the presents. Cecilia had given them a sewing kit and an aroma therapy oil diffuser. It could have been worse, Vanessa thought. Paul had given them an organiser bag for carrying electronic cords and charges and an iced coffee maker; both of which they'd use. Diana deliberately kept back her present for Vanessa until all the others had been unwrapped. They still had an hour to fill in before they needed to start out for the airport to catch their flight, when Vanessa was finally allowed to pull open the bow on her present from Diana; there was a small handcrafted sandalwood box inside the cheap Father Christmas paper. Vanessa grinned. This looked like it had come from Trade Aid. Inside the box lay a smooth circle of burnished rose gold, holding a diamond solitaire in a white gold setting; it was nestled on a bed of white satin. Its twin lay next to it.

"These are gorgeous Diana," she said, stunned. "Although I think you'll have to go to the bottom of the class for not sticking to the $20 budget."

Diana, kneeling in front of her, picked up one of the rings. "But maybe I'll go to the top of the class for loving you so much that I cannot imagine living without you. Vanessa, my darling, will you marry me?" She slipped the circle of gold onto the ring finger of Vanessa's left hand.

Tears began to slide down Vanessa's face. She took a moment to compose herself before replying "Yes, of course, oh yes." She got to her knees and pulled Diana Darling close for the longest kiss.

Paul said loudly, "Oh how wonderful. Congratulations to both of you. That's marvellous, isn't it dear?"

Cecilia made a sound as if she was choking and clutched at her heart, falling into the nearest chair. Waiting until her daughter and fiancé had pulled apart and were kneeling, beaming at each other, Cecilia said in a quiet controlled voice, "Get out of my house. I will not stand for it. You are no daughter of mine." She ran from the house in her high heels without her purse or keys and letting the front door slam behind her.

# Knowing

# Chapter Eleven

It was freezing. They stumbled off the plane at John F. Kennedy International Airport into a crisp temperature of one degree Celsius, in front of the huge terminal. It was 7.30 in the evening after a trip that had taken more than a day and a night. Having never been anywhere but Sydney, the enormity of what he was doing hit Clint the moment he stepped onto the tarmac in New York; a place so foreign he could have been on the moon except that most people here did at least speak English which you probably couldn't expect of moon-dwellers.

"You alright Clint?" Vishesh spoke through a gap he'd left in the hood of his jacket which was pulled tightly around his face.

"Sure. Just thinking about moon-dwellers."

Vishesh glanced at him again and Clint thought he was grinning. He seemed to understand, even though this was probably less overwhelming for him than it was for Clint. Vishesh had at least travelled around the world to University conferences as well as to India with his family. Clint was a novice. They followed a man's outstretched and pointing glove to a shuttle bus which would take them to the terminal. The temperature in Sydney would be 40 degrees Celsius right about now, Clint thought. He wondered if he had brought enough warm clothes.

It took more than an hour to walk through the terminal and get through customs, pulling their cases behind them. Vishesh had a small black hard-shelled case. Clint had bought a type of sports bag on wheels with a handle. Being two brown-skinned young men they created some interest at customs so there was extra examination of bags and clothes, a sniffer dog, questions about their intentions while in New York, a request for confirmation of their address while staying and close scrutiny of their passports. Clint had to suppress the strange feelings of guilt he experienced when anyone in authority questioned him. He didn't know why he felt guilty; there was nothing to feel guilty about.

Equally, however, he had no intention of mentioning his father, a weird religious cult called the Order of the Solar Temple or a Sydney murder. He and Vishesh had agreed that their reasons for being in New York for five days, if anyone asked, were to take a well-earned break after a hard year and the loss of a beloved family member to Covid-19. And if people wanted to assume that they were lovers; that was fine. Who cared? As well as the strange feeling of guilt, Clint also felt a simmering rage that they were being treated like criminals just because they were young brown-skinned men. It was a feeling he knew he needed to repress if he didn't want to be beaten up or thrown into prison. The unfairness of the situation, combined with their helplessness to do anything about it, felt scary.

Their single-room Airbnb was near Grammercy Park and East 19th Street. Although the room was tired and cramped, it opened onto an outdoor courtyard and had everything they needed including a bed and a convertible sofa as well as two electric blankets which they kept on all night. A sleep, shower and a takeout breakfast restored Clint's spirit of resolve which had flagged the night before. Although the morning was cold, the day was clear and sunny and was expected to be fairly warm later on. In fact, every day of their stay was forecast to have similar weather. Clint felt blessed as he and Vishesh sat at the wrought iron table in the courtyard in their Kathmandu jackets, which were all they could find in Sydney in the middle a heat wave. Vishesh wore a down-insulated bomber jacket and Clint a jacket lined with merino wool with stitched waterproof material on the outside. They sat drinking Starbuck coffee and eating breakfast burritos. Vishesh had called his family to report their safe arrival while Clint had gone in search of breakfast. When he returned with a bag of food, Vishesh conveyed Mrs Devi's good wishes. Clint had become an honorary member of the Devi family since Christmas day when he had earned kudos by eating the hottest curries, playing hide and seek with Vishesh's nieces and nephews and helping with the mountain of dishes.

"There's a Thai, two hamburger joints, a steakhouse and a pub all just up the street." Vishesh was checking out the local offerings using Google maps on his phone. They had bought American sim cards at the airport to avoid the cost of an Australian Roaming package and had accessed the Airbnb's wireless internet. "What's the plan for the day Clint? What do you want to do first?"

"Good question." Clint gathered up their packaging from breakfast. "It's just after 9am New York time on a Saturday and I don't have a clue about when wacko religious cults open their doors. I suggest we march right up to the building, check out if there are any lights on and push the bell. When someone answers we can ask them if they are at the headquarters of the Order of the Solar Temple and if they know Bekym Ryal." There was a considered pause and then they both laughed at the sheer stupidity of this idea; there was a hysterical edge to their laughter. "When that fails, I think we might have to do a stakeout, like the Police do, only we will be a bit conspicuous without a car to sit in. But we could take turns wandering up and down East 19th Street and keeping an eye on what is going on." Clint stared at the sky for a moment. "It is possible that someone may not appear before evening."

"Or at all," Vishesh supplied.

"True. So we need a Plan B. I did a person search using the online White Pages and there is a B. Ryal living at 81 Olive Street in Brooklyn, over the other side of the East River. There is nothing to say it is my dad, or that the address is current, and there is no phone number but we should check the address out. So the question is, should we split up or should we do a stakeout together at East 19th Street today and again on Sunday and then check out Olive Street together on Monday?"

"I reckon we should stick together, don't you?"

"Okay. Probably for the best. And then if Plan A and Plan B both bomb out there are a few other Ryals in New York we could follow up. That would be Plan C for Tuesday and Wednesday and then we fly out Wednesday night." Just a moment ago, five days had felt like a long time to fill in. Now, it didn't feel long enough. "Oh, and is there anything you want to do while we're here?"

"Hell yes. When are we going to fit in trips to the Statue of Liberty, the Empire State building, Grand Central Terminal and the 9/11 Memorial Site?"

Clint raised his eyebrows. "Okay, let's make a plan." Fair enough, he thought. All work and no play made Jack a dull boy and Vishesh had spent all that money on the airfare. It was fair enough that he wanted to see some of the sights. There was a knock at the front door to the apartment just as they had decided on their plans and were grabbing day packs to take with them. Clint's heart thumped loudly and he could feel his blood pressure rising. He and Vishesh shared a glance. Who the hell could that be?

"Who is it?" Clint called, his hand on the door knob, peering through the peephole. He could see very little; whoever was out there was standing to one side.

"NYPD. Open the door."

Shit. Was this really happening? With a panicky look shared with Vishesh and the realisation that they had no option, Clint opened the door. A small black boot was inserted into the doorway followed by a woman with thick blond hair pulled back in a ponytail. She glanced swiftly at Clint with eyes of blue ice before sweeping them around the remainder of the room and taking in Vishesh standing still with his hands up. Behind the woman stood two enormous men, shoulder to shoulder and dressed in blue police uniforms. All three had guns trained on them.

"Jesus Christ." Clint stepped back in the small space in shock, scraping the hard heel of his shoe down Vishesh's shin and stamping on his foot. Vishesh yelped and pushed Clint forward. As he fell towards the policewoman there seemed to be enough time for many things to stampede through Clint's brain including the thought 'I'm dead,' closely followed by 'she is gorgeous' and a renewed feeling of hysteria. He expected the gun to go off and for it to be classified as an accidental death. He'd seen that happen many times in the movies. Instead, the policewoman stepped back, her gun still trained, and Clint fell with a thud. His head hit the wall. Next thing he knew, the woman was pulling his arms behind his back and rasping on handcuffs before pulling him to his feet. The group moved into the room, shutting the door and pushing Clint to sit down on the edge of the bed. The woman motioned for Vishesh to turn around so she could handcuff him also, making him sit next to Clint. The two men continued to train their guns at their heads.

"I'm Detective Lilla Adams," the woman announced. "These are Officers Kelly and Sipowicz. We'd like a chat."

She pulled out one of the two dining room chairs in the room, turned it around and straddled it so that she was leaning with both arms across the back, surveying them. Without moving his eyes, Clint took her in from her black booted feet, her muscly legs spread in dark grey trousers cinched with a black belt around a tiny waist, and a fitting white top with a V neck under a short grey jacket that flared from the waist. This was definitely a detective's uniform, Clint thought; it's not how a beat cop would dress. Detective Adams had holstered her gun. A black and gold badge on the right hand lapel of her jacket reflected the light when she moved. She was young and fit with curvy lips and sharply defined eyebrows. Her hair was a shade of blond Clint had heard referred to as honey. It was parted to one side and pulled back tightly to keep it off her face. She wore gold stud earrings and a thin gold chain around her neck holding a tiny pearl. Her eyes were chips of turquoise under water and were staring at him. Clint knew that he was in trouble and yet all he was aware of right now was the heat from Lilla Adam's body mingling in the air with his and his heart thumping madly as if it wanted to burst out of his chest to join hers.

"Clint Ryal and Vishesh Devi, we are here to ask you about your intentions while you are in New York. Five days. You've come a long way for just five days. Are you planning to smuggle drugs into America or back to Australia? Is that why you are here? Or are you planning terrorist activity?"

Vishesh moved imperceptibly beside Clint. He was feeling some of that powerlessness and annoyance at their treatment that Clint had felt back at the border.

"If you know our names and our address while we are here, you will also know what we do back in Australia. I teach at the University and Clint is a journalist. Do we look like drug smugglers or terrorists?"

Clint could hear the edge in Vishesh's voice and noticed that, even sitting down, he was tall and imposing with a profile that said don't fuck with me. The word smouldering came to mind. Detective Adams presumably heard the edge in his voice also.

"Keep calm. Don't do anything stupid or you will be in a world of trouble," she warned. "I know all about you. I also know that Clint is the son of Bekym Ryal, a man I am searching for, so if it's all the same to you, I'll be the one to ask the questions."

Clint's heart gave another leap. He loved how authoritative her voice sounded with that rolling American accent. And she had information about his father.

"I have never met my father," Clint said calmly, trying to bring the temperature in the room down a notch. "He left my mother before I was born. An old school friend of his, a woman currently on trial for murdering her husband, asked me to visit her in prison and told me she had a crazy idea that my father was in New York." He took a deep breath and told his heart to slow down. He wanted to sound reasonable and truthful. "The year 2020 was a tough one for a lot of us with the global pandemic. My friend Vishesh and I decided we wanted a holiday away from Australia. I automatically thought of New York. It probably sounds crazy, but I thought I could try and find my father. We are also planning to visit the key tourist sites. Our first stop this morning was intended to be the Empire State Building." The detective's eyes did not move from Clint's face. "I did an online search and found a B. Ryal living at Olive Street in Brooklyn. I don't know if it's my father or even if the address is current, but we were planning to go and visit. There are other Ryals listed and we could visit those too. It's all a longshot, I know. We are only here for five days because that is all we can afford." Clint stopped talking momentarily but continued gazing at the woman. "Can we help you in any way? Why are you following my father? What has he done?"

Vishesh settled back beside Clint, less on edge. Clint noticed that the earlier smouldering aura of his friend had retreated to be replaced by one of calm confidence. Vishesh could see that this was all about the Ryals and that he needed to take a back seat.

"Your father's old friend in prison is Emma Costa? Bekym Ryal lived with the Costas about the time you were born."

"Yes." Bloody hell, she had done her homework.

"What made Emma Costa think Bekym Ryal might be in New York?"

"That isn't clear to me," Clint lied. He wasn't prepared to give that up just yet. "She seemed a bit mad to me, and a bit simple."

"A Bekym Ryal, who might be your father, is a person of interest to us in an incident that happened three days ago near the Empire State Building on 34th Street and Fifth Avenue. Two people, naked, chanting and with their hands stretched to the sky were killed by an unknown sniper. They had removed their clothes and left them folded in tidy piles. In the pocket of the woman's dress we found a folded page of a printout from an internet site about the Order of the Solar Temple. The picture was of a robed and hooded man standing outside wrought iron gates." Clint knew the picture well, having studied it online many times.

"A handwritten note on the paper included the name of Bekym Ryal. Didn't Emma Costa and Piripi Nosi also worship at the Order of the Solar Temple?" Okay, Clint thought, the game is up; it's time to come clean.

"Yes. And Vishesh and I were planning to visit the headquarters of the Order to see if my father was connected to it in any way."

"But how do you know where the headquarters are?"

"We don't know for sure, but we think it might be on East 19th Street next to a boxing gym and wellness centre called PowWow. We were going to check it out after we'd visited the Empire State Building."

Detective Adams' face remained stony but Clint could swear her body had softened. She glanced up at Kelly and Sipowicz and nodded. They holstered their guns and one of the officers removed Vishesh's handcuffs; he flexed his arms and rubbed his wrists in relief.

"Why were you going to the Empire State Building?"

"That might sound suspicious to you," Clint acknowledged, "But we didn't know anything about the shooting there."

Vishesh chipped in "It was my idea to do some sightseeing while we are here, not Clint's. Who knows when I'll ever be back here again? I thought that we should take a memory of the Empire State Building back home to Sydney with us."

Detective Adams had transferred her steady gaze to Vishesh momentarily and now swung it back to Clint. "What makes you think that the Order could be based near this place called PowWow?"

"I saw it online. I can show you if you like, on my I-pad." Clint nodded towards his day pack.

There was an unspoken signal between the Detective and her officers. One officer stood in front of the door out into the hallway of the building. The other took Clint's handcuffs off and then positioned himself to cover both the back door into the courtyard and the window. Clint rolled his shoulders; being required to keep his arms behind his back for so long had made him stiff. Vishesh remained sitting on the bed while

Clint and Detective Adams sat at the round table. He could feel her thigh next to his. Her arm brushed his as she leaned in to see what he was showing her on the internet, sending shivers of fire through his body. He loaded up the same site as the one she had mentioned in the printout at the scene of the shootings near the Empire State Building. There was a person, robed and hooded, standing at the gates with their arms lifted and holding a ball of fire. Zooming in, Clint pointed to the corner of the picture where there was a smudge of lettering.

"I had to use a magnifying glass," he told her, "but I'm pretty sure the lettering says PowWow and it is on the fence in front of the neighbouring property. I searched for the name and got only one hit: in East 19th Street, New York."

"Okay." She looked doubtful. "I'll get our tech guys onto it. Now," she turned to look at Clint again, "You are not to go near that place …"

"Oh but …"

"… What can you possibly do by visiting there except blow our investigation sky high? No," she was firm, "Your options are to go sightseeing or to be placed in custody until Wednesday; your choice. How were you planning to get in there, anyway?"

Clint already knew how feeble it was going to sound before he said it. "Knock on the front door or ring the bell."

Detective Adams, Lilla, as Clint was starting thinking of her, was confounded for only a second before she burst out laughing. Her officers jointed in. Clint could feel his face going hot.

"Absolutely no way," she said. "We will have surveillance on the building around the clock and I will know if you have broken my rules. Don't forget, I can have you arrested if you get in our way."

"But my father," Clint felt bulldozed. "How do I get to know about my father?"

"I will call you. Give me your numbers, both of you, and here is my card if you want to get in touch. By the way," the Detective remembered something, "There is no longer a Ryal living at 81 Olive Street in Brooklyn. We've already checked it out. Top marks for your sleuthing, however."

He felt abruptly inflated by the Detective's compliment. She placed her hand on his shoulder as she turned to leave and the heat of it exploded through him, making him shut his eyes with desire and tenderness. So, this was love at first sight, Clint thought. But pointless, stupid love with a cop in a faraway country for God's sake; I am doomed, yet again, for heartbreak. The silence crashed over them after the NYPD had retreated. Clint could hear a ringing in his ears like dozens of cicadas rubbing themselves.

"Did that just happen?" Vishesh asked dubiously? They stared at each other. "It's 11.30 already," he said, checking the time on his phone, "The Gramercy Tavern just down the road will be open."

"A beer? God yes, let's go," Clint agreed.

They planned to walk down East 19th Street for two blocks, turn right into Park Avenue South, and then left into East 20th Street to find the Tavern. Just before they turned into Park Avenue, Vishesh thumped Clint on the arm and pointed across the street. It was PowWow with a billboard now out on the pavement. Two people holding hands and wearing matching white trousers were walking up the steps. Clint's eyes moved to the closed wrought iron gate at the neighbouring property. His phone buzzed. It was a message containing only an emoji of a pair of handcuffs. Grinning, he held it out to Vishesh. They laughed, peering around in search of the hidden surveillance, before walking on and rounding the corner. Lilla was as good as her word, Clint thought, she was on to it.

Lunch at the Gramercy Pub started with craft beers: a Smuttynose brewed in New Hampshire, because that was the home of Jed Bartlett from The West Wing, and an Other Half brewed in New York. Feeling more grounded and less like they were about to blow into the sky like balloons released from a child's hand, Clint and Vishesh worked out how to catch the subway and made their way to the Empire State Building. They hadn't booked and, after two hours in the queue, the warm glow of the beer had worn off. When they finally got to stand on the observation deck and look across the United States of America, Clint had a sense of being utterly insignificant, but the building itself was extraordinarily beautiful.

They were weary and ready for an early night as they emerged from the 23 Street Subway and walked back down Park Avenue South. They decided to take a right turn into East 19th Street first to pick up some Thai takeout before wandering back down the length of the street swinging carrier bags of food, each lost in their own thoughts. Clint was thinking of running his hands over Lilla's body. He wondered if Vishesh was thinking about Bian. Clint knew Vishesh had emailed her last night and had been checking his messages regularly today. Had she responded or was she leaving him hanging? As they approached the now closed PowWow, Clint began looking around carefully in search of cops. It was as he moved his head to the left that he saw a movement behind a ground storey window in a building almost exactly opposite the Order's wrought iron gates which, he noticed with a leap of excitement when he turned his head to the right, were now open. The person behind the window had moved in a flash and out of his line of sight, but it reminded him of someone. It was a man with muscles rippling under a tight mohair jumper and he moved like a cat. It was someone who made him think of the smell of raspberry jam. It made him think of Arash. At that moment, his phone buzzed again.

# Chapter Twelve

*Keep Moving. Now* the message read. It was from a different number to the one Clint had received earlier with the handcuffs icon in it which, when he'd checked, was the number printed on Detective Adams' business card.

"Come on, we need to go," Clint murmured to Vishesh who stood peering over the road to the open gates, trying to see inside. He showed his friend the text.

With a sense of reluctance they forced their feet to keep moving; both of them were keen to know what was behind those gates. Although they glanced over their shoulders occasionally they could see nothing and nothing stirred. They ate chicken Pad Thai, a curried tofu soup, and Thai spring rolls for dinner, glad to get out of their jackets and turn on a heater. They collapsed onto their beds to read or catch up on emails for a while. Vishesh had taken a towel and gone down the hall for a shower and Clint was dozing, still fully dressed, on top of the bed when the back door into the courtyard opened slowly. The creak woke him from a dream involving running, screaming and being choked. A man stood next to the bed, reaching out an arm towards him.

"Aargh …" Clint's yell was stifled by a gloved hand over his mouth.

"Sssh. It's only me."

"What the fuck. Arash? You scared me half to death. What the hell are you doing here? How did you get in?" Clint stood up and Arash gave him a quick hug.

"Sssh. I haven't got long," he whispered. "What the fuck are *you* doing here?"

"I'm here with Vishesh. We're seeing the sights."

"And trying to find your father?" Arash's eyes were lumps of burning coal under a cap pulled down low.

"Well, yes. How did you know? What do you care?"

"Long story. Can't now ..." There was the sound of a door shutting down the hall. "Stay away from your father *and* from that good looking woman cop. I'll find a way to talk with you soon."

Arash slipped back out the way he'd come and Clint heard the lock to the back door being turned from the outside. He had a key? Vishesh returned carrying his clothes and wrapped in a towel tucked in at the waist. His body is a lean, mean machine Clint thought, glancing at him from under his long eyelashes.

"What does Bian see in you, mate?" he asked out loud, teasing. "You're bloody awful to look at."

Vishesh laughed and threw his wet towel at Clint as he pulled on a clean white T-shirt and eased a pair of striped Peter Alexander pyjama bottoms up over the graze on his shin, caused by Clint's fall at the feet of Detective Lilla Adam's.

"I'm ready for sleep; what about you?"

"Yes, I reckon. I'm too tired to shower now. I'll have one in the morning."

They went back to the 23 Street Station the next morning to take the half hour subway ride to Fulton Station. First stop was a visit to the World Trade Center followed by the 9/11 Tribute Museum. They had in the back of their minds to also visit Wall Street and the Stock Exchange, depending on how the day panned out. They had both woken early. Vishesh was excited to see what the day held. Clint was exhausted. He had slept fitfully, wondering if Arash was in cahoots with his father, if they were bad guys and if they were going to come back and murder him and Vishesh in their beds. The friends avoided the end of East 19th Street closest to Park Avenue South where Clint's father might possibly be and where the cops most certainly would be, walking up 3rd Avenue instead to have an omelette breakfast at the Bluebell Café. The food was delicious, the tables spaced and hand sanitizer was available. People were still terrified of a return of Covid-19. New York had been one of the hardest hit American cities. Even on the subway many people still wore masks. Clint was glad they had thought to bring a pack with them.

It was Sunday. If the premises of the Order of the Solar Temple were going to be occupied on any day wouldn't it be today, Clint wondered? He kept checking his messages to see if Lilla or Arash had been in touch. It wasn't until they were riding the subway back to their room in Grammercy, after a full day of awe-inspiring, humbling and emotional experiences, that anything happened. His phone buzzed. *I have news. Will send a car to pick you up in the morning.* It was from Detective Adams. He immediately felt refreshed and reinvigorated. A wave of happiness lifted him up from the exhaustion which had dogged him all day. He knew he'd spent the day being a drag on Vishesh's enthusiasm and now he felt guilty.

"What do you think about buying provisions from 21 Berry Deli, you know the deli on the corner, and eating-in tonight in front of the television? It's a huge flat screen for such a tiny room. We could find a liquor store and get a few beers too. Oh, look what just came in." Clint showed Vishesh the message.

"Great idea for dinner. If we get extra we'll have leftovers for breakfast. I notice your lady detective doesn't say what time the car will arrive." Vishesh grinned at him. Clint smiled. His admiration for Detective Lilla Adams had clearly not gone unnoticed. His friend stiffened. "Swap places with me Clint," Vishesh murmured.

"Okay. Why?"

"Help me out." They swapped. "There's a guy over there giving me the eye and it's starting to annoy me." Clint looked up from his new seat into the eyes of a good looking Latino man wearing a tight T-shirt with the sleeves cut-off and the shortest denim shorts Clint had ever seen on a man. Earrings marched up the sides of both ears and there was a piercing in his lip.

"Bloody hell," he whispered to Vishesh as he put his head down and pretended to rub his eyes. "He must be cold." It was still fine but the day was closing in and the evening chill was coming down. Clint was glad he had his jacket on, even in the subway. They shared a grin. When Clint looked up again, the man had lost interest and had turned his back.

"Heard from Bian?" Clint asked.

"Yes." Vishesh glowed. "There was an email waiting for me when I got up this morning. She's been kept very busy with preparations for her sister's wedding."

"You two are a definite item then?"

"I think we are. We have talked about finding an apartment together when we both get back to Sydney. She arrives back a day after us."

"Damn. That means we'll have to have to find another flatmate." Clint put his hand on Vishesh's shoulder. "I'm pleased for you. I really am." No wonder he was so bouncy today, Clint thought. It's amazing what love does to one's state of mind. He was looking forward to seeing Lilla again tomorrow, although he knew she could not possibly return the feelings he already knew he had for her. He abruptly remembered Arash's warning to stay away from the woman cop and wondered what the hell that was all about. He intended to use the bolts on the inside of both doors to their apartment tonight, not just the locks. He didn't want any more uninvited guests.

As predicted, Monday dawned as crisp and sunny as the preceding days and so they ate their breakfast of bacon and egg sandwiches in the courtyard, using ingredients from the Deli bought the night before. They'd spent the evening watching a basketball game over a Deli dinner and cans of beer, neither of them knowing the first thing about basketball but having fun even so. They were ready the next morning when there was a knock on the door. Officers Kelly and Sipowicz, as silent and burly as the last time they'd met, were waiting for them. Clint had assumed they were going to a local precinct but, when he asked, officer Sipowicz told them that Detective Adams was based at One Police Plaza. Looking at the signposts, Clint could see they were heading back towards the financial and Chinatown sectors where they'd visited yesterday. The car eventually turned off Park Row into the NYPD's headquarters just before the Brooklyn Bridge which loomed on the horizon. One Police Plaza looked like a gigantic cheese grater.

Detective Adams was sitting at the desk in her office when the officers let Clint and Vishesh into the room. "Good morning." She rose and motioned them to sit in front of the desk. She was beautiful with the sun coming through the window behind her and catching the highlights in her hair. She had lip gloss on and a touch of eye shadow which Clint had not noticed on Saturday. He felt nervous about being in her presence and about what he was going to hear.

"We visited the headquarters of the Order of the Solar Temple on Saturday night and again on Sunday. You were correct Mr Ryal ...," she faced Clint, "... about the location of the premises. Great detective work by the way."

"Thank you. Please call me Clint. And did you find my father?"

"Not yet Mr, I mean, Clint. We brought in twelve of the members of the Order for questioning. All of them told us a similar story: they are descendants of knights from the Knights Templar and they wear robes and take drugs while chanting in order to get close to God. They believe that if you are not close to God a demon in the form of an anti-Christ can enter your body. They all believe that they will be taken up in some way to meet God, when the time is right. This is a concept I've heard of before as 'the rapture'. Do you know of it?" They both shook their heads. "It refers to the end of time when people who are holy will rise up to be with God. There was the suggestion from the people we questioned that this might happen through the use of a UFO. We can confirm that the two people shot near the Empire State Building were members of the Order." Detective Adams looked at them solemnly.

"But how does this help you?" asked Clint feeling slightly frustrated. There wasn't much here that was new to him. "Do you know who shot those people and why? And where does my father fit in to all this?"

"There is more." She smiled at him quickly as if she wanted him to know that she understood his frustration and that he needed to be patient. "Some of the members know the High Priest of the Order as a man called Bekym Ryal but they do not know where to find him. Apparently he is often out of town or even out of the country. And we need to be cautious about the name," she added quickly as Clint's eyes opened wide. "Just because someone uses that name doesn't necessarily mean it is the man *you* are looking for. However, the people we questioned also say that he has a group of followers who come for private tuition and that these men all seem to be young Iranians."

Clint looked at her feeling scared. Could she be confirming his grandfather's fears about what Bekym was doing? "Are you saying that this man Bekym Ryal might be involved in Iranian politics or, alternatively, terrorism in America?"

"It's a possibility, and that possibility is reinforced by the type of weapon used to kill those people near the Empire State. Ballistics has come back and it was no ordinary weapon. It is generally used by the Russian or Iranian military." Her jaw was set and she looked grim.

"Shit. You're not saying that my dad killed those people, are you?"

"No. I'm not saying that but we do need to find him. Do you have any more leads you'd like to tell us about Clint?"

She knows about Arash, Clint thought, as Detective Adams' eyes bore into his soul. "Nothing, I'm afraid," he replied, remembering Arash's advice to stay away from her and surprised at how calm he felt in his lie.

She kept his gaze on him for so long he knew she didn't believe him.

"Vishesh, two doors down the hall is a kitchenette. Why don't you make yourself a coffee and Clint will be along soon."

She hadn't taken her eyes off Clint. Oh God, she's going to use a lie detector, she's going to break me, I'm doomed, Clint thought, his mind going a million miles an hour.

"Okay. See you in a minute Clint." Vishesh hesitated a bit, wondering if this was a good idea but deciding he had no choice.

"Clint. I know this is a bit unorthodox, but …" Detective Adams said after the door had closed, not looking at his eyes and with her cheeks flushing. "Um. I wondered if you'd have dinner with me tonight. My place."

He took a deep calming breath and told himself he could do this, surprising thought it was. "Dinner with you?" He felt himself sitting taller and grinned into those ice blue gems which rested on his ebullient face. "Try to keep me away."

As he put an arm around her in a hello hug, Clint felt an electric charge that was like nothing he'd ever experienced. They were at the door to her stunning apartment which, he noticed in a moment, had ceilings that soared 15 feet above them and windows that were the height of the walls and wrapped in blue silk curtains. He could smell something cooking with undertones of garlic, tomato and melted cheese. The soft music was classical, maybe Puccini. His senses felt like they were folding under her hug into a warm bed piled with puffy quilts. Her body against his was both strong and soft. He could feel her breasts pressed against his chest. The door was closing behind him as he let the wine bag slide gently to the floor, enclosing her with both his arms and meeting her lips. Their clothes fell from their bodies as they moved towards the pale pink damask settee with Lilla lifted in Clint's arms and her powerful legs gathered around his waist. Her wet lips parted and she welcomed him. Her long brown nipples, mounted on voluptuous breasts, found his mouth. They rolled through their waves of longing to the end and back again.

They lay entwined on the settee under a throw, smiling into each other's eyes. Clint trailed his fingers down Lilla's body.

"That was unexpected," she chuckled. "But very welcome," she added hastily as a cloud of apprehension crossed Clint's face. "I think I need to check on the dinner. Would you like a drink? I see you bought some wine."

Clint pulled Lilla closer into a two-armed hug. "I don't want to let you go. I want to stay like this forever."

"Well, I could show you the bedroom after dinner, if you like. We could try it again maybe, if you're not too tired."

"Oh you tease. Tired is not what I feel right now." Clint could feel himself stirring again against Lilla's thigh.

"I can tell," she laughed, slipping from his grasp and walking to the kitchen.

Lilla's firm buttocks were the colour of porcelain and swung as she walked in a way that only increased his ardour. He tucked himself into his boxers and jeans, telling himself to calm down, and retrieved the abandoned wine bag. He watched her breasts move as she checked on dinner and turned off the oven. He decided she was an angel fallen from the sky into his life. They ate cannelloni and salad, drinking Bordeaux, while sitting opposite each other at a small Tuscany table. The white bathrobe Lilla's pulled on did little to hide her figure from Clint's gaze and he tried to pull himself together.

"This is a wonderful apartment. And it's very apt that you live in a place called the old Police Building. Do you own it? What's the area called that around here?"

Lilla dabbed her mouth with a serviette. "This area is called Little Italy. It's a wonderful vibrant area and New York's best bakery is just over the road. And no I don't own the apartment." She hesitated and then decided to carry on. "My father is wealthy. We descend from John Quincy Adams the sixth President of the United States and, therefore, John Adams the second President and former revolutionary. We can trace our lineage in America back to the puritan Mayflower Pilgrims. My father is also in the advertising business, so he has his own wealth. This apartment is his and he lets me live here at the moment." She waved around the room. "I love it here but I'm not sure how long I'll stay."

Clint felt out of his league and wondered why he was here. He was so inferior to this extraordinary and confident woman from a solid and wealthy family. How could she possibly feel for him what he felt for her? He pushed his empty wine glass away and stood up.

"It has been a lovely evening but I think I should go now."

His voice was husky and sad.

"What? Clint, no, please don't go." Lilla stood up too, alarmed. "Have I said something to upset you? Please stay. Have another glass of wine and let's talk."

"How can I stay Lilla? Look at you. You are gorgeous and respected with a great job and family money and …" he took a deep breath, "… I think I love you. If I stay I can only get burned. Look at me Lilla. Look. I'm an unemployed Aussie brat of an Irish whore and a father who walked out on me as a baby, for Christ's sake. How can I possibly hope to have you in my life?"

His voice was stronger now, resolute. He was not going to be in a relationship that left him feeling inferior and heart-broken. Lilla poured wine into both their glasses calmly.

"Well, I am also the brat of an Irish whore and an absent father. Don't you think I know all about you and your background? Of course I do. Did you think I was toying with you, offering you a one-night stand? I don't do that. The things you feel for me, well I think I feel the same way about you. Please sit down Clint and let's talk."

Clint remained standing, feeling uncertain.

"Please?" she asked again.

The plea in her voice made him lower himself slowly into the chair and accept the wine.

"My mother came to New York from Boston to work in advertising. She'd been brought up in a hardworking, hard drinking Irish Catholic family. She struggled to find a job, was down on her luck and took to escorting. She was so young and very beautiful. She got pregnant to my father, the hot shot business man who took whatever he wanted." Her voice was bitter and scathing. "When my mother named me, she gave me his last name. We lived on welfare. It was only when she got cancer, about the time I joined the force, that she tracked my father down and told him who I was. That was just before she died. He demanded a paternity test of course. And here we are," Lilla spread her arms wide around the loft. "I was living in a one-bedroom apartment a bit like the one you are staying in when my father decided to acknowledge my existence. He even told his wife and other children, all of whom hate the very idea of me. I have never met them. Letting me live here rent free is my father's penance."

Clint stood once more and walked around the table. He lifted Lilla from her chair and gently took her in his arms. With her head resting against his shoulder he whispered in her ear, "I'm so sorry."

They talked about their lives as they soaked in the claw-foot bath, avoiding talking about the shootings or the possible role of his father. Lilla leaned back against his body and occasionally added more hot water from the antique gold faucet, using her foot to move the tap. Climbing from the bath, Clint reached for his lover's curvy moist body. He knelt in front of her to open her lips with his tongue. When she gasped and moaned in ripples, her fingers tangled in his hair, he lifted her into his arms again and carried her to the adjoining bedroom. Laying her on the bed he turned her over gently, lifted her hips and slowly lowered himself into her before retreating just as slowly. Only when she moaned for more did he plunge deep inside her until they both lay spent and panting. Clint was slick with sweat.

Lilla was sleeping, snuggled against Clint, when he remembered Vishesh. Reaching for his phone he noticed a message from the number he now knew to be Arash's. *Meet me tomorrow 11am at Hometown Hotpot. Two blocks over from Detective Adams place. 194 Grand St.* Clint returned an *Okay*. Bloody hell he's had me followed, he thought, and then messaged Vishesh. He had felt bad about going out for the evening without him but his friend had been relaxed about being abandoned.

"I'll spend the evening in a bar with a big TV and a game." He had sounded delighted at being let out on his own in New York. "And I'll stay up late," he told Clint, "To hear all your news."

*Don't stay up*, Clint now messaged. *Staying the night with Lilla. I have an appointment at 11am tomorrow. See you later in the day?* Vishesh must have been waiting to hear from him, because he messaged straight back. *Good for you. Have fun. I'll take a ferry out to the Statue of Liberty and Ellis Island tomorrow. Night.* Clint lay back under the duvets, smelling Lilla's skin and feeling like the luckiest man in the world. A cloud crossed his mind as he suddenly wondered where his father was and what he was up to.

## Chapter Thirteen

The modest exterior opened into a long brick-walled restaurant with marble-topped tables. Wall art made of black iron and depicting bucolic scenes of rural harmony in China hung the length of the wall. Open grills were cooking meat and vegetables on request. A man was sitting in the far corner where there was no light, facing both the front door and the stairs to the second floor; it was unmistakably Arash with his handsome face and strong shoulders, his head shaved and his penetrating coal-coloured eyes locked onto Clint's. Clint felt a chill and wondered what this was all about; he really wanted some answers. When Lilla had asked him this morning what his plans were for the day, he'd said something about meeting Vishesh and taking it from there but could tell from her eyes that she didn't believe him. He wondered if she'd have him tailed like Arash had, but he couldn't understand why either of them might care where he went.

Clint had woken to find Lilla already showered, dressed in lingerie and standing in front of the mirror by the bed brushing her wet hair. He had reached for her.

"You'll make me late Clint," she'd laughed, half-heartedly slapping his hands away.

He had pulled her down to him, kissing her neck and rubbing her nipples which lifted through her bra of ivory lace. He reached beneath her matching panties, using his thumb to play her like a delicate musical instrument. Her eyes thick with yearning, she repositioned her hips and guided him to her. He loved watching her breasts heave as she sat astride him, her mouth slightly open and her eyes closed. They exploded together with shouts of joy.

They'd eaten granola with berries and yoghurt for breakfast and drunk dark strong coffee. Lilla had held him before she left as if she might never see him again.

"Come to meet me after work at the office?" she asked.

"Of course, I'll see you about 5pm then. Have a good day."

Her full lips brushed against his so softly and stayed there for so long that Clint hardly dared to breathe. It was more loving and intimate than anything he'd ever known.

Arash stood and held a finger up to his lips as Clint walked towards him in the Hotpot, carrying his jacket; it wasn't quite cold enough to wear it now but he knew he would need it later. Arash shook his head as Clint opened his mouth to ask what was going on and waved his phone over Clint, making a small satisfied noise when it beeped over a pocket in his jacket. Arash took the coat and felt in the pocket, pulling out a small piece of metal which he placed carefully on the bench seat. Another sweep of the phone found another in his jeans pocket, which Arash replaced after examining it. He found Clint's mobile phone in the back pocket of his jeans, turned it off, and smashed it with his heel.

"Hey, no, what …" Clint was outraged.

Arash placed a gloved hand over his mouth, jerked his head towards the back of the restaurant and propelled Clint by the shoulder through a swinging back door, the storage area and out into the utilities lane that held the bins and people without hope who were sitting in the dirt clutching bottles. A black SUV waited with its engine running and a back door open.

"You've been followed. We're going for a ride."

"What do you mean? Why? Hey." Clint was pushed into the back of the SUV. It began moving as Arash joined Clint in the back seat and then took off at speed but with no sound.

"Arash, what the hell is going on?"

"Put your seatbelt on and I'll tell you."

Clint obliged with bad grace. "Have I been kidnapped?"

Arash looked at him and laughed mockingly. "You're not important enough to kidnap."

It was his tone of his voice that stung. Clint unbuckled his seatbelt and put his hand on the door handle. "Let me out," he said quietly.

"Come on mate. I'll tell you everything. I promise. Sorry I laughed. I'm a bit on edge. Come on Clint." The last words were spoken like the

Arash that Clint had thought he knew and so he gave in, settling back and buckling up. There was a moment of silence.

"Where are we going, anyway?" He was staring at Arash to see if he was going to tell the truth.

"I am taking you to meet your father." Arash had thought about how Clint might react to this news but had not anticipated his calmness.

Clint nodded his head. "I thought you two might be up to something together. Just what is that 'something'? Did you shoot and murder those Order members by the Empire State Building the other day?"

"No. Clint, look at me. Neither your father nor I have murdered anyone, directly. By the way, you know far too much about … everything."

"Directly," Clint said, honing in on what mattered to him. "What the hell does that mean?"

"Let me tell you everything I can before we get to your father. I work for ASIS, Australia's Secret Intelligence Service, which is why I am forever travelling around and am often not contactable."

Clint nodded again but didn't say anything. Somehow, it didn't come as any surprise to him. It was if he'd always known and just needed someone to put his knowledge into words and say it out loud.

"You don't look surprised," Arash said with a wry grimace. "I had a feeling you might be on to me. I am not allowed to tell anyone where I work or what I do, so I'm going to need you to sign a non-disclosure form. And ASIS will want to debrief you once you return home. I expect they will recruit you so that you have some skin in the game. And you won't be able to tell anyone about anything, including your lady Detective." Arash grinned at him mischievously and his voice changed. "You two really hit it off."

"What the fuck?" Clint scowled at the man he had thought was his best friend. "Have you been listening in on my life?"

"Yes. I planted a bug in a pocket of your jeans when I visited you the other night. I gambled you'd only bought one pair of trousers because I saw how little luggage you had when you arrived at the airport. And I was tracking your movements through your phone, as well."

Clint's face flushed as he sat back and stared out of the window away from Arash. Jesus, the things Arash would have heard. The car had roared at speed up the long straight road of Park Avenue and then crossed a bridge merging into, first, Route 87 and then Route 278. Clint was determined to follow where they were taking him.

"You planted two bugs on me?" he asked.

"Two?"

"Just now in the Hotpot, you found two bugs on me."

"Oh. The other bug must have been planted by Detective Adams. We left that one behind in the restaurant. And we gave Kelly and Sipowicz the slip too. I followed you and them part of the way from the Detective's apartment and then slipped through the back door of the Hotpot while you came in the front. I assume your lady is also tracking you by your phone, which is why we left it behind. By the way, I'm impressed that you didn't give me up to Detective Adams. I thought you might when you were in her office yesterday."

"I wish I had, now." Clint felt mutinous. The SUV swung left onto the Bronx River Parkway. Clint saw a large green park on his left and the clutter of tall brick buildings tightly packed into the Bronx on his right. They roared around a roundabout and took Route 1 out of the City.

"Ah. No you don't. I'm sorry Clint. This is my job. And it affects your father. Your father is also an ASIS agent; you've probably worked that out by now." He watched Clint closely as Clint tried and failed to hide his surprise. "Okay. Well he is. Actually, he is assigned to Five Eyes, which is an alliance between the intelligence communities of five nations including Australia and the USA. He is involved in obtaining intelligence from Iran. The Order of Solar Temple is or rather, was, merely a cover for his meetings with those Iranian men that Detective Adams told you about. He was hiding in plain sight, so to speak."

"Is this all true? Are you spinning me a line?" Clint put his head in his hands, trying to shift his mental picture of his father from loser, deadbeat dad to a James Bond figure. "If Bekym Ryal is a mastermind and a 007, how did he get involved in the murder of Tadeas Costa and the shootings at the Empire State? And why didn't he stay with my mother and me, or at least keep in touch?"

"To answer the first of those questions, your father was not involved with any of the murders. The members of the Order are an unstable lot and get themselves into some tricky situations. Bekym has now removed himself from the Order; it was putting him in harm's way. He will need to find another cover. With regards to the Costa murder, it looks like weird shit just happened. The shootings in New York look like they were carried out by the IRGC, the Islamic Revolutionary …"

"I know what the IRGC is, but why would they shoot two naked Order members?"

"We have only suspicions. The IRGC wants Bekym. Those naked Order members were second in command in the cult and knew Bekym. They just went over the edge and we hadn't anticipated it. The IRGC were one step ahead of us. In fact, they might have engineered the whole event including the shooting. We think they wanted the cops to learn about Bekym and take him in for questioning. The IRGC has infiltrated the NYPD and they want to, um, interrogate your father."

"Interrogate? You mean torture him?" Clint's heart froze.

"Well, yes." There was silence, broken only by the humming of the wheels. Clint looked out the window again, wondering where they were. They were still on Route 1 but Clint had lost track of how far they'd come.

"As for your second question …"

"My second question?" Clint turned to Arash.

"Yes. You asked why Bekym didn't stay with you or at least get in touch? I think that is a question you need to ask him yourself."

The SUV swung off Route 1 into Larchmont Avenue and headed southeast, coming to a stop at a beautifully preserved building painted grey and wrapped around with verandas; the sign said Horseshoe Harbour Yacht Club. The driver had remained silent, staring at the highway throughout the entire trip. He now got out of the car and stood with his back to it, staring back down the road they had just driven, a gun held across his chest with both hands. Clint shivered, then opened the car door and stepped out, pulling on his jacket. Arash had opened his door but remained sitting in the back seat. A man sitting on the veranda stood up and walked towards them.

"Hello." The man stopped a few feet away as if he was keeping out of reach of the length of Clint's arms, wary that Clint might take a swing at him. "I'm Bekym Ryal. And you are Clint Ryal, my son."

Clint struggled to breathe and to think. He stood staring at this man who was a version of himself; skin the colour of caramel, the same sharply defined jaw, slim build and thick black eyebrows, but Bekym's head was shaved and his eyes were deep brown. There were grey flecks in the stubble on his head. Clint was slightly taller. He took a step towards Bekym, who stood his ground and looked deep into his son's eyes. There was no apology, no plea, no sign of emotion. Not knowing what to feel or how to act, Clint lifted his right arm for a handshake and Bekym clasped his hand with both of his, holding on firmly. And then Bekym was hugging him, holding him tight and there were tears in both their eyes; tears that neither of them would let fall. Arash was beside them now, suggesting they move inside. He had brought lunch.

Clint was ravenous and devoured a falafel wrap washed down with a can of local beer while listening to Arash and Bekym converse quietly over their lunch about how to re-establish their cover in America. They occasionally glanced at Clint. They were using a small wood-panelled room at the front of the yacht club with big open windows, a table and chairs, and two armchairs near a bookcase. The numbness of a moment ago was leaving Clint, to be replaced with a jangle of jagged shards of anger, abandonment, grief and hate that were catching in his gut.

"So, he said at last, pushing his plate away as the food started to get stuck in his throat, "Are you going to explain why you left Pearl when I was a baby and why you have never made any contact; never tried to help either of us?" The empty can crumpled in Clint's right fist, which was shaking with anger. He could hear the pain in his voice and stared unseeing out of the window which opened onto the stunning beauty of sun glinting on the tossing waves and the greenery of the coast of Long Island in the distance.

Bekym took a breath and focused on Clint. "I am so sorry if you and Pearl, and my father have suffered Clint, I … no, please let me finish." He laid a hand over Clint's to restrain him from interrupting and Clint quickly sat back in his seat, removing his hands from contact. "I am sorry for you all, but the choice I made was for my country and I am not sorry about that. I would do it again if I had to."

Clint glared at this man opposite him; he was brutal. "You care more about bloody Australia than you do about your own son?"

"No. That's not it Clint. It's not about Australia. Please let me tell you my story. I need to do it justice." He paused a moment, breathing. "I left school with little in the way of skills or qualifications and so, later on, I started taking night classes in computer studies to gain a skill. I did not want to be a labourer all my life. I had always spoken Iranian at home with my father, Sunil, and at the mosque, but I was not proficient at reading and writing Iranian and so I took night classes in that too. I wanted to feel closer to my culture, my roots. I continued attending the mosque. And one day I was approached by someone who turned out to be a recruiter for ASIS. They showed me photos of what the

Ayatollah's people did to my mother and sisters in 1979; they talked about restoring order in Iran. They convinced me. I have been working for ASIS and for Five Eyes ever since. My work involves supporting Iranians to break free of the yolk of fundamentalism through the sharing of intelligence, in the hope of a return of the prosperity and freedom of the days of the Shah; the days that Sunil will remember."

Clint lifted his green eyes, the eyes he had inherited from Pearl, to the brown eyes of his father as the realisation hit him that Bekym did not know about Sunil. "Your father," he said, his voice cracking, "died a few months ago in the pandemic. He loved you." Breathing was difficult. "He told me, before he died, that he'd never given up hope of seeing you again. And," his voice was stronger now, "He knew. He guessed that you were behind the riots in Iran. He knew that you'd thrown away your family so you, you could … be a hero."

Bekym had lowered his head into his hands, his elbows on the table between them. "Not a hero." His voice was muffled. Lifting his head he said more clearly, "Peace, freedom and prosperity in my country is a noble goal and has nothing to do with me wanting to be a hero. Anyway, I am anything but."

"But I still don't understand." Clint leaned forward, gritting his teeth. "Why couldn't you have stayed with us and still been an agent for ASIS? Why did you have to choose?"

Bekym looked at him sadly. "It was to keep you all safe. Do you have any idea what the IRGC would do to you, or your mother and grandfather, if it had known that we were connected? They would have used you to get to me. And how could I possibly play happy families when I'm hidden away or travelling most of the time. Haven't you noticed that Arash is rarely around? How could I have explained all that to someone like Pearl?"

"Someone like Pearl?" Clint spat the words back at his father. "So, instead, you left someone like Pearl to look after a child when she was incapable of doing so. You left me to 'keep me safe' so that Pearl's boyfriends could beat the shit out me? Do you have any idea what my childhood was like?"

"I'm so sorry, but …" Bekym opened his hands with his palms up in entreaty.

"Yes, I know. You're so sorry I suffered, but you'd do it all again in a heartbeat. And," an idea had just struck him, "the IRGC *has* cottoned on to the fact that Sunil and I are related to you, despite you disowning us. A group of Iranians with Australian accents, presumably working for the IRGC, put Sunil in hospital before he died. They also confronted and hurt my landlord who is in his 80s, and searched my apartment. Sunil thought they were ISIS."

"Same thing, for all intents and purposes," Arash noted.

"Sunil said that too," Clint nodded his head, feeling calmer. At least he understood now. He may not like it or agree with it, but he understood. "But what I don't understand," he said out loud, "is why you are telling me all this *now* and meeting with me *now*?"

Bekym and Arash shared a look; it was Arash who answered. "Because you've been like a bloody dog with a bone," he laughed. "You weren't going to stop until you'd exposed us all and put the whole operation in jeopardy. You even sent Bekym an email at the Order of the Solar Temple for goodness sake. During the Covid-19 lockdown I had to come back to Sydney. A place was found for me on an air force plane. While I was there I slipped into your apartment when you were asleep. I gave myself remote access to your laptop because I was worried that the IRGC would find you. I've been watching your internet use, emails, your notes, everything. And so we could see your increasing interest in the Order of the Solar Temple; we could see where this was going to end."

Clint felt outraged again. That feeling was so close to the surface. And he also felt sullied. Nothing in his miserable life mattered to the man who was supposed to be his best friend or to the man who was supposed to be his father. They'd even listened to him making love with Lilla. Well, he may not matter to them but he mattered to Lilla.

"I want to go back to Manhattan," he announced, pushing his seat back. "I'm meeting Lilla at 5pm and I want to catch up with Vishesh first."

"Ah. Yes, we do need to get you back but you won't be meeting with Detective Adams, I'm afraid." Clint stood motionless, heavy, a weight across his shoulders trying to push him down into a small heap on the ground. "We have re-booked the flights for you and Vishesh, upgraded them to business class even, and we are taking you straight from here to the John F. Kennedy International Airport. Vishesh has been informed and he is currently back at your Airbnb packing the luggage, including yours. He will then be transported to the airport too. You will meet him there. He enjoyed his sightseeing trip this morning, by the way."

I should have known, Clint thought. Something good comes into my life, and some bastard connected to my father takes it away.

"Try to understand," Arash went on, leaning forward, "Detective Adams was using you to get to Bekym. We need to get you back to Sydney. We will also give you protection back home; protection from the NYPD but also from the IRGC now we know that they've tracked you down."

"Lilla was not 'using me'," Clint snapped. "She cares about me. I care about her. I can't just disappear."

"She knows by now that you found the bug she planted on you and that you've abandoned your phone." Arash said gently. "She will already be aware of the change in your flights. She'll have officers waiting for you at the airport, so you and Vishesh will need to be escorted into the airport by a back route. If she finds you she will arrest you until you give up Bekym."

"Let me call her," Clint whispered, steadying himself with one hand on the table.

"I'm sorry Clint."

Clint stood straight and forced himself to sound calm, determined to match the flint and steel of his father and his friend. The way they had used and manipulated him disgusted him.

"You are both dead to me. I never want to see or hear from either of you ever again. If you ever contact me, I will find a way to go to the police."

He knew he was dreaming. They'll have me followed, he thought, they'll bug me, access my laptop and my phone; they'll control my life. If I put a toe out of line, they'll probably have me killed. I am, after all, expendable. I do not matter.

## Chapter Fourteen

The four flatmates at 16 Oxley Street had become close friends and their farewells the previous day at the now empty apartment had been emotional. Each was starting a new chapter in their life which made the parting feel more final. Graydon had also come down from his flat to say goodbye. Clint returned on his own early the next morning for a last visit and check through the rooms. The March morning was warm and sunny and he could hear birds chirping. Voices were calling out in the children's park nearby. He had felt the need for a solitary goodbye to the now hollow space that had once been the centre of a life that had felt stable and normal; a feeling that had been new to him and one to which he'd clung.

Standing alone, Clint wondered what was next for him. Nothing felt normal now. He had moved to Sunil's old apartment in Wingello Street, which he now owned, and this made things financially easier than they might have been. Although he was unemployed and didn't know what to do next, he at least had most of his severance pay still to live on and some cash that his grandfather had left him. But living in Sunil's apartment increased his awareness of his beloved grandfather's absence and the sorrow that accompanied it. Shane and Megan had bought an apartment down by the Tramsheds; Clint reminded himself that they weren't that far away. Vishesh and Bian were setting up house in one of Samuel's rentals on Darling Point which had a modest rent. That was a kind and generous gesture from Samuel, Clint thought; it would help the couple start their life together without financial stress.

Six weeks had passed since he and Vishesh had landed back to the scorching heat of Sydney, a day earlier than they had expected. On the way to the airport from the Horseshoe Harbour Yacht Club, Clint rode in the front passenger seat of the SUV next to the driver leaving Arash sitting on his own in the back. The sweet raspberry jam smell with a tangy undertone, which Clint had assumed was a soap Arash used and which had always meant friendship to him, now made him feel nauseous. Clint had stared straight ahead as the SUV moved away from the yacht club, ignoring the man, his father, standing on the veranda with his hand held up in farewell. They took a different route to the roads they'd used when leaving the City, turning off Route 1 onto 95 and then moving to Route 678 through Queens to arrive at John F. Kennedy International Airport quicker than Clint had anticipated. The trip was heavy with silence.

Clint was ushered through a back entrance with the driver walking on one side of him and Arash on the other: two muscle-bound men with shaved heads and clad in black shepherding the smaller Clint between them. He was still wearing yesterday's clothes after his night with Lilla. Clint felt like he was a child who needed an adult to hold his hand. It was humiliating and he felt resentment building in his chest. Coming in through the back entrance had avoided the main terminal and security and taken them straight to the departure gate. Vishesh was waiting for him in the lounge, reading a book by the political activist Noam Chomsky. Arash handed Clint a print out of his ticket.

"Your luggage has been sorted and your boarding card. You will be safe now. Good luck Clint. I'm sorry if this seems unfair …"

"It doesn't matter." Clint turned away and walked over to sit next to his friend, not saying goodbye or even looking at Arash. Vishesh put his book down and gave him his signature one-armed hug. Clint was glad to see him.

"Well, this was a surprising turn of events. What has been going on?"

"I'm sorry about our trip being cut short," Clint said. "What did they tell you?"

"Two burly guys came to our room this morning before I went out and said that you were likely to be in trouble with the NYPD if we didn't get out of New York. They said we needed to leave and they had transferred our tickets. I was allowed to go sightseeing but they trailed me, and then they brought me out here after I'd packed up our luggage. I left the keys in the lockbox at the entrance to our Airbnb."

Clint looked up at where Arash and the silent driver had been standing a moment before. They were gone. He thought carefully about what he could tell Vishesh. "It turns out that my father is alive and well and involved in all sorts of things. Arash, who I thought was my friend," his voice was bitter, "is also involved. He believes that Detective Adams is using me to track down and get to Bekym. I don't really understand." He knew he couldn't tell Vishesh much more. "I think it is all mixed up with national security somehow. Anyway, Arash said we will be met by the authorities at Sydney airport to be debriefed before being allowed to go home."

Vishesh whistled. "Jesus Clint. That is heavy shit. Well, the less I know the better." He is a clever man, Clint thought. "Just so long as you're alright." He put a hand on Clint's arm. "Are you alight?" He didn't ask about Clint's night with Detective Adams.

"Not really."

A lump formed in Clint's throat and he couldn't say any more. Soon, their flight was called for boarding. Clint was weary in the aftermath of too many emotions and slept for much of the long journey home when he wasn't staring blankly out of the plane window, his headphones on but listening to nothing. As they disembarked and made their way through Sydney's customs, they were asked to bring their meagre luggage and follow a uniformed officer who took them to adjoining rooms. He searched Clint and his bag thoroughly, removing his I-pad and asking why he didn't have a phone, before leaving him alone. Clint assumed he would do something similar with Vishesh and felt very sorry that his friend was caught up in this. He tried the door handle; he was locked in. It wasn't long before the door to Clint's room opened and a woman wearing a cool linen dress and carrying an enormous blue leather handbag stepped in. She had short spiky hair and a petite heart-shaped face.

"Hello. You can call me Deidre."

She shook Clint's hand and then cleaned them with hand sanitizer from a bottle on the table. Clint did the same. He wondered if he had brought Covid-19 back with him from New York and immediately felt dirty. They stayed in that interrogation room for three hours, going over and over the same things, even the same questions; all of it recorded by Deidre. At one point, when Clint had thought he couldn't stand it anymore, Deidre left the room but soon returned with coffee, bottled water and packets of sandwiches. He was grateful for that. He knew she was only doing her job. He understood also that this wasn't really about him; they just needed to know that he wasn't a security risk. She required him to sign a non-disclosure form as well as another form that made it clear he was now working for ASIS on an as-needed basis. The financial sanctions and prison terms, if he so much as disclosed a whiff of anything sensitive, were explained. Deidre gave him a new phone which he looked at suspiciously.

"Yes, it will track and monitor you. But this is not about invading your privacy; it is about keeping you safe."

Clint kept his mouth shut but was determined to buy a phone for himself as soon as possible and hide this one in a drawer. When Deidre had finished with him, she suggested he catch an Uber home. "Your friend Vishesh is waiting for you outside." Vishesh and Clint had not spoken about the debriefing since and soon Bian returned to Sydney, taking Vishesh's mind off everything else.

Clint closed the last kitchen drawer in his final check through of 16 Oxley Street. The trial of Emma Costa and Piripi Nosi was starting at 9am today and Clint needed to get going if he was to get a seat in the courtroom. He left the empty apartment, locked the door and deposited his keys in the letterbox. He didn't look behind him and so didn't see Graydon watching him out of a back window as he walked up the street to the bus stop. He felt naked without his satchel but he didn't need to carry it now that he was unemployed; he no longer needed to cart around a laptop and I-pad. Those devices were both firmly turned off and sitting in a drawer in the apartment at Wingello Street next to the phone from Deidre.

He had bought himself a new phone but turned off the location function, which made a few of the apps quite useless. He kept the phone close to him at all times. Even when he was asleep and the phone was charging, it lay under the covers in bed next to him. He now rarely used anything electronic and had found that there was something liberating about leading a more simple life. He'd also spent a considerable amount of his grandfather's money on improving security at the apartment. He had started by installing a dead lock, two large bolts and a heavy-duty chain for the door. He then had dead locks fitted on the inside of every window as well as to the sliding glass door to the balcony. A monitored alarm system was installed that would pick up anyone entering the apartment while Clint was out. As well, CCTV cameras were now positioned on the landing outside the door to the apartment and the CCTV system was linked to an app on his phone that beeped if there was any unexpected movement. Arash can probably get around all of that, Clint thought, but I'm sure as hell not going to make it easy for him.

Waiting for the bus on Glebe Point Road, Clint's mind wandered, yet again, to Lilla. It would be mid-afternoon the previous day for her in New York. He thought of her going to the kitchenette down the hall from her office to make herself a coffee before returning to close her office door and look out of that huge window behind her desk as she drank, thinking about Clint. This was all very fanciful. Would she even give him a second thought, he wondered? Was she really just using him as Arash had suggested or had they forged a connection? It would be so easy to find the number of the NYPD, place a call and ask to speak to Detective Adams. But would she take the call? And what could he possibly say to her? If he called, the topic of his father would come up. He didn't want to lie to Lilla but he knew he must if it came to that. And there were some questions for her that he didn't want to ask because he was afraid of her answers. Clint knew that it was fear that was preventing him from taking any action; fear of learning that Arash was right about Lilla's motivations for spending time with him; fear of being used, fear of rejection. And yet he longed to be with her.

Arriving at courtroom 11A, Clint saw Deidre sitting to one side with a cap covering her spikey hair and pulled down low over her brow. He wondered if she was here to report back to Arash if there was any mention of Bekym Ryal. The Order of the Solar Temple was bound to come up. Her roving eyes found his and she made a small nod of recognition, looking at him searchingly as if to remind him of the forms he'd signed.

The Crown prosecutor, Josephine Moss, was reading her notes and preparing to begin her opening statement as soon as His Honour arrived. She felt exhausted and the mirror this morning had confirmed she looked it. There were dark smudges under her eyes. She had pulled her brunette hair into a knot at the back of her head and applied foundation, eyebrows and a rich brown mouth. When she smiled, the jowls drooping from each side of her mouth disappeared and helped give an illusion of youth and vigour. But her role as prosecutor meant there were few opportunities to smile and so the photos of her that were bound to be released throughout the trial would reveal a woman past her prime. She hoped they wouldn't also somehow reveal her current crisis of confidence; she wanted to keep that well-hidden if she could. She was unsure of her efficacy these days and no longer found satisfaction in her job. After 30 years of juggling a marriage that had gone bad, raising children and forging ahead in her career, she felt she had (to steal a term mentioned by athletes, of whom she was not one) 'hit a wall'. Josephine glanced over to the defense table. Ms Raine and Mr Abara were conferring briefly while they waited for the Judge. Both looked cool and in command, personifying every ounce of the intelligence and compassion attributed to them by articles that had appeared in the Sydney Saturday World soon after the initial plea hearing with the Registrar.

With Emma Costa and Piripi Nosi now in the dock, and with the Judge-only trial finally about to start, Clint was as interested as everyone else whether battered women's syndrome would be produced as one of the reasons for the murder of Tadeas Costa, as had been hinted in George Bakker's articles nearly eighteen months ago. Having been on the scene on the night it happened and with all the things he'd learned since, Clint thought that something else was actually going on. He had started to build a theory.

There was a rustle of movement in response to the call "all rise." Once Judge Malcolm McNeill was seated, all others in the courtroom sat too except for the accused and their guards, who remained standing. Clint looked over to the row of seats filled with journalists and noticed the Friar's fringe of hair around a pudgy face that he associated with George Bakker, his old colleague. George's head was already sweating in the heat and his nose was wrinkled with his customary look of disdain. Clint felt a stab of bitterness. He had tried to be a journalist but his attempt had failed. Like dozens of others in the courtroom, he was here out of curiosity rather than because of his career which made him feel unimportant and a bit useless. He slouched down in the chair and adjusted his sand-coloured chinos so they didn't bite into his groin. He'd let his hair grow a little over the last year, revealing its natural dark wave. It offered him a small degree of anonymity if he let it slip over the sides of his thin face, partially concealing his Arab nose and his startling green eyes which were a legacy from his mother. He kept his eyes lowered to the floor while the reporters settled. The Judge spoke briefly to the prosecuting and defense lawyers up at his bench and then directed Josephine Moss to begin. The prosecutor took a position near her bench.

"Thank you Your Honour. Mrs Emma Costa and Mr Piripi Nosi are jointly charged with murder. The prosecution will show that on Friday November 8, 2019, Piripi Nosi (then aged 19) and Emma Costa (aged 46 at the time) killed Mr Tadeas Costa (aged 75) after prolonged torture." A horrified gasp and shudder undulated across the courtroom. This was new information. "Evidence will be shown that Mr Costa was bound, water boarded and had fingers removed with a serrated object. After which," Ms Moss continued, "Mr Costa's body was cut into pieces as the life drained from him. Eventually, his body parts were set alight in a bonfire in the backyard. Sparks from the bonfire are suspected of having set the house alight. Conditions at the time were hot, tinder dry and breezy. If the house fire had not occurred, it may have been sometime before Mr Costa's disappearance was noticed. As it was, Fire and Rescue was called at 6 pm on the evening in question. Mr Costa's beagle named Basil was seen by the fire crew to be pawing at the base of the bonfire, uncovering what was found to be, on inspection, the femur bone of an adult human. The remains of Mr Costa's body were subsequently excavated by police from the fire pit. The defense may argue that Mr Costa treated his wife Mrs Costa and their border Mr Nosi badly, and that these simple and defenseless people were victims as well as perpetrators, but the prosecution will disprove that. There is no defense for the actions of the accused. We will prove that the jointly accused intended to inflict grievous bodily harm on Mr Costa; intended to kill Mr Costa; and did kill Mr Costa. They are both guilty of murder."

Journalists were already rushing for the doors to submit their breaking stories as Ms Moss resumed her seat. Not bad for an old biddy, Josephine thought, her face showing no emotion. There might be life in the old girl yet. Conversations had broken out all through the courtroom, causing His Honour to bang the gravel and demand silence with a level of sternness in his voice not usually heard. The physical distancing caused by the seating arrangements meant that conversations were louder than usual; people were unable to huddle.

Judge Malcolm McNeill was well aware of the weight of the task ahead of him; his face with its large jaw and high forehead was set and grim. No trial is ever cut and dried but this one looked to be even less straightforward than most. What people did to each other was appalling. He had often wondered how far he would have to be pushed to be able to kill another person. Were there any circumstances under which he could torture someone and then murder them? He thought of his own father who had taught geography for 40 years before retiring and almost immediately succumbed to dementia, dying slowly and in confusion. How could anyone hurt a defenseless older person who had given his best years to society?  Judge McNeill took off his glasses and rubbed his clean-shaven face and eyelids with his left hand as if to wash away any impure thoughts and so remain impartial. He gave the reporters an opportunity to resume their seats before he invited Ms Raine to give her opening address in defense of Mrs Emma Costa.

Emma stared straight ahead. There was a buzzing in her head and she felt sick. All those people in the courtroom hearing what she was supposed to have done; it would be in the newspapers and on the TV as well. She now understood she had been bad when she couldn't stop Piripi and she should be punished, but she didn't know what more she could have done at the time to stop him. She hadn't wanted Tadeas to be hurt. She had loved Tadeas. When she left school at 16, he had given her a job serving at the counter of his souvlaki shop. He kept that shop until he was 70 years old, making a good living and selling it for a good price. He had taught her how to work out the change for notes and to be nice to people. It was the first time anyone had shown her any attention. She was charmed by the way he spoke to customers with such interest and kindness, how he remembered their names and how he sang snatches of Greek songs while the Greek radio station played in the hot kitchen and he wiped the sweat off his face with his apron. She was charmed by the poetry he recited when they sat out the back of the shop after hours with a bottle of beer and the kitchen hand listening with a look on his face that said he didn't know what to make of it all. Tadeas had said he was speaking words written by ancient Greek poets with names she couldn't remember and, anyway, couldn't say.

It had felt like life was coming right. She could put behind her the years of not knowing her parents, the string of dismal foster homes with adults and children who had beaten her and the schooling that made no sense. Her life was starting. And so when he went down on one knee, almost 30 years older than her, his hair already thinning and going grey and his belly hanging over his trousers, she had said yes. He had immigrated to Australia 20 years before, throwing himself into establishing a shop and making good money. He had wanted a wife and children, he was Greek after all, but no woman had wanted him. His misshapen head with its bulging forehead over the left side of his face had left him undesirable and miserable. Money and kindness hadn't been enough. But the package of Tadeas was enough for Emma. And in return he had offered his heart, his life, and everything else to his Emma. Little Emma with light brown curls to her shoulders and wary grey eyes, a profound need for protection and a tiny waist he could put his slabs of hands around, joining his fingers and thumbs at front and back.

Vanessa Raine stood, the tips of her fingers touching the light wooden bench in front of her. "Your Honour. My client, Emma Costa, is not guilty of the charge of murdering Mr Costa. I will show that she loved her husband, Tadeas, and has done for all the years she has known him. On her own admission, she is a simple person who had a tough start to life in foster homes. She achieved no educational qualifications at school. Mrs Costa's simplicity makes her vulnerable to being persuaded by others and this was the case in the murder of her husband. She came under the spell of a religion called the Order of the Solar Temple as practised by Mr Piripi Nosi, her then boarder at number 14 Forsyth Street. The cult is said to have been responsible for murder and mass suicide in the 1990s. A defining characteristic of the mass suicides was fire. A resurgence of interest in the Order is said to be occurring currently. The revitalized religion promotes days of naked fasting, chanting and drug taking to achieve spiritual awareness intended to pave the way for the second coming of Christ. Central to the religion is the desire to block the antichrist who can otherwise settle in your body or in someone close to you."

As Vanessa paused for breath, Clint glanced along the rows of people who sat silent and motionless as if stunned, with wide eyes and slack jaws. Someone was heard to exclaim "What the fuck?" and the spell was broken. Judge McNeill stared severely down at the offender and those giggling around him and motioned the attorney to continue.

"I will show that my client came under the influence of Mr Nosi who was convinced that Tadeas Costa had become possessed by the antichrist and intended to do them harm. I will also show that Mrs Costa did not participate in any way in the torture or death of her beloved husband Tadeas. Mrs Costa is not guilty. Thank you."

The reporters did another scramble for the door so they could call their editors. Following her opening statement as defense attorney in Mrs Costa's trial, Vanessa Raine sat down feeling as if she hadn't really 'nailed it' and was somehow working blind. Like many clients, Emma Costa had struggled to explain to her lawyer what had happened on the evening of her husband's murder. There were gaps in the story and inconsistencies. Emma was inarticulate during their sessions on possible motives for the crime and neither her relationship with Piripi Nosi nor her commitment to the Order of the Solar Temple was clear. It was also not certain that this strange religion was actually the cause of the tragic events at number 14 Forsyth Street. Ms Raine could find very little about the religion as it was practised today and there was no response to her query to the Order which she sent through the contact form on its website.

Vanessa did the best she could with the information at her disposal and had decided to use the oldest defense in the book; going on the offensive. She was placing the blame squarely at the feet of Piripi Nosi in support of Emma's plea of not guilty. She had the strange feeling, however, of waiting for the other shoe to drop. Her career to date had progressed on the path she had mapped out but she had an eerie, shivery feeling that she might have met her match in Lubanzi Abara. She also wondered, however, how much of this uncertain feeling was due to the case and how much due to the things in her personal life churning below the surface. She suspected that her worries about her mother and Diana Darling were affecting her rational thought processes.

Lubanzi Abara was not surprised when Vanessa Raine blamed the death and dismemberment of Mr Costa on his own client. It was a good tactic. But he intended to make it irrelevant. This was a case he felt strongly about and he had some cards up his sleeve. Watch out Ms Raine, he thought, as she resumed her seat and he waited for the Judge to call for his opening statement on behalf of Mr Nosi. Just watch out.

## Chapter Fifteen

Diana Darling Croswell had helped Vanessa prepare for the Costa/Nosi case, researching case law and talking through a strategy. On the first day of the trial she sat at her desk back at the office, her mobile within reach, waiting to hear how it was going in court. They had agreed that she should stay back in the office in case Vanessa needed any research to be carried out at short notice. This was the sort of trial where things could turn on a dime. It was hard to know what direction the case might take and so Diana was feeling tense; she did not want to let down the women who was both her boss and her lover. Vanessa had messaged her earlier to tell her that the attorney for Mr Nosi had also come to court without his assistant, so that person too was presumably sitting at a desk somewhere poised for possible action.

Finding it hard to concentrate on other work, Diana had resorted to flicking through intelligence law because Vanessa had said it might come in handy. But her mind was wandering back to life in Summer Time, the stress-free community in which she had grown up. Summer Time was very different to the highly charged atmosphere of the law firm she was now working for. The commune was a place where you could be alive to all possibilities, find your own way, learn what you wanted to learn, participate in adult conversations about big issues, have a voice, be oneself and know what that was. The commune had weekly meetings where they discussed how to be even better at living and working together. It was slow, orderly and caring. She didn't want to live there anymore but Diana loved going back and spending weekends talking with her mother, teasing her younger sisters and tending the vegetable beds. Taking breaks there refreshed her, so that she could keep up with the manic pace of her new life. She was glad that Vanessa had now visited the commune and met her family. It was important to her.

A memory surfaced in Diana's mind of the furore at Summer Time when she was aged about 15. The commune was investigated by one of Australia's intelligence agencies as a potential domestic terrorist cell. Eventually, it came out that a former member, who had been asked to leave the commune after stealing the petty cash and trying to force himself on young women, had made false allegations about the group. He had made a report to the police, who handed the case to … what was it called … ASIO? Yes. The Australian Security Intelligence Organization, which handled threats to security that came from inside the country. The disaffected man from the commune had reported to the authorities that the commune was actually a camp run by Islamic fundamentalists who were training young people to become ISIS members. The commune had been raided very early one morning by waves of men and women carrying guns and dressed in riot gear including flak jackets, helmets with visors and batons. The commune residents had been scared. The raiders were searching for piles of incendiary pamphlets, Qurans, guns and ammunition, false passports and wads of cash. They didn't find anything of interest. They did, however, find quite a bit of weed which they unaccountably ignored. They were also looking for men wearing long gowns and with long beards, which they found, but they weren't the right sort. Diana laughed out loud at the memory. The adults were kept for hours in the main quarters and were grilled, separately, about their activities. Some were almost naked and all were hungry. The children were herded into a cabin and watched over by a woman in full riot gear. Diana's youngest sister asked her if she was Darth Vader and the woman had smiled. The raid eventually dispersed. Diana had the idea that her mother asked them if they'd like to stay for breakfast. Did she actually do that?

Anyway, Diana Darling thought, if the commune was of interest to the *national* intelligence organization, could the *international* intelligence branch be interested in a strange offshore religion that was connected to a crime in Australia? But wouldn't that be the police's domain, not intelligence and security? She turned her focus back to the law. What if the religion was a cover for a terrorist cell that had moles planted in Australia? Yes, here it was in section 8 of the Intelligence Services Act; the Australian Secret Intelligence Service known as ASIS could gather intelligence and undertake activities relating to an Australian who lived overseas. It could do the same where the person overseas was not Australian but was doing things that might affect Australians. And here, in section 9, this was particularly the case if the activities of this person presented risks to someone's safety or they were acting on behalf of a foreign power. Good God. Diana Darling froze, her finger marking the clause on the computer screen. Could the Order of the Solar Temple be a front for terrorists, even ISIS, and, if so, could the Costa/Nosi case have some connection to terrorism? She looked at her watch. No, there was no point trying to contact Vanessa now, she'd just disturb her; she didn't have anything concrete after all, just questions. She'd do more research and wait for Vanessa to contact her.

Piripi Nosi was raised tending the pigs and growing vegetables on his family's land in Goroka in Papua New Guinea. His parents Namax and Kepari were clever farmers who used regenerative agricultural techniques to improve the soil. Their crops and income from the market thrived while some of the farms in the highlands struggled from generations of over-cropping. His parents were generous. When there were rumours that Namax used sorcery or sanguma on his crops, and those rumours reached the ears of Piripi's father, Namax invited the elders for a visit and took the best part of a day to walk with them around the farm and explained his techniques. He showed them the worms in the moist soil compared to dry brittle soil with no life in an unloved corner of the farm. He said he would help the other farmers put similar techniques in place if they wished. He drank Jungle Juice with them to consolidate their friendship.

"Ren i save – it is science - no sanguma," Namax told the elders.

But a child on one of the neighbouring farms was sick with a cough that rattled and husked and, the next day, little Ato died. Cries went up that sanguma had crept from the Nosi's farm into the neighbouring properties.

"Why are you here?" Namax asked a rabble of men coming onto his land as Kepari shooed the children into the house and told them to hide under the big bed. She was scared and her voice was different; high and tight. It was the strangeness of her voice that made them obey her in fright.

"Bilong yu sanguma daiman pikinini Ato."

The men came with the smell of the local Jungle Juice made from fermented fruit and spat buai. The father of the dead child pointed at Piripi's parents and said "Kuk-im emtupela"; the others took up the chant. The men bound Namax and Kepari, forced water down their throats, splashed them with oil and rolled them on sheets of corrugated tin heated with hot coals from the fire that Namax had been feeding. They were driving out the demons. Much later, with his father dead and his mother critically ill from the torture, the children had been found, rushed to immediate safety at Port Moresby and then taken away to an Uncle living in Sydney. The neighbours took over the Nosi's farm as payment for the loss of their daughter Ato. Piripi was remembering all this. He stood unmoving in the dock, accused of torture and murder, staring with big eyes at Mr Abara. The Nosi history was locked inside Piripi and was not something he would tell. The big man who was fighting his case rose to give his opening remarks.

"You have heard from the Crown prosecutor that Mr Tadeas Costa was tortured and murdered. And you have heard from my co-counsel that Tadeas's wife Emma Costa is innocent on all charges, having come under the influence of my client, Mr Nosi. Piripi Nosi comes from a different land and a different culture to ours. It is because of the chasm between our deeply embedded cultural beliefs that I believe it is difficult to try Mr Nosi under the laws of our Western culture. What I will show in this trial is how the beliefs and natural laws learned as a child are enduring even in a new land with different beliefs and laws. I will show that my client's beliefs are based on a foundation of compassion and spirituality rather than a foundation of hate. I will show that the death of Mr Costa was a tragic accident rather than premeditated murder or even killing in the heat of the moment. I will also show that the co-accused was jointly involved in that tragic accident. Piripi Nosi is not guilty of murder but admits his guilt of involuntary manslaughter."

Vanessa Raine continued to stare at the stack of papers in front of her, not noticing that Mr Abara had glanced her way as if to check her reaction. She had not expected Lubanzi's client to enter a plea of involuntary manslaughter; she had assumed that card had been played and lost when it was found that Piripi Nosi was fit to stand trial. Lubanzi Abara was playing the game she so often played for her own clients and she felt wrong-footed. The Judge asked the prosecutor to move to call her first witness. Clint sat up straight in his seat as his former flatmate Megan walked to the witness box and took an oath to tell the truth about the events at 14 Forsyth Street on the night of Friday, November 8, 2019. Dressed in her police uniform, her hair pulled back and her back like a steel rod, Megan looked every inch the competent policewoman.

She was calm and concise in her answers while being questioned first by Josephine Moss, and then by each of the defense attorneys. She was then dismissed for the time being.

Clint had learned nothing from Megan's testimony he didn't already know; he had been there, after all. Josephine Moss next called a grey-haired man with a short mottled beard and thick glasses with black rims who had led the forensic investigation. He stated his name and job for the record: Dr Ewan Farthing, forensic scientist with the Sydney Police's Clinical Forensic Medicine Unit. The warm room made Clint yawn and he closed his eyes momentarily as he relaxed into his chair. Sleep the previous night had been fragmented as his head buzzed with thoughts about Detective Lilla Adams and his old friend Arash, as well as questions about his new life without his grandfather and without employment.

"… eventually we recovered every bone in the skeleton of an adult male aged 75 to 80 years, I'd estimate," Dr Farthing was saying when Clint tuned back in. "My opinion is that the victim's fingers on his left hand were sawed off before death. I say this because there were signs of a struggle, with the striate, or marks from the saw, crossing each other. The cut went from the distal area of the little finger to where the proximal of the index finger meets the metacarpal." The Doctor held out his left hand, palm down. Using his right index finger, Dr Ewan Farthing drew an imaginary line from the fingernail of his little finger diagonally across to the point where the left index finger joined his palm.

"How do you know a saw was used Doctor?"

"We found a pruning saw in the fire along with the victim's bones. The teeth of the saw match the striations on the phalanges, fingers, exactly.

"And what else did you find?"

"Other body parts were also cut off; all of them at joints such as knees and elbows and all with an axe. The cuts were clean with no sign of a struggle. My assessment is that this dismemberment took place after, or at the time of, death. An axe head was also found in the fire and the dimensions of the axe head matched the cuts on the recovered bones. The axe handle was lost in the fire."

"So the saw and the axe must have been in the fire for some minutes in order for the axe handle to be thoroughly burnt?"

"Yes."

"There would not have been finger marks remaining to indicate who might have been the perpetrator or perpetrators of this crime?"

"That is correct."

"Did you find any evidence that Mr Nosi and Mrs Costa were involved in the torture and death of the victim?"

"When police arrived at the scene, after the bone in the backyard had been discovered by firefighters, the accused were asked to provide their clothing for analysis."

"The accused were both naked when the fire department arrived, and this was before the police arrived. Was their clothing lost in the fire?" Ms Moss asked.

"No. They had already removed their clothing. It had been dropped into two separate piles in the front yard and was unharmed by fire. Mr Nosi's body and clothing was later found to have blood spatter consistent with standing up and standing close to an arterial spurt that came from a person who was seated. The blood splatter on Mrs Costa was minimal and largely on her neck and head rather than on her clothes, indicating that she was at a distance from the body while the blood was spurting and was probably sitting down. The accused were then taken to the police station and fingerprinted. They were swabbed for their DNA and material was scrapped from under their finger nails. The DNA of Mr Costa was found under the finger nails of both of the accused."

Clint was starting to feel nauseous and a bit light headed but he managed to continue sitting through the Doctor's explanation of where the arteries were in the hand which, if cut, would cause a spurting of blood and the cross-examination of his testimony by Vanessa Raine. Ms Raine focused on three points. The first point was that Mr Costa's DNA could be expected to be found under Emma Costa's fingernails because she was his wife and would have touched him regularly, which was not the case for their border Mr Nosi. The second was that her client's diminutive size suggested that she would not have the strength to hold her husband still in a struggle or cut his body into bits with an axe. Third, the splatter on Emma's clothes indicated that she was at a distance from the murdered man as the events were unfolding. Lubanzi Abara declined the opportunity to cross-examine the Doctor, which made Vanessa Raine frown.

Clint stayed in his seat to hear the evidence from the pathologist Dr Shimada in support of the statements of the forensic scientist, Dr Farthing. Dr Shimada sat small and upright on the edge of the chair, his short black hair sprouting in tufts around a face that looked perpetually surprised.

"Are you, as a pathologist who has worked both in Japan and in Australia, able to throw any light on the amputation of Tadeas Costa's fingers?" the prosecutor asked.

"There is a Japanese yakuza or gangster tradition of amputating the left little finger as an act of penance and presenting it to the 'boss' of the mafia. It is something I saw from time to time as a pathologist in Japan. It is possible that this ritual became entangled in the religious creed and cultural beliefs of Mr Nosi."

"Objection. Speculation." Both defense lawyers were on their feet. His Honour waved them down. "Yes. Yes. I know. I'll allow it this time but be careful Ms Moss."

"Yes Your Honour." Josephine bobbed her head to show deference to the Judge and to hide a small smile.

Megan returned to the stand to provide evidence of the statements made to the police by the accused when they were arrested and charged on November 9, 2019, the day after the murder. Mr Nosi had been willing to explain to the police that he believed Tadeas Costa was inhabited by a demon and it was this which had caused the bulge deforming Mr Costa's head. The best way to force a demon to come out of your head, he had told police, is to fill the body with water until there is no room left for the demon while also cutting off a body part so that the demon has somewhere to come out. This conviction came from Piripi's understanding from childhood that sorcery and demons existed, combined with the views of his more recently acquired religious faith."

"The Order of the Solar Temple?" Ms Moss asked.

"Yes," Megan confirmed. "According to Mr Nosi's statement, that sect believes that the antichrist, a type of demon, can inhabit your body or the body of someone you know."

"In their statements to the police, did either of the accused say that Mr and Mrs Costa were devotees of the Order of the Solar Temple or believers of Mr Nosi's other doctrines?"

"Both of the accused stated that all three participants were of the same mind. Mr Nosi also stated that Mr Costa partook of the rituals voluntarily. Mrs Costa could not be drawn on that point."

Ms Moss next called Polly Beauchamp to take the stand. She lived at number 12 Forsyth Street, adjoining the house owned by Tadeas and Emma Costa, and was in the stand in her capacity as a character witness. Yes, she had lived next to Mr and Mrs Costa for a long time because she had bought the house about 15 years ago. Yes, she had come to know Tadeas and Emma; only to talk to, mind, when they met at their front gates or when she was watering the pot plants on the front step. No, she had never heard any arguments or shouting from number 14 Forsyth Street. She had observed Mr Costa sometimes putting his arm around little Mrs Costa out in the back yard, with a fond look on his face. No, she had not noticed any change in their relationship since their new boarder had moved in. Gently, Josephine Moss showed His Honour that a defense of battered wife syndrome for Emma, if her counsel was intending to go that route, could not prevail.

Clint was relieved when the Judge banged his gavel and announced a lunch break before the defense for Mr Nosi began. The morning of the trial had moved quickly. Clint was fascinated by Vanessa Raine's tactic of accepting that torture and murder had happened the night of November 8, 2019 but that the blame rested entirely on the shoulders of Piripi Nosi; her defense was that Emma Costa was innocent. Lubanzi Abara, on the other hand, indicated joint guilt but was of the view that in Mr Nosi's case, at least, the verdict should be involuntary manslaughter rather than murder. That had been followed by evidence from the forensic scientist and the pathologist that was so gruesome it had made him feel sick. He needed some air.

Lubanzi Abara did not eat lunch. The trial was proceeding with extraordinary haste. Ms Moss had already finished calling her witnesses. She obviously thought it was a slam dunk and, after all, why not? The witness testimonies had been pretty damning. Lubanzi took five deep steadying breaths, visualised his whole body filled with warm, gold sun as he had learned to do through meditating, and thought about his two young boys. They were carbon copies of him but with Cara's curly hair and he loved them so much he had to clutch his chest with the hurt of it. He had wondered many times if the reason he worked so hard to help young rudderless men full of hate and confusion was because he wished every boy growing up had had the life his parents had given him;

the life he was now giving his own boys. He knew the love and the sacrifice of his parents; they supported him in his endeavours. He also had the deeply embedded Namibian heritage of looking for peace. He wanted to hand that peace baton on but it was hard, so hard. Most of his clients couldn't see the baton he was offering them. Those who could see it didn't usually want to take it.

The experience of being beaten almost to death, many years ago now, had changed Lubanzi. Still at Law School, he'd been walking home from the University gym one evening and thinking about Cara, the most beautiful and intelligent black woman he'd ever met who was also studying law, when he was surrounded by a pack of white skinheads.

"What's in the bag, black boy?"

He had gently placed the bag on the ground a little in front of him. "Gym gear. School books." He could see three men pacing in front of him. The one who had spoken was acting like their leader. His face was dominated by wide pupils, flaring nostrils and chin lifted like an animal staking its claim to a female on heat. A swastika was tattooed into his shaven head and he was skinny with jeans that slipped down his backside. I could outrun this guy, Lubanzi thought.

"Books. Shit." There seemed to be a loss of pride associated with having bagged only books and smelly gym shoes. "Where's your wallet? Your phone?"

"In my trouser pockets. I can pull them out for you if you like."

"Nah. Jules." The leader flicked his head at one of the other skinny white boys who approached him with apprehension, to retrieve the contraband from his trousers. The boy smelt bad: dirty drugs, dirty clothes and dirty skin, Lubanzi thought, possibly sleeping rough. He lifted his head up and to one side so he didn't have to breathe the boy in.

"You a proud arse? Think you're better than us?" The leader stepped closer to Lubanzi but his attention was diverted by a jubilant sound from the boy who smelt bad; he held up the wallet. Lubanzi took this moment to turn and run. He would have made it too except that two other boys had hung back behind him out of sight and they now tackled him to the ground. The world went dark after boots whacked his head onto the concrete, over and over. Here was a living example of the people who will become my clients, he thought as he began to fall into a small circle of light. This is a hate crime: hating someone who has some advantages in life but who also has features considered by some to be inferior. After it was done, he heard some fear in the voices above him that they might have gone too far, might get caught. "Leave him Cody." There was the sound of fast feet receding.

His next memory was of the hospital, days later, when he came out of the coma. His parents were beside him. His father was holding his hand with his head bowed as if in prayer. His mother was reading the newspaper to him out loud. She said later that she hadn't wanted him to wake up and not know what had been going on in the world. His father was unable to say anything, his eyes bright with tears. His parents had worked hard for all the years he'd known them as they provided their children with routine, love, explanations, food and opportunity. He and his brother and sister owed them everything.

To begin with, he couldn't understand why he was in hospital and what had happened but it slowly came back. Eventually, the descriptions of the three boys he had seen clearly and the two names he'd heard, Jules and Cody, combined with information about the location of the attack and the fact that the boys were stupid enough to try to use his ATM card, meant that the police could track the boys down. They were already known to the police. Everyone involved was a little taken aback when Lubanzi Abara chose to drop all charges if the perpetrators would agree to restorative justice.

Cara came to visit him. "You're trying to change them?" she asked, as he talked it over with her.

"I guess I am. I'm trying to show them another way. Trying to show them that it is not people like me they need to hate; its society. And they can choose to try and change that, and themselves, if they want."

But they didn't want. His clients usually expected him to get them a lesser sentence as if it was a God-given right, and then carried on being the same people and doing the same things. Lubanzi sighed. There was something different about this trial though, he thought, trying to settle on his strategy for Piripi Nosi. It did not seem to be about hate or even about sexual jealousy. It seemed to Lubanzi to be about the clash of cultures and religions. He paced the alley behind the court building and marshalled his thoughts. It was his turn up next in front of the Judge and he intended to refer to South African case law. In one case an employee was dismissed after she took non-sanctioned leave to train as a traditional healer. She was convinced she had been called by her ancestors to attend the course and believed she would die if she did not go. She had requested unpaid leave from her employer in order to attend the course but the employer had refused to allow it. The court subsequently found in the favour of the employee; it held that she was sincere and her cultural beliefs were reasonable.

In another case, traditional dispute resolution practices between colleagues failed. The employer, on learning about the dispute resolution attempts, dismissed one of the participants for bribery. The court found in favour of the dismissed employee, stating that even though employers may not be bound by the same cultural traditions as their employees they cannot simply ignore the existence of those other beliefs, especially in instances where the cultural traditions aim to achieve something good.

Abara's client was sincere in his belief that his landlord Mr Costa wanted to be rid of the demon that had lodged and bulged in his head since he was a little boy, so that his wife would find him more attractive. Mrs Costa had seduced Piripi and was having sex with him but Mr Costa had found out and wanted her to stop. Mr Nosi was of the view that Mr Costa understood that the use of water and cutting rituals would be involved. But Piripi, so he said, was not clever enough to know that Mr Costa would lose so much blood so quickly or would stop breathing because of the water forced relentlessly into his mouth. When he realised that Mr Costa was dead, he believed it was important to burn his body to stop the demon from departing the corpse and entering Mrs Costa or even his own body. They had also burned the tools not to hide their crime but as offerings to appease the demon. Piripi had been raised knowing about demons and seeing their work. He was attracted to the Order of the Solar Temple religion because it fit with his cultural beliefs and boyhood experiences. The Leader of the Order had sermonised in YouTube videos that if any of his flock was ever in trouble they should cleanse themselves, pray, and wait to be lifted up. That was why he and Emma Costa had cast off their bloody clothes and waited, praying, in the front yard for a UFO or some other type of transportation. Lubanzi came to the conclusion that he needed to call Piripi and Emma to the stand one after the other, and he also had a cultural expert from Papua New Guinea on standby to testify about the role of sorcery in PNG. He was ready.

## Chapter sixteen

Lubanzi Abara marched back into the courtroom, leading with his chin and clear about what he was going to say.

"Your name is Emma Costa? Married to Tadeas Costa and living at 14 Forsyth Street, Sydney?" Mr Abara began

"Yes sir."

"How long were you married?"

"Oh. Well, we met when I started working for him when I left school. I must have been about 16 years old then. We married before I was 20.

I'm 47 now." She looked expectantly at Mr Abara, struggling with the maths.

"So, at the time of Mr Costa's death, when you were 46, you had been married for at least 26 years."

Emma was relieved. "Yes sir. That would be right."

"How did you feel towards Tadeas Costa?" Emma looked puzzled. "I mean, when you married him, did you love him?"

"Yes of course."

"And nearly 30 years later, did you still love him? Were you affectionate and kind to each other in the weeks and months leading up to the death of your husband? Or did you argue and fight?"

"We never fought sir. Tadeas was so gentle, loving and kind to me always, and I loved him always in return." Emma was weeping silently now.

"If your feelings remained loving to Mr Costa throughout nearly 30 years of marriage, despite the deformed lump on Mr Costa's head, can you explain why your husband thought it necessary to have the demon in that lump exorcised in 2019 in order to retain your love, and so agreed to be water boarded and have his fingers cut off?"

Emma balled a handkerchief against her eyes and then blew her nose. Her head hanging, she spoke to her hands, "He knew that I was attracted to Piripi and he was worried that I might leave him."

"I'm sorry, we didn't quite catch that." The lawyer stood very still.

Emma repeated her sentence with her eyes staring at the back wall of the courtroom.

"Piripi. Mr Piripi Nosi who was boarding at number 14 Forsyth Street at the time?"

"Yes."

"And did you have a sexual relationship with Mr Nosi?"

Emma's head hung again and she seemed unable to respond.

"Please answer the question Mrs Costa."

"Yes."

Clint looked at the back of Vanessa Raine's head and wondered if her stiff posture was her way of containing surprise at this information.

"You slept with Mr Nosi?" Lubanzi pressed.

"Yes."

"How many times?"

"Objection. Relevance?" Ms Raine was on her feet.

"Yes, yes. Mr Abara," the Judge said, "Please confine your questions to the matter at hand."

Lubanzi bowed slightly to the Judge. "So your husband had cause to be worried that you might leave him?"

"No. I loved Tadeas. I would never leave him. It's just that Piripi liked to have sex with me and he wouldn't take no for an answer. Tadeas, um, couldn't have sex anymore but he didn't want me to have sex with anyone else."

"And so you would have us believe that even though you would never leave your husband, Mr Costa thought you might leave and so he asked you and your lover to torture him?"

Emma was confused. "No. It wasn't like that."

"Then what was it like Mrs Costa? Didn't you plan to get rid of an older husband who was getting in the way of your relationship with a new lover? Someone you had seduced? Wasn't that it? Didn't you suggest to Mr Nosi that he help you tie Tadeas down and kill him?"

"No. Not at all. It was Piripi's idea; all his idea. He said that the Order of the Solar Temple channelled light through him and that he could send demons away; Jinn, he called them. And Tadeas agreed to try it."

"You would have us believe that your husband wanted to be tortured and that your boarder wanted to torture him? Your husband didn't matter to Mr Nosi. And Mr Nosi could take or leave having sex with you. But it annoyed you that Mr Costa was there in the house interrupting your sessions of sex with your lover. In fact, wasn't it true that

Mr Nosi told you he might need to leave you for another woman if Mr Costa didn't leave you both alone? Wasn't it true that you were desperate to keep Mr Nosi living in that house with you and desperate for Mr Costa to go away?" Lubanzi Abara was laying his questions down thick and fast. He was insistent.

Emma became incoherent with confusion and despair at this and had to be led away. Lubanzi's witnesses and questioning, with Vanessa's and Josephine's follow-ups, went quicker than any of them thought possible. The Judge decided to adjourn for the day and it was Vanessa's turn the following morning to put her witnesses on the stand. The bang of the Judge's gavel and the words "all rise" were still echoing as Vanessa and Josephine hung up their wigs and gowns and moved towards the steps leading from the court house. This was all moving much faster than normal and neither of them liked where it was going.

Josephine Moss was intrigued by Abara's notion that cultural norms could be used as a defense against the law and might support a manslaughter charge for his client instead of a murder charge. To her way of thinking it was a bit like using the defense that someone didn't know what the law was. Ignorance is not a defense. There was nothing in the Crimes Act that allowed for different considerations for people from different cultures; that would be a nightmare given the number of different cultures now living in Australia. Josephine was not aware of any case law in the country that allowed different cultures to be treated differently under criminal law. Furthermore, because she was cautious by nature, she had made sure that Piripi Nosi had been arrested using the same processes that were required for Aboriginal and Torres Strait Islanders in case he was found to be descended from the Aboriginal or Torres Strait Islander people. After all, the islands in the Torres Strait were very close to Papua New Guinea and it hadn't, at first blush, been apparent what Piripi's ethnicity was or where he was originally from. Josephine Moss was thankful that she had been cautious enough to cross all the 't's and dot all the 'i's. But she was going back to the office right now to kick off her shoes, increase the layer of fat around her waist with a bag of potato crisps and a glass or two of red wine, and search for case law relating to cultural beliefs, just in case. She hoped her assistant was still in the office.

Vanessa Raine was well aware of all the same matters as Ms Moss but was decidedly less dignified as she ran up the street clutching her black lawyer's bag with the broken clasp, her mobile clamped to her ear and her red hair escaping from its pins. She had read examples in America where cultural defense was used as a shield for violence; usually when men from other countries killed their wives or daughters for reasons of disobedience, married a woman 'by capture', raped a woman, or allowed damage to occur to their daughters. Some Judges (wrongly, to Vanessa's way of thinking) allowed the notion of cultural defense to influence which charges were upheld as well as the severity of any sentencing.

"There is no place in a court for a cultural defense," Vanessa mumbled to herself, causing a passing couple to giggle and cling to each other. She didn't notice them. She was thinking that if an action is defensible according to culture-of-origin, then it should be enshrined in the law as such and shown to be what it is: different laws for different people in the same land. Ms Raine had admired Lubanzi Abara for many years but his use of cultural defense left her cold and a bit scared. She intended to fight him by changing the premise. She would not let this trial degenerate into one that hinged on cultural defense; over her dead body.

"Diana Darling." Vanessa said into her phone. "I need everything we can find on the spiritual beliefs of the Papua New Guineans, especially relating to sorcery and demons. And although we know some of the history of the Order of the Solar Temple, we need to find out more about how it operates today; if the headquarters really are in New York, for example, and who really the Leader of the Order really is. It's going to be a long night. I'm on my way." Diana Darling was ready for her and had her own ideas about the Order of the Solar Temple to throw into the mix.

It was the substance of Lubanzi Abara's argument that decided Clint on a course of action after the first day of the trial. With Mr Nosi on the stand, Clint watched Mr Abara spin a story of a simple boy brought up in Papua New Guinea on a diet of demons and how to exorcise them, with these beliefs consolidated by the religious cult he now followed. Clint could see that, if the Judge bought Lubanzi Abara's defense, there was the potential for Piripi to be found guilty of only manslaughter while the guilt of Emma might remain uncertain. In his bones Clint felt that there was something wrong. A defense based on a person's cultural background felt, to Clint, that anyone from another country could come to Australia and flout the law. Why bother having laws if they only applied to some people in a country and not to all? He also found it difficult to believe that Emma Costa was capable of the things Mr Abara claimed when he called her to the stand.

As the Judge banged his gavel to end the hearing for the day, Clint moved outside and sat out on the steps leading down from the courts. It was still blazing hot outside and he found some shade to one side of a pillar. He searched the internet on his phone using the search engine DuckDuckGo rather than Google so that his searches could not be traced and an idea began to form. It was then that he looked up Vanessa's number on the Sturgess, Diamond and Co. website and dialled the number. Lubanzi Abara walked past Clint as he was talking on his mobile phone in a low voice. Lubanzi was feeling good about how things were going, was looking forward to having dinner with his gorgeous wife and his boys and did not notice Clint. When Josephine Moss walked out, feeling angry that Mr Abara would use culture as a defense for his client, she saw Clint sitting on the steps and talking into his phone. She had noticed him in the courtroom and had wondered what his interest was. He was clearly not a reporter and neither was he likely to be a family member. Family tended to sit in the first row behind the barriers, whereas this young man sat near the back. Josephine Moss was an old hand at this and had learned to trust her instincts. Those instincts were on high alert right now. She wondered what tomorrow would bring.

Clint reached the imposing glass front doors to Sturgess, Diamond and Co. at the same time as the pizza that had been ordered by Vanessa. He felt like he was walking into a TV series about the exploits of a legal firm. Vanessa was at the door to take the pizza boxes and let Clint in. She had tamed her flaming hair under its clasps and looked coolly sophisticated in a trouser suit with wide stripes and big lapels. They took the lift together up to the 12th floor and Clint was introduced to Diana Darling Croswell, Ms Raine's assistant. Watching their hands touch briefly, Clint thought they might also be something more. He noticed that they wore matching engagement rings. Diana was wearing a fitting cream dress with a large bow at the back, together with deep blue slip-on shoes that matched her broach and earrings. The office, Clint noticed, was huge and wrapped around with glass windows. He gazed at the still bright sun on arching greenery in Hyde Park and the spread of blue beyond that was the ocean.

"What a view."

"Wait until the sun goes down and the lights come up; it's magical." Vanessa was opening a pizza box on a glass coffee table and Diana was seated in a nearby chair covered in fawn suede with a tumbler of sparkling water in her hand.

Looking around at the glass on three sides of the room, Clint felt like he was in a fishbowl. "Do you ever feel exposed?" he indicated the glass walls and windows.

Vanessa shrugged. "You get used to it. Would you like a slice of pizza?"

Clint moved to the table, helped himself and sat on one of the soft chairs. "Thank you."

"So, you think you might be able to fill in some gaps in the Costa/Nosi case?" Vanessa took the lead.

"It's possible. I don't want to waste your time, but I have been doing some research which may be of some use. The research began for a story to be published in the online newspaper the Sydney Saturday World but has increasingly become something of a personal interest; especially since I got fired from the paper." Clint grinned.

"We could use all the help we can get. You were in court today?" Clint nodded. "So you will have heard that the defense for Mr Nosi is weaving a tale of a simple man and a scheming woman. I know that Emma has withheld information from me …"

"The fact that she was sleeping with Piripi?"

" … yes, that. But I also think she doesn't have the capacity to be a 'schemer'. You've met her. What were your impressions?"

"My impression of Emma is that she loved her husband and is remorseful about what happened to him. She must also be simple or a bit crazy to get hooked into the Order of the Solar Temple."

"Diana has been wondering if the Order of the Solar Temple is a front for terrorist activity and if the murder of Tadeas Costa is somehow linked to that." Vanessa spoke between mouthfuls of gooey cheese.

"I was thinking along the same lines," Clint confessed, "And so I took a trip to New York to check out the headquarters of the Order."

"Crickey, you were thorough." Vanessa looked impressed, wiping her chin of dripping oil. "Was that after Emma told you that your father might be the Leader of the Order and might also be in New York?"

"Yes. I touched base with the NYPD while I was there, too, because the police were interested in what the Order was up to." I'm walking a fine line here, Clint thought. I must steer clear of anything to do with ASIS. "It turns out that the Order attracts many people who are slightly unhinged and Order members had been murdered in New York, so the cult was being investigated. The leader of the cult has disappeared so it is anyone's guess if it was my father." Clint took a deep breath. "I doubt very much if the murder of Tadeas actually had anything to do with terrorist activities or even the Order. I think that is all a smoke screen. I have been thinking about and researching another possibility. I have a theory to put to you which is far more prosaic, if you are interested."

Vanessa and Diana drew their chairs closer to Clint as he began to tell them his ideas. Darkness had fallen outside and the lights of Sydney were displayed beneath their feet before they called it a night. Vanessa was excited. Clint's ideas had captured and convinced her. That strange feeling had gone of not being on top of this case. Together, the three of them had drawn up a new strategy for her questioning tomorrow and had contacted an expert who was willing to be called as a witness. They had decided that Diana should also attend the trial and sit at the defense table as Vanessa's assistant while Clint would remain as inconspicuous as possible unless he was needed, and would continue to sit near the back of the courtroom.

# Being

# Chapter Seventeen

Clint woke to a beeping near his left ear. He hadn't managed to fall asleep until well after midnight because his brain was working overtime after the evening of strategizing with Vanessa and Diana Darling. It was his second night in a row of not inadequate sleep. It was a few moments before he understood that the beeping noise was coming from the mobile phone clutched in his right hand, resting under his pillow. The CCTV app had been activated. It was 2am and the app's real time video showed a grey shape in a hoodie on the landing outside his apartment, fiddling, it looked like, with the door handle.

Clint sat up without making a sound and eased out of bed. He picked up a pair of jeans folded over a chair and pulled them on over the boxers he'd slept in, before padding to the doorway of his bedroom. There was a click as the lock gave in to the ministrations of the intruder, followed by a small sound as the door handle turned. The door did not move, contained by its bolts. Clint watched the figure on the video give the door a soundless push and a shake of the handle. There was a moment's pause and then the figure stared straight up into the CCTV camera, staring at Clint, but with his face still shaded by the hood. Mere suggestions of other figures lurked behind him. Clint knew that the shadowy form could not see or hear him but realised he was standing as still as stone, holding his breath. The figure, or was it figures, retreated. Pumped with adrenaline, Clint moved to the sliding door to the balcony which overlooked the gates to the complex and watched movement ripple through them. Was it more than one shadow of movement? He wasn't sure.

If that was Arash, Clint thought, as he re-locked the door, he will try again during the day when I am not here and the bolts and chain are off. Or he could try to gain access through the sliding door by climbing the balconies up the wall. The locks that had been installed on the glass door to the balcony and on the other windows were on the inside, however, and so Arash would have to break the glass to get in. It was possible, of course, but it would be more visible and noisier than marching through the front door when the apartment was empty. In that eventuality, though, the CCTV would still provide an alert to what was going on even if Clint was out. And entering the apartment when I am not here comes with the risk that the monitored alarm would go off, with security guards turning up to see what was going on, Clint thought, although Arash would probably have ways of getting around alarms. But was the intruder actually his old friend? Clint replayed the video. The person in the hoodie seemed thinner around the shoulders than Arash. Clint moved back to the window and peered out, looking down the street for any sign of a shadowy figure or even more than one. Nothing moved.

The second day of the trial was scheduled to resume at 9am. Vanessa Raine and Diana Darling Croswell were at the courthouse early, feeling both nervous and confident. As she wigged-up, Vanessa glanced over at the slow and imposing figure of Lubanzi Abara pulling on his gown. It looked like nothing could faze him. Lubanzi smiled at Vanessa with a look of unruffled calm in his large eyes.

"Clint does not seem to be here."

Diana Darling had scanned the crowd and was puzzled by Clint's absence. It wasn't essential that he attend but they had agreed that he could be called to the stand to give testimony if it was needed. She had tried to call him but his phone had gone straight to voicemail. Vanessa felt a niggle of worry. Clint had done the leg work for this case and it would be strange for him not to turn up. She hoped he was just running late. Someone else had noted Clint's absence. A woman carrying an enormous blue leather handbag and with short hair sticking out from under a cap flicked her eyes around the courtroom and frowned. She left the room briefly, pulling out her phone, with her head kept down.

The attendants closed the doors behind her as she returned to her seat. There was the usual call of "all rise" as the Judge entered.

After the aborted attempt of an intruder to enter his apartment, Clint had struggled to return to sleep despite the exhaustion that quickly followed the pumping of adrenaline through his body. It was some time before he fell into a doze of agitated dreams and jerking limbs. He woke with a start, his ears straining for a sound over the hum of the aircon, something that was essential in the hot summer nights of Sydney. He could tell that it was no longer early morning from the light which crept around his bedroom curtains and sliced onto the carpet in the sitting room which he could see through the open bedroom door. What had woken him? He slipped his legs to the floor from under the covers, sat up and was about to stand when he was surrounded by people. Someone kneeling behind him on the low bed had one hand over his mouth and an elbow around his neck in a stranglehold. A second person stood in front of him, legs apart, pointing a gun at his head. There seemed to be a third figure at the very edge of Clint's peripheral vision, standing by the door. He wasn't sure if there were more. Clint stayed very still and made no sound, although the thump of his heart and his desire to scream were all he could think about. Stay calm, he told himself, and keep breathing through your nose. He wondered if he should bite the hand over his mouth but decided not to; they would beat him up if he did.

"We meet at last Clint Ryal." The man by the bedroom door walked into Clint's vision. "Now, be a good boy and we won't hurt you. Scream, or try to make a run for it, and we will hurt you. We surely will, and it won't be pretty." The man had something in his hands that Clint thought might be a Taser. Shit. "You've made some clever attempts to keep us out of your apartment but they are not clever enough." He stood directly in front of Clint, positioning himself next to the man holding the gun. He jeered down at Clint. "If you make a run for it, you won't get far.

The bolts and chain are still on the door and they'd slow you down. Anyway, if you try to take off, I will Taser you. If you shout or scream, I will Taser you. Do I make myself clear?"

Clint nodded slowly. He was scared. The man holding him from behind took his hand away from Clint's mouth but tightened his neck brace. This forced Clint's back to arch slightly and his head to go up. He had to look down his nose to stare directly at the man with the Taser. "Who are you?"

"You don't know?" All three gave muted chortles of laughter. The man holding the gun and the person whose face was jammed up against Clint's had scarves covering their mouths. All three intruders had hoodies up over their heads which cast shadows of protection over their eyes. "All that running around seeking your father and you don't know who we are?"

Clint did not respond.

"We work for the Islamic Revolutionary Guards Corps. We defend our country against external threats and, this will come as no surprise to you, your father is a threat. He is inciting revolution and riots in our country; our great country that has cast out the ways of the infidel." The man's voice was gruff and low. Try to remember, Clint said to himself. Try. It was an Australian accent he was hearing.

"But you sound Australian," Clint ventured.

Quicker than saying 'hello, goodbye' the man holding the gun stepped forward and smacked Clint across his right temple with the butt of his gun. "Fucking shut up," he snarled through a scarf. Clint caught a glimpse of brown skin, a large Persian nose and bloodshot whites of the eyes as if the man was jacked on drugs. *His* voice was raspy and higher pitched than the other man's. Clint tried to commit all this to memory as the gun crashed, as his head was flung to the left, and as the hold on his neck momentarily loosened a little. He heard himself moan. His brain hurt. Amid the thumping ache he felt a trickle of something warm down the side of his face as well as warmth in his groin. "I've pissed myself," he thought angrily. It was this loss of dignity, more than anything, which steeled his resolve to get the better of these bastards. At least Arash wouldn't do this to me, he thought or, rather, I don't think he would. He took a deep breath and tried a different line of discussion.

"How did you get in here?"

"We climbed up the outside of the building from one balcony to the next under cover of darkness and cut a hole in the glass of the sliding door to your apartment. Did you think those puny deadlocks would keep us out? We've been here for some time, going through your things while you tossed and turned. We thought the sound of the glass cutter would wake you but you were exhausted, I'd say. And we didn't want to ruin your beauty sleep. We are in no hurry. No one knows we are here. No one cares where you are. You are a 'man alone' aren't you Clint? You are so very alone." There was a flash of white teeth from the guy in charge, as Clint was now thinking of him, which was presumably a smile. "No more questions," he snapped abruptly; his playful voice returning to a tone that meant business. "I am asking the questions. Where is your father?"

"I don't know."

Clint's body convulsed as the Taser hit. His muscles cramped and he could feel his mouth stretched into an empty scream. If he thought he'd experienced the pump of adrenaline earlier that night, it was nothing to this. The man holding him around the neck had let him go and he slumped off the side of the bed onto the dark grey carpet as the electric shock retreated. The main in charge took him by the shoulder and turned him over, peering into his face. Clint wished he could kick out and grab the Taser or run and throw himself out the hole in the window. Death by falling might be preferable to hours of prolonged torture. But none of his limbs worked.

"Now, now," the man soothed, moving strands of hair back off Clint's wet face and stroking his cheeks with the hand not holding the Taser. "I thought you were going to be a good boy for me. And ..." his hand ran over Clint's right shoulder, across one dark nipple erect with pain and fear, and down his flat abs, slipping his fingers playfully just under the waistband of his sodden boxers "... you are such a good looking young man. I don't want to hurt this fine body, this fine face." The man moved his hand to his own groin and rubbed it suggestively, undulating his hips so that the bulge in his pants came and went close to Clint's face. "We could be friends, now, couldn't we? I could look after you. We heard you with that whore detective in New York; that slut. I could make you moan with pleasure far exceeding anything you experienced with her."

Jesus Christ, Clint thought, his anger rebuilding. Was there no sodding person in the world who didn't follow and listen to me while I was in New York? I'm not some bloody plaything. At that, he turned his head and vomited up the partially digested pizza from the evening before. The man jumped to his feet and backed out of the way.

"I'll take that as a rejection." The voice was cold and gruff again. "So, let's try this again."

Two arms lifted Clint from the floor and sat him back on the side of the bed. He saw the sides of a brown shaven skull under the hoodie and thick black eyebrows above the scarf covering his mouth. Clint stared into the man's small beetle-black eyes for a moment, noting a look of concern or fear. Okay, I've made a connection, Clint thought. When the man resumed his place behind Clint with an arm around his neck, it was more relaxed. Clint found the warmth of the man's body reassuring against his own. Glancing under cover of his long eyelashes, now beaded with moisture, and out through the partially closed bedroom door, Clint could see brilliant sunshine and dust motes playing across the carpet in the sitting room. It was another hot day and yet he was shivering with hurt and the terror of what might happen next; shivering in his darkened bedroom with its curtains still drawn.

"So, Allah Akbar, you will tell us where your father is. When did you last see your father?"

"I cannot remember ever meeting my father. He left my mother, maybe even left Australia, about the time I was born."

The man with the gun now slammed the butt into Clint's left temple. Clint felt his brain slosh from side to side against the walls of his head. "Wrong answer. You met him in New York."

"I *thought* I might meet him. I *wanted* to meet him, if he was there, but the NYPD banned me from going into the headquarters of the Order of the Solar Temple, which was where I thought he might be. The NYPD said there was no sign of him. The police were not even sure that he had anything to do with the Order and neither was I, to be honest." Clint raised his aching head a fraction and watched the two men in front of him exchange looks. "Um," he continued, thinking feverishly, "I mainly went to New York to help the Costa/Nosi murder trial. I wanted to find out if Piripi Nosi, the co-accused, was telling the truth when he said the murder was the accidental result of the religious beliefs of the Order. I wanted to help Emma Costa if I could. I am helping her legal team. You can ask them if you like."

Clint had been going to say that he wanted to help Emma because she was an old friend of Bekym's, but managed to stop himself in time. If they didn't know that already, he shouldn't tell them. Clint had also just remembered that, according to Arash, the IRGC had infiltrated the NYPD. He needed to make sure he didn't say anything that could be disproved by the infiltrators. The two men in front of him had turned to each other and were murmuring in low voices. The pressure around Clint's neck had eased even further. His mind returned to the fact that the IRGC had heard him making love to Lilla but didn't seem to have heard anything else he had done in New York. That was a good sign, he thought. It might mean that they weren't bugging me; they were bugging Lilla or her flat. But that may also mean she is in danger, Clint realised. Damn.

A loud beeping from under Clint's pillow made them all jump. The man holding the Taser reached over and threw the pillow out of the way. The CCTV app had activated again, although the exposed video didn't seem to be showing anybody outside the door to the apartment. Clint sat very still, thinking fast. Was it a neighbour or had someone come to find out where he was. If they had, they had managed to remain concealed. The clock on his phone said 9.30am. He should be in court and maybe he had been missed. Could Vanessa have sent someone to find out if he was okay? Clint hoped it was someone with large shoulders, a big gun and lots of street smarts.

"Lion." It was the first time the man holding Clint had spoken. "We need to leave. What do you want to do? Take the lad with us?"

The leader looked steadily at Clint while Clint stared back knowing from the look in Lion's eyes that he was not convinced by Clint's answers and also wasn't ready to give up on playing with him sexually, although he knew that they might be at risk of being discovered. "Leave him," he said at last. "He has nothing for us right now." He picked up Clint's phone, considered it for a moment and then dropped it on the floor, grinding it under his boot. Bloody hell, Clint thought, not another one. Lion extracted some zip ties and tape from the pocket of his hoodie. The men tied Clint to the slats in the bedframe and taped his mouth. All three of them took out their guns and, without a backward glance, left the bedroom. Clint heard them undoing the bolts and chains on the apartment door followed by a small click as the door was pulled shut behind them. He lost no time in leaning his face close to his bound hands and ripping the tape off his mouth. Taking a deep shaky breath he was about to shout for help when he heard the apartment door click again. His stomach turned to ice and he sat motionless, straining to hear.

Had they returned to finish the job? The barrel of a gun appeared soundlessly around the doorframe followed by eyes of coal that darted around the room, before resting on Clint.

"Clint, thank God." Arash moved across the room, withdrawing a blade from a trouser pocket, flipping it open and slitting the zip ties. His arms caught Clint into a hug.

Arash had refused to immediately discuss what had just happened; quickly making a hot cup of tea instead while Clint got out of his boxers and found a bathrobe. Clint's face screwed up at the sugary drink but understood why Arash was forcing it down him. A plate of scrambled eggs and toast was then pushed in front of him. He ate ravenously, his hands still shaking, while Arash looked at the wounds and bruises on his head. His saviour had made an impromptu cold pack out of a bag of frozen peas and held it awkwardly against the worst of the bruising while Clint ate.

"Shower next," Arash said, shooing Clint into the bathroom that opened off the end of the hall.

Arash had already checked to make sure that no intruders were hiding in there or in the hall cupboard that housed the laundry appliances. Clint found himself standing in the bath, leaning against the tiled wall with the hot water from the large shower head falling over his back and tears streaming down his face. The beating was not nearly as bad as it might have been and certainly no worse than some of the beatings he'd taken as a child from his mother's boyfriends, although the tazering was something new, but the entire experience had left him feeling vulnerable and useless. He seemed to be incapable of looking after himself as an adult. Clint emerged from the tiny bathroom with one of Sunil's old raspy towels of faded blue wrapped around his waist. Two strangers were sitting next to Arash at the small dining room table. Arash stood up smiling.

"You look better already. This is Amy; she's going to take a look at your wounds and make sure you're not concussed, and then she'll leave." Arash could see that Clint was a bit overwhelmed by all the people. "This is Tom who is here instead of Deidre. Deidre is at the court house today so couldn't be here. Tom and I will listen to your story of what happened, if you're up to it."

"Okay. I'll just get dressed." His bedding had been stripped and the wet boxers gathered up. Clint could hear the washing machine chugging behind the door to the laundry cupboard in the hall. It looked like the mattress had been turned over for the time being, too, so that he wouldn't have to sleep on the soiled patch. His broken mobile phone and the vomit had been cleared away. It occurred to Clint that he had made few changes to the décor or the furniture since this apartment had become his and maybe now was the time to replace Sunil's things, including the mattress. His memories of Sunil would remain with him irrespective of whether or not his grandfather's things were still in the apartment. Once he had dressed in fresh fawn-coloured shorts and a blue T-shirt, Amy tended to his wounds in the bedroom. After giving him medicine for the pain and a local anaesthetic, she put a handful of stitches in the right temple which had taken the brunt of the force. She checked his vision and ability to move his neck, then handed him a bottle of pain medication for when the anaesthetic wore off. She gave him the all clear.

"No sign of concussion," Amy announced as they returned to the sitting room, "But his head's going to hurt like hell for a few days and getting to sleep will be rough. No matter which side you lay your head, it's going to ache," she told Clint. "Keep taking those pills," was her parting shot as she left the apartment.

Clint felt a wave of exhaustion knock him over and sat heavily in his grandfather's favourite beige chair with its high back and enclosing arms. Arash silently made coffee while Tom moved to the matching beige couch to be closer to Clint. A small wooden coffee table from a charity shop sat between them, covered in circles from hot mugs. Arash placed the remains of three small metallic objects on the coffee table next to Clint's coffee. The objects had been smashed into small bits.

"I did a sweep of the apartment and found these; courtesy of your intruders I imagine. I'll check the bathroom too in a minute, before we hear your story. I know this is tough, Clint." Arash could see how weary Clint was. "You probably feel like crawling into bed and sleeping for the rest of the day, but its best if you tell us the story now. I promise you'll feel better once you have and then we can leave you alone if you like."

Clint gazed at the sliding door onto the balcony which now had an oblong of glass removed. Did he want to be alone? What if those thugs came back?

## Chapter Eighteen

"Mrs Costa, can you please tell the court what happened in the events leading up to your husband being killed on Friday, November 8, 2019? Remember you are under oath and must tell the whole truth." Vanessa was on her feet, taut with tension.

Emma was in the stand. She thought she might be executed in an electric chair if the Judge got to hear how bad she'd been. Her lawyer had told her that Australia didn't do that, but Emma didn't really believe her. Anyway, she understood that she had to tell the whole truth, no matter how bad it made her look and no matter the consequences, and so she would.

"Tadeas had been to the shops. He came home early and found us in bed …"

"That's Tadeas Costa, your husband? And when you say 'us' do you mean yourself and Mr Piripi Nosi?"

"Um. Yes. Yes. Piripi wanted to have sex with me all the time even when I said no. I knew it was wrong."

"Why do you say that having sex with Piripi was wrong?"

"I didn't love him. Piripi. I loved Tadeas." Emma slumped and a guard helped lift her straight again.

"Would you like a seat Mrs Costa?"

"Yes please."

There was a pause while a seat appeared and Emma was settled.

"Please carry on with your story. Tadeas came home and found you in bed with Mr Nosi. What happened next?"

"Tadeas cried. He sat at the kitchen table with his hands over his face and moaned, asking me where he had gone wrong and why I didn't love him anymore. I said 'No, no. Of course I love you.' Tadeas wanted Piripi to leave the house and never come back. But Piripi sat down at the table too and finished smoking a joint; as casual as you like. He said that the demons, the Jinn, that lived in the bulge on Tadeas's head were taking over his body so that he was unable to have sex with his wife ... me, anymore. He said that the rituals he'd learned from the Order of the Solar Temple could help him drive out the demons if Tadeas wanted him to try. He said he'd have to tie Tadeas down because the Jinn would put up a good fight but if he was successful then Tadeas would be a man again and then Piripi would leave the house." Emma stopped to breathe and to remember and to let the tears fall unchecked down her face.

"And what did Tadeas say in response to that?"

"He said that he was willing to try because he wanted to make me happy, but he wanted Piripi to go away after that, no matter what happened."

"And did you say anything then?"

"I said that Piripi should just go and not try to do any voodoo because I loved Tadeas no matter what. But then Piripi went into a trance. His voice changed and his hands began dancing in the air near Tadeas's head. I didn't understand what he what saying. When he came back to being normal again, he gave a little shake and said that the Jinn was getting restless; it was now trying to possess Piripi and next it would be me. So Tadeas said we should try the exorcism. Piripi found some ties that Tadeas used when he grew tomatoes out the back and he bound up Tadeas's hands and legs to the kitchen chair. Piripi put a hand on Tadeas's forehead and forced his head back. He poured water into his throat. Tadeas was thrashing around and choking and trying to shout and I was screaming 'stop, stop'. But Piripi didn't stop. The water went all over the floor. When Tadeas went limp and his head fell forward Piripi said that was a good sign and that the demon was now weak. He said he had to let the demon out by cutting Tadeas's body and he picked up a pruning saw that was in the corner of the kitchen. I don't know why it was there because it should have been in the box of tools we kept in the back porch. When Piripi cut Tadeas's fingers, he, he twitched and seemed to come alive again, he was choking, but then the blood spurted everywhere; it went everywhere," Emma's voice rose to a thin wail, "And Tadeas slumped down again."

There was no sound in the court, no movement. Emma sat gazing at the handkerchief twisted in the hands clutched in front of her and the drops from her eyes that were splashing into her lap. She was wearing the same oversized blue top, now spattered with tears.

"Mrs Costa, I and my team …" Vanessa indicated Diana Darling Croswell sitting at the defense table, "… have researched the Order of the Solar Temple and have found reference to demons, but never to them being called Jinn. Neither does the term Jinn appear in Papua New Guinean religious beliefs. Do you know why Piripi referred to the demons in your husband's head as Jinn?"

"It came from the High Priest of the Order of the Solar Temple. We saw videos on YouTube. *He* referred to demons as Jinn."

"For the court," Vanessa turned to address the Judge, "Our investigator found the High Priest of the Order in New York and discovered that he has an Islamic background. This unknown High Priest has now disappeared. Demons are often referred to as Jinn in the Quran. Now, Mrs Costa," Vanessa turned back to face Emma, "Can you tell the court what you were doing while the torture of your husband was going on?" She wanted to move on quickly before Emma could offer information about the identity of the High Priest. It was not relevant to the case and she didn't want it mentioned. When the word "Islamic" was mentioned, a small woman in a cap at the back of the court had leaned forward, her elbows propped on her thighs and her hands clasped. Now, she relaxed back into her seat.

"Me? I, I ..." Emma rubbed her eyes, " ... I was scared. I had crouched down on the floor in the corner near the rubbish bin. I was crying and saying 'stop' and calling to Tadeas but he didn't answer me." She gave a huge shuddering sigh as if relieved to finally have the opportunity to tell the whole story, the whole truth.

"And what happened next, Mrs Costa?"

"Piripi went out of the room. The blood was still spurting but slower. I moved slowly towards Tadeas but I was scared and then Piripi came back into the kitchen. He said we needed to destroy the Jinn by putting it into fire. He cut the ties holding Tadeas and his body fell to one side. Piripi lifted him up over his shoulder like firemen do on the television and he took Tadeas out to the backyard. I followed them, pleading with Piripi to save my Tadeas. He was dripping blood through the hall. There was a big bonfire in the backyard and Piripi had an axe. He cut off my Tadeas's head ..." Emma dissolved into moans and sobs, making the words hard to make out, "... and he put ... bits of my Tadeas and the tools he'd used ... into the fire." She gave a long wail.

"Thank you Mrs Costa. I'm sorry you had to relive that dreadful night for us today. I have no further questions Your Honour."

Lubanzi Abara stood up and Judge McNeill nodded to him to go ahead and cross-examine the witness. The Judge was pale. He used the sleeve of his black gown to mop the sweat that had formed on his forehead and upper lip; it had got hotter in the courtroom while Emma was giving her testimony. Lubanzi walked up close to Emma, standing to one side so that the court could see his proud profile under the white wig and hear his every word. He smoothed a hand down the black gown covering his powerful chest as he leaned in to talk to the accused.

"Mrs Costa. Your story is very sad. Were you scared for your own safety?"

Emma removed the sodden handkerchief that had been trying to stem the flow from her eyes.

"My safety sir? Why no. It was Tadeas that Piripi hurt; it was Tadeas that had the demon, not me."

"You say that you watched Mr Nosi torture, kill and dismember your husband but admit that you were never afraid for your own safety? Isn't that because you were a willing helper in the events not a bystander? Isn't that because you wanted your husband dead and out of the way so that you and your lover could carry on having sex?"

"No, no, not at all sir." Emma looked horrified.

"And," went on Lubanzi, barely pausing, "Have you any evidence, a video recording on your phone for example, of the events of that night?" He was now leaning his towering bulk towards her in the witness stand.

"No I …"

"And so it is only your word against Mr Nosi's about what took place that night. And after your husband's body had been consumed by flames you happily let your lover take you to the front of the house and remove your clothing, to wait for something to lift you up and take you away from the old man you never really loved and who you were now leaving behind. Isn't that so Mrs Costa?" The last words boomed over the courtroom as Lubanzi strode back to his seat looking huge and angry with the strength of his words shining on his dark face.

"I loved Tadeas," Emma crooned, her whole body rocking now. "I loved him. I didn't know what to do. I loved him."

"No further questions Your Honour."

The judge turned to Emma. "Thank you Mrs Costa, you may step down."

Vanessa was on her feet again. "I'd like to call Piripi Nosi to the stand." The black lawyer's gown on Ms Raine looked stylish and sliming. She wore high-heeled black pumps and long black drops in her ears. Her ring finger flashed as she used her left hand to push a wandering strand of hair the colour of flames back under her wig.

The defiant face of Mr Nosi stared into the distance just to the left of Ms Raine. The whites around his small black eyes sat under the hoods of his lids and were not dominant today. Piripi did not want to look into the woman lawyer's eyes and stood still and proud, his jaw defiant as usual. He wore a suit jacket over a round-necked T-shirt today. The tattoo on his neck was not entirely concealed. After the preliminaries, Vanessa turned briefly towards Diana Darling with a question in her raised eyebrows. Diana shook her head; Clint was still not in the courtroom and was not answering his phone. Resigned to proceeding without him, the lawyer turned back to the accused.

"Mr Nosi. Your defense attorney claims that the events at 14 Forsyth Street on the night of November 8, 2019 were the result of your cultural upbringing in which it was common during the exorcism of demons to use water, cutting the body and fire. Your parents were tortured and killed in that way while demons were being exorcised, were they not?"

Mr Nosi made no move to look at his questioner or to respond. A murmur and a ripple of interest drifted around the room. Mr Abara froze; he might have missed something.

"Answer the question please, Mr Nosi," The Judge said with a note of command in his voice.

"Yes."

"Can you tell the court about when your parents were killed, Mr Nosi?"

"Objection." Lubanzi was on his feet. "Relevance?"

"I'll allow it," the Judge said without elaboration.

Piripi's eyes finally moved to rest on Vanessa Raine. "A little girl, a neighbour, died. It was because my parents had used sorcery. The villagers came to exorcise the demons. They poured water down my parents' throats while they were singing songs and chanting." He stopped.

"And where were you when this was happening Mr Nosi?"

"I was in the house with my brothers and sisters. We had crouched below the window but sometimes peered out."

"And what did you see?"

"There was a bonfire in the front yard. My father had been burning the rubbish and the prunings from his crops. The villagers put some tin in the fire and rolled my parents on it." His voice was small and toneless.

"Your parents died?"

"My father died immediately and my mother died sometime later."

"And what happened next?"

"I was taken away to Australia. The other children too."

"Tell me about the house and the land of your parents. Was your family poor or was your farm prosperous?"

Piripi gazed at her and Vanessa could see hatred rising in his eyes. "My father was a clever farmer and his soil was good. He grew lots of crops and raised pigs. We were not poor."

"And what about the farmer next door, whose little girl died? Was his farm prosperous?"

Piripi looked at Lubanzi who rose and objected again, asking about the relevance of the question. The Judge looked at Ms Raine who said, "This line of questioning is highly relevant to the matter Your Honour, as I will demonstrate shortly."

"Get there quickly," the Judge advised and Vanessa asked the question of Mr Nosi again.

"The next door neighbour's farm was not prosperous," he replied with reluctance.

"After the death of your parents, what happened to the farm and the house belonging to your family?"

"The next door neighbour took the land and the house as payment for the loss of his child."

"How does that make you feel Mr Nosi? That the land and house owned by your family was taken from you."

"It is the culture." Piripi had resumed his gaze off to one side and away into the distance; the whites of his eyes now showing.

"Thank you Mr Nosi. I have no more questions for now, but may wish to call you back to the stand shortly."

The Judge motioned to Lubanzi Abara who said he had no questions and so Mr Nosi was asked to step down. Vanessa stood again.

"I call to the stand Dr Kepano Morgan."

A man, possibly in his late 30s or early 40s, walked quickly to the stand. His dark hair was cropped close to his skull and around his chin. Wrinkles radiated from the corners of his eyes, giving him a look of gentleness. He wore a short-sleeved shirt that was such a light colour of blue that it was almost not blue at all, and pale coloured slacks.

"Dr Morgan, have you been a human rights advisor to the United Nations?"

"Yes. I was the United Nations' human rights advisor to Papua New Guinea from 2013 to 2018."

"Are you from Papua New Guinea yourself, Dr Morgan?"

"Yes, I was born there and brought up there."

"Can you please tell the court the subject matter of your PhD?"

"My PhD is on the role of sorcery in modern day Papua New Guinea."

Vanessa could hear murmuring and restlessness in the courtroom behind her but did not look round.

"Can you briefly explain to the court the substance of the findings of your PhD?"

"I found that modern sorcery attacks in PNG are a brutal way to redistribute power. People who feel disenfranchised can enhance their power by accusing successful members of the community of sorcery and gaining community support for their accusations. Essentially, an accusation of sorcery is a way to give voice to jealousy and greed. Acting on those accusations with violence is the way that people with little wealth or power can take revenge on those with more wealth and power. Childless widows I studied, for example, were accused of sorcery so that extended family members or neighbours could take control of their land."

"I'd like to ask you some questions, given that you are Papua New Guinean yourself and you are an expert in sorcery in Papua New Guinean culture. You've heard the testimony of Piripi Nosi here today about the torture and death of his parents. Can you tell us anything about the motive for that tragedy?"

"Oh yes. I included Mr Nosi's parents in my research. Their deaths were unequivocally the result of the neighbour's jealousy."

The murmuring in the room was louder this time and Judge McNeill banged his gavel once, sharply.

"Does your research consider the ripple effects of torture and murder based on accusations of sorcery?"

"My research found that where a family is accused of sorcery and their property taken, the next generation, or even the wider family, believe it is appropriate to accuse someone *else* of sorcery in an attempt to gain back property and wealth. They, we, call it revenge."

"In your professional opinion, Dr Morgan, is revenge the cause of the torture and death of Mr Tadeas Costa?" Vanessa's voice rose over rising babble. "Do you believe that Mr Nosi coldly killed Mr Costa to claim Emma and the property at number 14 Forsyth Street and the Costa's savings from the sale of the Souvlaki café in order to gain back property and wealth because his family's was stolen when he was just a child?"

"Quiet, quiet in the court." The gavel came down twice.

Mr Abara rose to shout "Objection. Speculation."

The Judge allowed the line of questioning because it was the witness's area of expertise and Dr Morgan answered "Yes. That is my opinion. My research indicates that such murders are premeditated and are considered by the murderer to be their 'right'."

"And what is your opinion of Mr Nosi's claim that his belief in demons was consolidated by the religious cult he followed, and that he was trying to help Tadeas Costa recover his sexual prowess with his wife."

"That is nothing more than a fabrication."

"Objection Your Honour," Lubanzi Abara was on his feet. The Judge waved him to sit down and Vanessa Raine recalled Mr Nosi to the stand.

## Chapter Nineteen

"A glazier will be here shortly to fix the sliding door. The glass of the door and the pane next to it can be replaced with material reinforced with fibers that are very difficult to cut through," Arash said. "We would also like to install roll-up steel guards on the inside of your widows and the sliding door, if you have no objection. We've got the all-clear from the body corporate for the apartment block to install them inside the building, just not outside, but that's okay."

"Won't that make it harder for you to get in too?"

Arash grinned at Clint. "I just have to knock and ask if I can come in."

"Thank you for coming." There was a lump in Clint's throat. "How did you know something was wrong?" He sipped his coffee to hide his emotion.

"It was Deidre. You weren't in court this morning and she could see that the defense lawyers for Emma Costa were looking for you too. She had a hunch that you really wanted to be there and that something big must have kept you away. I said I'd check and came round here. I quickly realised that you might be in trouble when I looked up at your apartment from the outside and saw the hole in the sliding door. I set off the CCTV alarm to your phone by throwing a rolled up newspaper along the landing, being careful not to get into the line of sight myself. In order to observe what might happen next, I retreated to the ground floor and tucked myself under the stairwell. I didn't really know what to expect. As the men came down the stairs I decided not to confront them but my colleagues have followed them. We may now be able to find their headquarters, which would be very helpful. You were my first priority so I didn't go with my colleagues. I thought I'd find you dead or, at the very least, in a far worse state. You did well, Clint, to keep them calm and to get out of this alive."

Arash smiled at him proudly and Clint could feel his self-disgust easing a little. They talked through the events for about two hours before Clint could talk no longer. Tom and Arash were particularly pleased with the descriptions of Clint's assailants and their voices. The name Lion seemed to mean something to them; "Arsalan," Tom proclaimed. He went on to explain that it meant lion in Persian and that they'd had someone in their sights for a while who went by that name. "Someone nasty," he added. Arash sucked in a breath when Clint recounted the conversation about IRGC and their search for Bekym.

"If they were prepared to give so much about themselves away to you Clint, it is a surprise that they didn't kill you."

"I have the feeling that Lion wanted to recruit me or, at the very least, take me as a lover," Clint admitted, feeling his face going hot, but the other two just nodded sagely.

"That means he's likely to be back," Arash commented.

One thing bothered Clint. "I'm worried about Lilla. Detective Adams. It sounded from what Lion said that they have her apartment bugged. Is there anything you can do to ensure her safety and get rid of any bugs?"

Arash looked at Clint for a long moment. "I'll see to it," he said finally. "Ah, here is the glazier. Why don't you try and get some sleep while you can Clint? I'll stay here," he added. I'm not going anywhere."

Once the bed was remade with fresh linen taken from the shelves in the wardrobe, Clint climbed into it with a sigh. He liked his grandfather's bed. It was quite low to the ground and slatted like a futon base but it definitely needed a new mattress. Even if he hadn't wet it, it was too thin and lumpy for his liking. He looked around the room as if seeing it for the first time. He liked this room. It was the room he had grown up in. It was situated in the corner of the apartment block and so had large windows on two walls. Because this corner of the building faced north (the prime position for housing in the southern hemisphere) the room was flooded with light and warmth whenever the curtains were pulled back. Today, the curtains were closed.

With the events of the night behind him, the bedroom and its shapes and colours looked strange, as if he was seeing them for the first time. The old chest of drawers was small and probably bought second hand 30 years ago. It had once been painted white but was now discoloured and peeling. When he moved into the apartment, Clint had bagged up his grandfather's clothes but the bags still sat in the corner. They were shapeless lumps of another time which, now he looked at them, niggled at his sense of neatness and order. The time was finally right to take them to a charity shop. The walls of the bedroom were bare of art and the bedside tables were made from wooden boxes, each containing a pile of old paperback novels. There was only one bedside lamp with a faded grey lampshade. Next to the lamp, someone had plugged in the phone Deidre had given him, allowing it to charge its battery. Other than that, little had changed in this room since Clint first came to live with Sunil when he was a young boy. Even with the pills, Clint's whole body ached from the cramping effects of the Taser and the after effects of the adrenaline. His head thumped as he laid it gingerly onto the pillow. It was a relief to know that Arash was in the other room and would keep watch. He was thinking about Lilla, hoping she would be alright, when he fell asleep.

Sun was still displayed around the edges of the curtains when Clint woke. The room was stiflingly hot and he must have thrown the covers off while he slept in an attempt to cool down. The cool air from the aircon could not reach from the sitting room into the bedroom with the door shut. Feeling groggy and a bit sick, Clint sat up, wincing at the pounding in his head. He pulled back on the shorts and T-shirt he was wearing earlier in the day, grimacing as the neck of the shirt rasped against his stitches, and opened the door. A man in overalls was packing up a bag of tools near the sliding door. Arash was sitting on the couch scrolling through something on his phone.

"Hello. How are you doing?"

"I'm okay I think. I'll be with you in a sec."

He needed to pee and he wanted to take pain killers and have a drink of water. As he sorted himself out, the glazier finished up and said goodbye. Shortly afterwards, a team of three workmen arrived to install the window guards and Arash talked them through what was required.

"Hey Clint," Arash came to stand next to Clint who was looking at the new sliding door with mesh laid between dual panels of glass. "This team is here to install the steel roller-guards over the windows and sliding door. Apparently they can let the light and air in when they are in position, but keep people out. And you can always roll them up out of the way if you wish. The installation will take a few hours and will be a bit noisy. Do you fancy taking a stroll with me to have a late lunch? My treat."

Clint reached for his phone in his jeans pocket to check the time and remembered it had been smashed. He looked over at the clock on the stove. It was 3pm. "Food sounds good. I'll just put some shoes on. Um …" he paused, "… how much is all this costing?"

"Well the cost of the glazier isn't much and you might be able to claim it on insurance, although, as we haven't reported the break-in to the police, maybe not. The real cost is in the steel guards and we are paying for those."

"Really? How come?" Clint didn't need to ask what he meant by 'we'.

"We feel responsible for putting you in harm's way." Arash smiled grimly. "I'll ask Tom to come back and keep an eye on the place while the installers are here, shall I? Oh, I pulled out the mobile phone Deidre gave you, by the way, in case you want to use it for a while."

Clint grinned. "I saw it in the bedroom. Thank you." Deidre had been right when she'd given him the phone, he thought. She'd told him that tracking his movements was about keeping him safe rather than invading his privacy. Maybe it wasn't such a bad idea after all if someone knew where he was at all times.

They ate platters of grilled lamb and chicken with hot Persian sangak bread, grilled tomato, onion and fresh mint with yoghurt at the Sangak Bread Bakery and Restaurant only a few blocks away. The tiny restaurant blared Middle Eastern music in an attempt to attract customers, which was a bit loud, but the restaurant offered aircon which was welcome. They looked out from the shade into the heat of the day, each lost in thought and saying little. Arash's phone buzzed.

"That was Deidre," he said as he finished the call. "All the arguments in the case have been put, including the closing arguments from the two defense lawyers and the prosecutor, and the Judge has retired to consider his verdict. She said that the lawyer Vanessa Raine was very compelling and she wouldn't be surprised if Emma Costa is found not guilty. Did you have a hand in her defense strategy?"

"What makes you think that?"

"You were seen going into Sturgess, Diamond and Co. yesterday."

Clint could think of nothing in response to that. He was an unwilling player in this cloak and dagger stuff and it felt smothering.

"I was thinking of going to the mosque tonight," he said instead. "I feel like I need some calmness and spiritual healing. Would you like to come?"

Arash sighed and put down his fork. "I don't know Clint," he said with concern. "It might not be a good idea. Sunil was attacked right outside a mosque, possibly the same thugs that got to you. Some imams are hand in glove with the IRGC. You could be in danger."

Clint put his head in his hands, his elbows propped on the table, and then wished he hadn't; his head hurt. Arash was right of course but the restrictions on his life and his movements were becoming galling. "I know," he said wearily. Arash was relieved that his friend hadn't shouted at him in protest. "I might call Graydon and see if he'd like a visitor. He's the nearest thing to a grandfather I have now." Arash nodded in understanding and picked up Clint's phone; he wanted to download the Wingello Street apartment's CCTV app onto this phone before he let Clint out of his sight, as well as ensure that the phone held all the necessary numbers in his contact list.

Vanessa Raine and Diana Darling Croswell snuggled up together in their apartment. The square-shaped sofa upholstered in honey coloured leather, complete with leather cushions in complementary colours, suited the style of the room; contemporary and minimal with pops of colour. Looking around the open plan sitting and dining rooms which led into the kitchen, with the walls taken back to the original brick and the ceilings low with light-timbered rafters, Vanessa realised how happy she was here. She had seen the apartment advertised a few years ago. It was marketed by the agent as being in the style of a New York loft. She didn't know how true that was but, nevertheless, had loved it and bought it immediately. Her colour scheme for the reception rooms revolved around yellows and tans. It had been decorated long before Diana Darling had come into her life but the décor now made Vanessa think of Summer Time colours.

The Costa/Nosi trial was almost over, unless there were appeals to come following the Judge's verdict, and Vanessa had left all work back in the office tonight in an act of light-heartedness. After today, Diana Darling would be shifted to work on cases with one of the other senior partners at Sturgess, Diamond and Co. This was something they'd agreed with the firm after their engagement became obvious in the New Year. Tonight, they were celebrating a milestone in the Costa/Nosi case and the start of a new era in their working relationship. They clinked their glasses of smoky Pinot Gris from the Adelaide Hills and kissed.

"Job well done," Vanessa said, leaning her head on Diana's shoulder.

"I'll say. How long will it take do you think for His Honour to deliver the judgment?"

"Difficult to say. It's a high profile but complex case. A few weeks?"

"And how are you feeling about it?"

"I feel positive. I do hope we get a good verdict for Emma's sake. She's a pretty vulnerable person."

"And," Diana Darling reached sideways to place her glass carefully on the floor. "Have you heard from your mother at all since Christmas?" Diana had decided to wait until after the trial to ask.

Vanessa's face darkened as she reached up to unclasp her hair, letting it tumble over her shoulders. "Regularly. Cecilia calls to talk *at* me rather than with me. I realise now that my mother is completely irrational; she has blocked out the events of Christmas day altogether and seems to assume that my relationship with you is a fancy that will pass. She's invited me over for Easter, without you, to meet the eligible son of a Cabinet Minister." Vanessa scowled and Diana tried not to laugh.

"I hope to hear all about it afterwards," she teased, turning to look into Vanessa's face.

"As you will have guessed, I have no intention of going. Dad is great. I talked with him the other day and he asked if we had set the date for the wedding. What do you think about when we should get married?"

"How about sometime in the spring, although I suppose it depends on our workloads a bit."

"I've been thinking about that." Vanessa placed her glass on the floor too. "What about staking out our claim now? We could book two months leave in, say, September and October. We could have the wedding at Summer Time if the commune agrees and then maybe we could hire a camper van and go on a trip around Australia."

"Oh Vanessa, what a great idea. I love it. Simplicity itself."

"That's what I thought too."

Graydon was delighted to have an early evening visitor. He was momentarily startled by Clint's battered face at the front door and gave him a searching look before motioning for Clint to precede him up the stairs and into the sitting room. Alice bounded over to him with joyful japs, standing on her hind legs and scrabbling at him with her front paws. He rubbed her all over while she shivered with delight and tried to lick his ears. She was very interested in the antiseptic around the bandage on his right temple. Graydon fetched a pot of tea and a plate of savouries.

"I wasn't sure if you would have eaten," he said in response to Clint's thanks.

"My eating patterns *have* been a bit strange today." Clint grinned.

"So," Graydon settled into a blue covered chair with a curling wooden frame and high back. "Did those thugs finally catch up with you?" He pushed a cup of tea towards Clint and indicated that his guest should help himself to savouries.

"Is it that noticeable?" Clint hadn't seen his own face since he'd showered that morning and had assumed that the small bandage covering the stitches on his right temple would not excite much interest.

"Take a look." Graydon pointed at a large silver-framed mirror hanging on the sitting room wall next to a row of photos with matching frames. Clint put down his cup and obeyed.

"Crickey." He was stunned. Purple and black bruises radiated down both sides of his face from each of the spots that had connected with the butt of the gun. "Okay. That looks more alarming than I had realised. But I'm okay," he assured Graydon as he returned to his seat and put two bacon and egg savouries on a delicate square plate that looked antique. It was painted in a blue pattern of weeping willow trees, bridges and pavilions with curved roofs; the painting made Clint think of China.

In the end, Clint ate five savouries washed down with two cups of tea. He told Graydon that the thugs, as his old landlord called them, had beaten him to try and discover the whereabouts of the father he'd never known, a man called Bekym Ryal. "Ah," Graydon had responded, putting down his cup. "Yes. No one close," he said, quoting Clint's response when Graydon had once asked him if Bekym Ryal was a relative. That was almost eighteen months ago, just after Graydon himself had been attacked by the thugs looking for someone called Bekym. Now he understood. Clint was impressed by his memory.

"But I don't know where my father is, so I couldn't help them. They weren't that impressed. Anyway, no need to worry, I've had security installed in my apartment now and I should be okay."

Graydon nodded and asked no more. That was one of the things Clint liked about his old landlord. Not only was he intelligent and interested in everything but he knew what to say, when. He also knew when to leave well alone so that people could be themselves.

"So how have you been getting on?" Clint asked. "Does living in this house remind you all the time of your wife? It must be hard."

"Yes. Everything reminds me of her. We had such a pleasant and civilised life together. But all things pass, don't they? There is nothing more certain than change. And, you know," he looked at Clint, "It is so important to allow yourself to follow your heart."

Clint tipped his head slightly to one side and considered Graydon. "What are you saying?"

"Well, I am pleased you no longer work for that online newspaper, for example. I got the feeling you were not happy there. You have the opportunity now, hopefully, to do things that give you a sense of joy and satisfaction."

Clint waited. He had a feeling that his old landlord had more to say.

"My wife Selma and I loved each other and were happy together but my real love was directed elsewhere all my life. Oh, in my case that love always was, and continues to be, unrequited," he moved his head from side to side and flicked one of his hands as if banishing thoughts. "Anyway, I did not fight for it. But if *you* find love Master Clint, I hope you fight for it a bit. Oh I'm not talking about stalking and forcing yourself on someone who doesn't want you, but standing up for yourself and making a case." He thumped a veined and freckled hand on the arm of the chair as if banging a gavel in court.

Returning through the darkened streets to Wingello Street in an Uber, Clint had a lot to think about. He was careful to check for movement as he climbed out of the car with his house key clutched in his hand, the sharp point pocking out through his knuckles. He deactivated the CCTV app before he reached the landing and reactivated it once he was inside, then locked and bolted the door. The steel guards had been installed; they were rolled down and locked. He felt very secure. Turning the aircon on, he sat in Sunil's chair with a Tooheys and let his mind wander. He had a memory of his grandfather saying to him as a boy something like "every child needs his own space to grow and dream; he must also be able to shut out the demands of others by closing and locking a door." Well, that might also be the case for adults, Clint thought, resting his head back against the chair. What a wise man his grandfather was in many respects. Without warning he was flooded with love for Sunil, for the extraordinary old man Graydon, and for his oldest friend Arash Esfandiari. He thought of Vishesh Devi, Bian who had been so kind to him, and Vishesh's lovely mother who treated him like a son. He thought of his friends Megan and Shane.

"I am so lucky," he said to the empty room which was silent except for the hum of cold air being forced into the room and the faint sound of cars moving through the streets somewhere out there. He knew he had a community, a family of sorts, and he was grateful. And then he let himself think about Detective Lilla Adams, the woman he thought he loved. He didn't have the energy to fight for her right now but he would find a way to do so soon. She was worth fighting for.

# Chapter Twenty

Laughter rang around the apartment. Clint was sitting at the dining room table, facing the balcony and the sprawl beyond of houses, people and lives. His laptop was open. Since his rescue by Arash, Clint had abandoned his previous stance of avoiding technology that could track and monitor him; he was checking his emails. The weeks since the night of the invasion of his home had gone by quickly. A reporter from the Sydney Morning Herald, an old and well-known newspaper, had approached Vanessa Raine for a comment on Judge Malcom McNeill's verdict on the Costa/Nosi case. The Judge had found Emma Costa not guilty of murder and not guilty of accessory to murder. She was released into the care of a shelter for people unable to live completely independently. Piripi Nosi was found guilty of murder and sentenced to life imprisonment without parole. While being interviewed by the Sydney Morning Herald, Vanessa Raine mentioned that her ability to prove the innocence of her client was assisted by the relentless investigation of Clint Ryal and so Clint had been contacted. He was commissioned by the newspaper to write a piece on his investigation and paid handsomely for it.

The email he was now reading came from his former boss Kelly Harper at the online newspaper the Sydney Saturday World; it had precipitated the unrestrained laughter bouncing around his home which was now bathed in autumn sunshine, replacing the cool of the early morning. Autumn and spring were Clint's favourite seasons. *Hi Clint. Read your piece in the SMH. Well researched and well written. Post Covid-19, the subscriptions for the Sydney Saturday World have picked up again and so the newspaper is able to take on more staff. I wonder if you are interested in having your old job back. I've tried to call you but your mobile number has been deactivated. I sent George Bakker around to your apartment in Oxley Street to talk with you just now - he's*

*a big fan of your work by the way - but he rang to say that you appear to have shifted. An old man on the premises didn't seem to know how to get in contact with you. I hope you receive this email. Give me a call. We're all very excited about the idea of having you back on board.*
Clint read the email through once more and then deleted it without replying, a grin still etched on his face. Vanessa Raine had hired him on retainer as an investigator for Sturgess, Diamond and Co., which was all the work he needed right now. Mr Raine's next case was already underway and he was busy coming up to speed.

Josephine Moss, prosecutor in the Costa/Nosi trial, also read Clint's article in the Sydney Morning Herald. A small photo of the author was displayed to the left of the heading which read *Becoming Real: the truth about the torture and murder of Sydney man Tadeas Costa as revealed by Clint Ryal.* Josephine scrutinized the photo as she sat in her office drinking her first coffee of the day. She recognized the face; it was the young man she had noticed in the courtroom and on the court house steps. Good on you, she thought, as she folded the paper and filed it in the recycling bin. She finished her coffee and reminded herself that she was only going to have one more that day and it needed to be before lunchtime if she was going to be able to sleep that night. Ms Moss had decided to take herself in hand. She'd stopped drinking alcohol which she knew she'd used all her life as a way to suppress her emotions. This was forcing her to find ways to deal with feelings of inadequacy that had dogged her all her life and which were now raw and exposed. Like Emma, Josephine's childhood had been marred by dysfunctional parenting. She'd gone on to form relationships with dysfunctional men who belittled and abused her psychologically to hide their own inadequacies, because that was all she had known. Now, living on her own and her children grown, Ms Moss had the choice of sinking or swimming. She hoped she wouldn't sink. She was eating better, exercising more, finding joy in small things outside of work and was thinking about her options. Did she want to continue with the grind of her job which dealt with the underbelly of society? Unlike Emma, Josephine had managed to claw her way into a well-paying job as an adult but only now realised it was one she had never really wanted. She was taking her time to think about what might be next in her life.

Lubanzi Abara was at his office after an early morning jog and a simple breakfast. The file for his next case lay in front of him but he was looking out of the window at the leaves on the trees in the park nearby; their edges were turning yellow. He had let himself be taken in by Piripi Nosi who was, clearly, a very clever man. It was a shame Piripi hadn't been able to use his cleverness for the betterment of society and for himself. Lubanzi felt a sense of self-disgust as he recognised that he had been motivated to win the Costa/Nosi case by whatever means necessary. He had not searched for the truth and had not done himself justice. He hoped he had learned from it.

After the Costa/Nosi case, Judge Malcom McNeill had gone on holiday to Adelaide with his wife. They did not talk about his work much. Even after all these years, they liked nothing more than walking hand in hand along the sand as the sun waned at the end of the day. They visited the farmers market up in the Adelaide hills and ate in pubs as they talked with fondness of their grown up children and their grandchildren.

The CCTV app on Clint's phone beeped, showing a slight figure on the landing nervously clutching a purse with one hand and the other reaching out to knock on the door. No knock came. Ceasing the beeping on his phone, Clint strode over to the door to unbolt and unlock it. Pearl O'Leary stood there, stiff and scared.

"Mum."

"Clint. Hello. Um," she lowered her hand and then lifted it again to run red-tipped fingers through her hair which looked brittle and sparse as if it was shedding. "I read your article. About Emma. I, um …"

"Yes?"

"Well, I wanted to … I don't know …" Pearl fumbled for a cigarette in her fluffy pink bag.

"You can't smoke here mum." Clint relented. "Come in. You can smoke out on my balcony."

Pearl scuttled into the room and looked around with bulging green eyes, tilting and swaying on the red stilettos attached to bony legs wearing tight three-quarter length denim. The heels had lost most of their colour and Clint thought they might be second hand. She looked like a long-legged bird. The clash between his mother's vulnerability and her clever manipulation tended to make mincemeat of Clint's emotions and today was no exception.

"Your grandad left all this to you then? You must be doing okay." He heard, not for the first time, the hungry, grasping note in Pearl's voice that wanted to suck him dry of any little success or joy in his life. "This is a nice flat, isn't it? Much nicer than my flat. My flat has mould and the Department won't do anything about it. It's bad for my lungs." Pearl coughed. The attempt was pitiful to begin with but the playacting soon changed into the hack of a smokers cough. "See?"

"I don't see how your flat can be mouldy mum." Clint said with one of his rare attempts to expose his mother to rational thinking. "We live in a hot dry climate. Do you open a window in your apartment every now and again? You don't think that your cough has something to do with your smoking instead?" Clint knew full well that there was nothing about his mother for which she would take responsibility.

"I don't smoke that much Clint." She took a cigarette out of her purse and looked expectantly towards the balcony.

Clint unlocked the deadlock and pulled the sliding door open so she could step out. He sat at the table just inside the sliding door to shut down his laptop and gather papers into a brown-covered folder. What he was working on was confidential. The smell of smoke wafted in through the door and so he went out on the balcony, pulling the door closed behind him to avoid his home being contaminated.

"What is it you want mum? I didn't know you read the newspapers."

"I heard people in the supermarket queue talking about Emma's trial. They mentioned a newspaper article written by Clint Ryal. I wanted to tell them 'that's my son' but they looked snooty so I didn't. What would they care anyway?"

Clint took a deep breath, tuned out her voice and looked over the wide expanse of hot roofs. He waited for her rant of self-pity to pass.

"… and so I bought a newspaper and found your article. Emma Costa was a sad little thing and I always thought she wanted to have Bekym instead of that old man she married. It's a good thing you helped to save her at the trial. I'm glad." She didn't sound glad. "Did the information I give you help your case?"

Clint thought back to Pearl's visit to him at work all that time ago when she had told him about the connection between Bekym and Emma. At the time, he was disconcerted that she hadn't asked for anything from him. But he now realised she'd been playing the long game. Now we're coming to it, he thought and said, "Yes, thanks mum."

"Well you probably got well paid for that investigation but I was a source wasn't I?"

Clint pulled out his wallet and found he had fifty dollars in cash. He rarely used cash anymore but had withdrawn some on impulse thinking he might shop at the local farmer's market this weekend. It had occurred to him that the urge to shop at the market might have something to do with wanting to engage more with the local community.

"Have it. It's all I've got."

Pearl clutched at the money and stuffed the notes into her handbag. Her mouth was pursed with triumph; she'd got one over on her son.

"You need to go now mum. Oh, by the way, how did you know I live here now?"

Pearl glanced at him out of the corner of false eyelashes.

"I met Sunil in the supermarket before Covid-19. My benefit had been cut because the Department said I was living with a man and I had to find somewhere else to live if I was to get the benefit back properly. I asked your grandfather if I could stay with him. Sunil said I couldn't stay with him. He told me that when he died he would leave everything to you. I suppose he just told me that because he thinks I haven't been able to do anything for you. What a thing to say. When I think of all the bad luck I've had in my life and all the things I tried to do for you. If my Lotto numbers ever come up I'd share the prize with you, you know I would." Her voice was wheedling now. "Well, after I read your article in the newspaper I went back to the office where I saw you last time but they said it was a different newspaper," Pearl frowned in confusion, "and that you didn't work there anymore. They also told me that they'd tried to visit you at your flat but you had moved out. I thought you might be here. Your grandfather is dead then?"

"Yes."

"Oh well. Stupid old bastard. He never liked me. Tried to keep Bekym away from me."

"You need to go."

Clint locked and bolted the door behind Pearl. There were familiar feelings of rage and self-hatred for allowing Pearl to manipulate him and get to him, as well as grief and the desire for love. The feelings wrestled and exploded in his chest so that he had to shout through gritted teeth and pound his fist into the bench top. He could still smell cigarette smoke and saw through the window a mangled butt, still smoking, on the balcony. Clint moved to get rid of it.

The old flatmates from number 16 Oxley Street were meeting for a pot luck dinner at Bian and Vishesh's apartment in Darling Point. It was the first reunion of the flatmates. Clint had put off seeing anyone until the bruising had receded from his face and the stitches in his temple had dissolved. He had picked up a six pack of Tooheys to take along. As Clint prepared Thai fish cakes and sweet chilli dip for tonight's gathering, he tried to calm himself and recover from the meeting with his mother. He knew he needed to break with his mother altogether. As long as he let her into his life he would suffer but he seemed unable to banish her completely. In that case, he needed to find better ways to deal with the emotions that resurfaced at each encounter. He knew it was up to him.

That evening, it felt to Clint that the flatmates had never moved apart. They ate looking over the lights of the harbour, caught up on news and watched the bliss of Vishesh and Bian. Clint felt the eyes of Vishesh on him a couple of times and knew what Vishesh wanted to ask: had he made contact with Lilla? Clint had finally decided just that afternoon that, even if she rejected him, he needed to let Lilla know that he missed her and was probably in love with her. He had rung the NYPD and left a message with his contact details. He hadn't yet heard back.

On the following day Clint found he couldn't keep his mind on work and so decided to finish painting the apartment. Over the past few weeks he had donated most of Sunil's belongings to charity shops feeling both sad at the severing of this physical link with his grandfather but also knowing that it was exactly what Sunil would have wanted. He had then discovered the joys of Ikea. Boxes were delivered and furniture assembled. New appliances were installed and kitchenware unpacked.

The comfort Clint gained from the new order in his life was huge. He had kept Sunil's bed base and his favourite old chair but almost everything else had been replaced. The sofa was a grey three-seater with no arms and large puffy backrests which could be turned into a sleeper. Clint had bought a new mattress and fresh bedding with covers striped in blue and white. The curtains would need updating at some stage but he decided to hold off on that until there was more money in his account. Clint had already given most of the rooms in the apartment a fresh coat of paint called Winter White and there was only his bedroom left to do. As he was cleaning his brushes that evening, the windows opened wide to let the fumes dissipate, he realised that Lilla had still not responded to his message. Clint decided that enough was enough. He needed to focus on work instead of mooning over a woman. She obviously didn't feel love for him like he did for her. He knew he needed to pull a steel roller door down over the swelling in his heart.

The next case he was coming to grips with for Vanessa Raine involved an Australian man with Nazi ancestors who was accused of murdering a Jewish family and desecrating a Jewish cemetery. Clint read and re-read the file that Vanessa had sent him but felt at a loss to know where to start to make a difference in this case; the evidence appeared cut and dried. The app on his phone beeped and Clint turned away from the files to pick it up with reluctance, hoping that Pearl had not returned. He wasn't sure whether or not he had the strength to ignore her. The CCTV video revealed a woman on his landing but it was not his mother. This woman was young and curvy with hair that cascaded down her back. Clint threw himself across the room and unlocked the security.

"Hello Clint."

"Lilla." His throat seemed to have dried up but his eyes felt moist.

"May I come in?"

Clint shut the door and reassembled the security. He turned to find Lilla standing very close; looking straight into his eyes. Her face was soft and her eyes glowing. She reached out her arms and Clint pulled her into a hug. They held each other carefully for some time as if each thought the other might break if held too tightly, before moving away from the door and into the sitting room. They lowered themselves into the sun that lay on the carpet like a sheet as it shone through the glass leading onto the balcony. Lilla unbuttoned Clint's shirt to run her hands over every inch of the warmth and tautness of his chest and back, reminding herself of his touch and look and smell. Clint closed his eyes and basked in her touch for a while. When he opened them, their eyes locked with love. The intensity of his desire scared Clint; he didn't want to hurt Lilla. He slowly unbuttoned her pink and white checked shirt, moaning softly as her white breasts tumbled out, unrestrained by a bra. He laid her on her back and gently removed each article of clothing. Her pink satin panties trimmed with lace slipped down her legs like hot butter.

He began to lick her, to lick every inch of skin across her front and her back, making her hips lift and her back arch in longing in the warm rays of the midday sun through the glass. Her arms stretched above her head with her hands clutching and spreading. Clint breathed softly on the delicate skin under her arms and around her neck. Lilla groaned with longing, her breath ragged, as he lifted her hips towards him. Clint's tongue found her and she cried out, her body wracked in spasms of surrender, her face transported. Lilla reached for him and, locked in desire, they rode waves of bliss together.

It was only afterwards as he and Lilla lay entwined in the fading patch of sun on the carpet, breathing in unison, that Clint wondered if Arash might have replaced the bugs he discovered in the apartment with his own bugs. After a moment, Clint decided it didn't matter. Good luck to him, he thought. He looked down at Lilla with her head resting under his chin. Her white skin contrasted with his caramel colour; their bodies looked like art. There were many things they needed to talk about. Why he left New York in a hurry, for example. Why neither of them had been in touch and, Clint took a deep breath, why she'd had him followed and bugged. Clint needed to know, too, whether he meant as much to her as she did to him, and how they might traverse the globe to be together. But they didn't need to talk about any of it right now. There was time enough later. Right now, Clint couldn't think of anywhere he'd rather be than nestled against Lilla's warm body. The mobile in the pocket of his shorts rang in the tangle of their clothes. He scrambled for it and the display told him it was Vanessa Raine.

"We need to talk. There has been another murder of a Jewish man."

"Really? Another Jewish murder. Well it can't be pinned on Helmut can it, because he's in remand, unless he's pulling the strings from afar?"

"The problem is; Helmut has escaped from prison."

"No shit." Clint sat up, every hair on his body standing on end; he felt electrified. "How did that happen? Bloody hell, that's rare."

"Can you come down to the office?"

"On my way."

Lilla was already getting dressed. "I heard the bit about Jewish murders," she said sounding business-like and ready for work. "We've had a spate of them in New York too. Should we join forces?"

Clint gazed at Detective Lilla Adams, gorgeous and desirable but so very professional, and thought his heart would burst. He adored her.

"Joining forces is exactly what I had in mind."

Within minutes they had secured Clint's apartment and were on their way out.

# A. YEOMAN

# BECOMING JUST

BOOK TWO OF *THE BECOMING CHRONICLES*

# Available early in 2021

### Becoming Just: Book Two of The Becoming Chronicles

A series of vicious murders and the desecration of a Jewish Cemetery send Clint back to New York and on to Germany. He is in search of evidence to prove the innocence of the murder accused, Helmut Fischer.

His investigations for the lawyer Vanessa Raine from Sydney firm Sturgess, Diamond and Co. uncover the work of former Nazi officers recruited by the CIA at the end of World War II: work which is being continued today. The CIA and Australia's own intelligence organization add complexity to Clint's every step as he closes in on the truth. In the process Clint must save the woman he loves, the NYPD's Detective Lilla Adams, and protect his father from brutality.

Clint wants to prove to himself that his previous success in solving the Costa/Nosi murder case was not just luck. He also wants to prove to others that his skills can help those who are in need.

A ruthless campaign of hate and manipulation is undone; justice is done.

Printed in Great Britain
by Amazon